CITY OF DEVILS
13 Tales of the Uncanny, Unlucky & Unholy

Short Stories

by

STACI LAYNE WILSON

Copyright © 2018 by Staci Layne Wilson

Published by Excessive Nuance in paperback
ISBN-13: 978-0-9675185-7-2

Also available via Kindle & Audible

praise for
Staci Layne Wilson

With enviable ease, Staci Layne Wilson manages the difficult trick of combining edgy eroticism, knowing humor, and unflinching horror into one delicious package. Like some bizarre ménage à trois between Stephen King, Candace Bushnell, and Sarah Silverman, her fiction explores every aspect of the Forbidden. – Peter Atkins, screenwriter of the Hellraiser and Wishmaster films, author of Morningstar

Staci Layne Wilson is an expert at creating believable characters, a chilling scenario, and a roller-coaster-ride-of-a-story that doesn't put on the brakes until the very last page. – James Newman, author of Ugly As Sin and The Wicked

Staci Layne Wilson knows how to write. Read her books and you'll see what I mean. But it just doesn't stop with good writing... there's an underlying hipness to everything that's going on, and while the suspense builds, you can't help but notice the sexiness, the rock and roll, the creativity spurred on by the innate sensibilities she clearly possesses. Her characters breathe the same airs we do, their fears are as real as they get. Her phrases... they send shudders of guilty pleasure across the raised skin on your back as you absorb them one delightful word at a time. – Michael Laimo, author of Deep in the Darkness and Dead Souls

For seasoned and new readers of the genre, treat yourself to the masterfully written mind tweaks of Staci Layne Wilson, whose haunting descriptions and endings that scream 'Move over, Rod Serling!' will keep you up all night long! – Cass Andre, author of El Chupacabra

Staci Layne Wilson's writing and her choice of stories go together like rich red wine and deep dark chocolate—and its effect on the reader is the same: You mean to only have a sip and nibble, but before you know it the hour is late and your cravings are satisfied. – Jen Lacks, author of Kill Me If You Can

contents
CITY OF DEVILS

*previously published

He Was Asking For It

Howard Wexler tossed restlessly in his bed. He moaned in his semi-sleep state. It was the nightmares again. The memories of childhood that he could not shake. The taunts from his classmates:

"You're so fat, you could sell shade!"

"If I had a face like yours, I'd sue my parents!"

"You're so ugly, when your mom dropped you off this morning she got a fine for littering!"

He remembered the admonitions from his teachers, telling him to stop crying. Lashes from his father's belt for desperately wanting to avoid the bullies, to stay home feigning one illness or another.

Howard came awake now, coated in a clammy sweat. He reached for his wife, then remembered he was alone in yet another hotel room. Where was he? London, Paris, South Africa… No… Santa Monica. On the beach. Not that he'd ever see the golden sand and waves of azure blue. When it was deal-time, Howard stayed in his suite and let them come to him. The directors, writers, actors, lawyers, wheeler-dealers and desperate pitch presenters.

As his eyes fluttered open to the dark room, blackout curtains drawn, he wondered if it was day or night. Not that it mattered. He worked day and night.

Howard reached for his phone and saw dozens of missed texts and as many unread emails. He sighed. Sure, he had an assistant. Several, actually. But he hadn't become the most powerful producer in Hollywood by delegating—he prided himself on being hands-on.

He sat up, swinging his thick, hairy legs over the edge of the bed. His bare feet touched Italian marble floor while his bare ass slid off of Egyptian cotton sheets. He stood, glanced down at his belly and his mouth curled in disgust at the size of it. He couldn't see any body part past it. He really should shed some pounds, he thought… but then again: Why? He was rich, powerful, had a gorgeous Russian trophy wife, several mansions and villas and movies currently at #1 and #3 at the box office.

And he did love to eat. His appetites were many, but fine food was at the top. In fact, that reminded him: He'd better order breakfast and get on with his day.

Howard did just that and then padded, naked, to his robe and slippers. He put them on. This would be his attire for today's meetings. That's how powerful he was—he gave no fucks about his appearance at all.

But he did brush his teeth.

He looked at himself in the bathroom mirror. "Ugly as a bridge troll," was one insult that had stuck with him. Someone posted that on his company's Instagram in the comments section after the scandal broke out. Howard was realistic. He knew he wasn't exactly Brad Pitt and no amount of power, money or influence could change that. But he'd grown to *like* his ugliness. His eyes were small, piercing and dark. His nose was huge, his lips thick. He felt his size and his looks made him more intimidating. It was about time he was the bully. His temper and his tantrums were legendary—Howard loved being thought of as the modern-day equivalent of Louis B. Mayer or Harry Cohn.

Well, he *used* to love it. The tide was turning in Hollywood. Scandals stinking of sexual misconduct were breaking all around him. Even within his own H.W. Productions; he'd fired a scapegoat just last week.

As for himself, he wasn't worried. He was the big boss, the titan, the star-maker, the mogul. Nobody would dare screw with him— their success depended on him.

When he was younger, just coming up, Howard read everything he could on Old Hollywood and the studio system. He remembered a line from Marilyn Monroe's memoir, when she talked about meeting movie producers and listening to their rhetoric: "You saw Hollywood with their eyes—an overcrowded brothel, a merry-go-round with beds for horses." Instead of being moved by her plight, he was motivated by it. He modeled himself after those guys and it worked wonders for his career and his sex life.

Oh, sure. At first, he kept his true self concealed. In fact, he remembered with an inward snicker, he even advocated gender sensitivity training for his employees. This was back in the late 90s, making him a trailblazer of sorts. Hell, he even attended one of the classes. He watched with amusement as the high-priced tutor erected an eraser board, drawing the male symbol on the left side, female on the right, then etched a crooked line down the middle.

The woman, whom Howard assumed was a lesbo, spoke to the gathered employees. "For the men only: What steps do you take on a daily basis to prevent yourselves from being sexually assaulted or harassed?"

There was a long silence. Then a titter of laughter from a couple of them. Finally, one of the junior executives said, "Nothing. I guess I don't think about it at all."

Then she turned her attention to the few female employees—assistants, receptionists, secretaries, publicists—and asked the same question.

Immediately, hands went up.

"When I walk to my car, I hold my keys as a weapon," said one.

"I don't get on the elevator with only one man, or a group of men," said the next.

"I avoid wearing heels higher than three inches, in case I've got to run," added another.

Don't jog with earbuds in. Own a big dog. Look in the backseat before getting into a car. Avoid eye contact. The litany went on and on.

Howard listened and stored the information away for future use. Phrases he could use to sound like he understood, like he was an ally. To exploit fear, whittle into their weaknesses, then pry their legs and mouths open.

He'd done it many times, in this very suite.

The hotel was supposedly haunted. It gave him an extra thrill, wondering who might be watching him from the so-called Great Beyond. He wondered if ghosts got horny, then remembered a movie from way back in the 80s called *The Entity* which was about that very thing. He liked the idea of still being able to get some, even after death.

His morbid reverie was broken by a gentle tapping sound. "Room service," came a muffled voice of indeterminate gender.

Robe open, yellowed toenails hanging over the edge of his satin slippers, he opened the door.

It was a young man behind the silver service cart. It usually was; hotel management had learned his ways years ago and stopped sending female servers. Still, Howard felt the disappointment grumble in his groin.

"Over there," he pointed at the rumpled bed.

Set up was quick and efficient and a hundred-dollar tip was pressed into the server's eager hand. The employee left with an obsequious "Thank you, sir."

Howard sat on the edge of the bed and spooned caviar onto his lightly scrambled eggs. He was just bringing the Christofle Sterling

Marly fork to his slavering maw when he heard another knock.

"What, the tip wasn't big enough?" he grumbled as he set the tray aside. He got up and went to the door.

On the other side was a smoking hot girl. She had a short brunet bob, a slim boyish figure and long legs.

"Mr. Wexler," she said, her voice breathy. "I hope I'm not too early?" She glanced at his body through the opening of his robe and blushed. "I'm Antonia… here to talk about the role…?"

"Oh, yes. Yes!" Howard chuckled deeply, stepping back and sashing his robe. He put on his most avuncular expression. He really didn't remember her specifically, but there were so many aspiring actresses coming and going in his line of work. "Come on in. I'm just having breakfast, hope you don't mind if I eat while we talk."

They walked through the sitting area and into the bedroom.

Antonia stepped in and took a seat across the room while Howard finished his breakfast in bed. They chatted and she told him about some of her most recent roles. He'd never seen them, but he sure liked what he saw in her. She was so fresh-faced, pretty and meek. She wasn't right for the role, he decided, but she was good for right now.

Howard put the serving tray aside and patted a spot on the bed next to him. "Come closer, dear," he said. "I can't see you very well from way over there."

"Um, do you have glasses here?" she asked, glancing around the suite.

"Eh, somewhere," he shrugged. "Come on, I won't bite. I'm a married man. I just want to look into your eyes. There's going to be a lot of close ups in this movie and you've got to be able to emote."

Antonia did as she was told, clutching her purse to her side.

They talked a bit more and as they did, Howard let his robe fall open again. "Do you like this?" he asked huskily, touching himself.

Antonia stood. Her eyes went wide. "What are you doing?!"

"I want you to watch me."

She turned, but Howard took her wrist and forced her to look at him. She did, in open-mouthed shock and he quickly finished. He let go of her wrist and as if nothing was amiss, he took the napkin from the serving tray and wiped himself off.

"If you're going to be in this business, kid, you've got to get tough."

"I'm tough," she whispered, sounding just the opposite.

Antonia reached into her purse and before Howard could even register what was happening, he saw the glint of a straight razor and felt a whoosh of cool air at his groin. Then he saw the blood. So much blood and a gaping hole where his prized penis had been. He was too stunned to scream. As his hands dove to stanch the flow, he felt the razor slash his throat.

The last thing Howard saw was a blurry smile on the face of the apparition of Antonia Lowe, up-and-coming star of the Silent Era who'd committed suicide after being violated by a Hollywood producer.

The next thing Howard saw was his place in the afterlife: The hotel suite he'd never escape and the vengeful female spirits with whom he would be forced to spend an eternity.

Based on a true story.

"At first, I thought it was a mannequin… but I could smell the blood. There was this metallic tang in the air. This was no joke," said the waifish woman, weeping into a wadded tissue.

The police interrogation footage was grainy and the camera was static, stuck to an upper corner of the bare, boxlike room—but Natasha could still see shock, anguish and fear in the woman's glassy eyes.

Just a few hours before, Denise Martin had found her roommate on the floor of their small apartment in Hollywood, riddled with stab-wounds.

Denise had gone out for a night on the town and didn't get home until daybreak. That's when she saw the carnage.

"Torey was faceup, her eyes were… dead."

Prompted by the almost mechanical monotone of the detective, Denise told the story.

Blood bloomed beneath Torey's body. It was trailing from her nose, matted in her hair and had drenched the baby blue silk pajama set she wore. It looked like Torey was about to go to bed, then had been surprised in the hallway between the living room and her bedroom by the knife-wielding madman who'd sexually assaulted her before murdering her.

Denise said she ran from the apartment and used her cell to call 9-1-1. She waited in the manager's office until authorities arrived. Ambulances and fire trucks came and of course the police. LAPD Detective Jorge Ramirez noted the victim was a twenty-something Caucasian female, last-known to be alive at 9 p.m. the night before, when Denise said "See you later," and left to meet her boyfriend. Ramirez noted no forced entry, no weapon on site. Nothing appeared to be missing.

An external examination of Torey's lifeless body revealed multiple stab wounds, seven of which were deemed fatal—but it was probably the perforation to her throat that did it. Her neck suffered extensive trauma; so much so that her head had been partially severed from her spinal column. Though the puncture to her right eye might have done it. She'd been stabbed in her head, face and neck.

"They stabbed her in the fucking head!" Denise wailed. "Who does that?"

There were slashes to Torey's once-beautiful hands and her fingernails were bent back, torn and broken, showing she'd fought hard for her life. Still, she lost.

The official M.E. report wouldn't be filed for another ten days, but the manner of death was obvious: Homicide.

And her roommate Denise was a suspect. Or at least a person of interest.

Using the touch-screen, Natasha scrubbed the video back. She had to see this again. And again. If she was going to portray Denise Martin correctly, she had to study and absorb every single nuance from the way the woman wiped her nose to how she said Torey's name.

The crime—crimes, actually—had happened five years ago and been solved. Now it was Hollywood's turn to dredge it all back up. Sure, there had been a lurid Lifetime Channel movie of the week about it before the bodies were even cold, but Natasha had been cast in the big screen version. A more serious and grand reenactment of the horror.

Problem was, Denise refused to meet with Natasha. Natasha had plenty to read and watch, but that wasn't good enough in terms of her process. Her goal was to win an Oscar and secondhand news simply wouldn't help her get the job done. She'd have to get devious if she was really serious about this.

"I'm so very sorry," fretted Natasha. "I didn't want to do this, but you left me no choice."

Denise, bound to a dining room chair and gagged with a silk Hermes equestrian-themed scarf, glared at her captor.

"Look. I need the story from *you*. The whole story. How can I play you unless I know exactly what you were thinking? What you were feeling? How he smelled, what he said. Everything."

Denise looked at Natasha as if she were contemplating whether it would be more satisfying to sew a skirt-suit made out of her skin or to scatter chopped-up pieces of her carcass into the Pacific Ocean. "Mmmmph! Grrrr!"

"OK, OK," said Natasha. "It doesn't matter anyway. No one can hear you up here." Natasha loosened the gag and it flopped out of Denise's parched mouth.

"Heeeeeelllllp!" Denise yelled with more gusto than Natasha would have expected.

Silence greeted the ear-shattering plea.

Natasha had owned this cabin on Big Bear Mountain since she got her first flurry of residual checks from her one-season stint on *Teenage Penitentiary*. The show was tawdry fluff, set in a juvenile detention center in the 1960s. But it was immensely popular, especially overseas. Especially in Asia. To this day Natasha couldn't even walk the streets of Tokyo without being mobbed.

They were far, far from Tokyo now—the secluded, upscale cabin might as well have been 5,474 miles from Los Angeles too. There were no neighbors nearby, and with the snowfall even the seasonal residents were keeping away.

Denise didn't cry. She didn't whimper. Not like she did on that police interrogation tape, five years before. No. What she had been through following that, Natasha figured, had made leather of her soul.

Denise was a person of interest in her roommate's death. But there was no evidence. Mainly because she didn't do it. The cops didn't know that then, but still: They had to let her go. Her boyfriend picked her up and took her home, back to the bloodied apartment, to collect some things. She couldn't stay there of course, even though it was no longer an active crime scene. All the evidence that could be gathered, had been.

Details on what happened next are murky, but Denise's boyfriend came to with a goose-egg bump on the back of his head and he was sprawled, otherwise unhurt, in Torey's dried blood. Denise was missing.

She was in the clutches of the killer. He had unfinished business. His goal was to snuff out the lives of *both* of the beauties in Apartment 117. A two-fer. He'd been dismayed to find only Torey at home the night before but he'd made the best of the situation. With Denise, he'd take his time.

Denise's boyfriend had called the police reporting her missing, but he got the impression they thought he was lying and Denise had actually fled. She did, after all, have a history of clinical depression.

Natasha sighed. "I'll get you some water."

Denise glowered.

Natasha opened a bottle of electrolyte-infused smart water, knowing she had to keep Denise alert and refreshed if she was going to get the details she needed. But Denise mustn't be too comfortable. It was a razor's edge she'd have to walk. She brought the bottle to Denise's lips. The woman took three long pulls, then turned her head.

"What did you think when you saw who it was? Did you suspect him? Were you scared?" Natasha asked, her words tumbling over one another.

Denise looked down, her expression grim.

"When he tied you up, was it like this? Did I get the knots right?"

Denise stayed silent, a petulant expression on her otherwise pretty, if gaunt, face. Her hair was swept back into a messy ponytail and she wore the jogging outfit she had on when Natasha had taken her.

It was risky doing it like that, in broad daylight at Griffith Park. It's not like she'd tackled Denise or overpowered her—that's something a man would have done. No, Natasha had hoped she could talk some sense into her quarry. She had hoped she would not have to go to Plan B. But Denise stubbornly refused to cooperate, coldly telling Natasha to leave her alone.

Natasha jabbed the woman in her butt, the needle going in so quickly and smoothly that Denise didn't know what happened until it was too late. She fell to her knees, woozy but not unconscious. Natasha guided Denise, who seemed faint—or maybe even drunk—to her car. No one recognized Natasha, thanks to the baggy clothes and dark oversized sunglasses. In fact, no one noticed the women at all.

But now, in the cabin, Denise was alert. However, her face betrayed no emotion. Maybe a little anger; Natasha couldn't be sure. But she took note of the expression—it was a good one and she could use it when the cameras were rolling.

Natasha sauntered into the kitchen. The cabin, like most, had an open floor plan. The dining area, where Denise was tied to the chair, was adjacent to the fully-equipped chef's kitchen. The dark wood floors, paneled walls and shadow-hugging vaulted ceiling could make the place feel either cozy or creepy. Since Natasha had not built a fire, it was leaning more toward creepy at the moment.

Natasha went to her butcher's block. She contemplated her options. The narrow, pointed boning blade certainly was menacing. The serrated bread knife was huge. The meat cleaver would definitely get anyone's attention. But it was a butcher's knife he had used and so, Natasha decided, should she. She extracted it with a flourish. She held it aloft.

Denise looked over. Her expression remained stony.

Natasha returned to the dining area. She stood in front of Denise and brought the knife's point to the pulse of her throat. There was the betrayal—her fear showed in the flush of her skin and the almost imperceptible quickening of breath.

"Look," said Natasha evenly. "You tell me what I need to know and I don't cut you. OK?"

Denise swallowed. "OK."

The story didn't unfold quite as grippingly as Natasha had hoped. Most of it was just a regurgitation of stuff she already knew.

Just the facts, ma'am, she thought bitterly to herself. The only reason she knew how to quote *Dragnet* in her mind was that she'd done a movie with Dan Ackroyd a few years back and he loved reminding everyone on set of his signature roles. *Well*, Natasha said to herself, *this will be my signature role. Even if I have to kill for it.*

Denise recounted what happened after she and her boyfriend entered the apartment. The landlord, Rudy Bonfiglio, saw them go in and immediately knocked on the door.

"Are you sure you want to go in there?" he'd called from outside.

"We're OK," Tom replied. He never did like the way the guy looked at his girlfriend.

"Can I come in?" Rudy called, knocking again.

Denise opened the door a crack and what happened after that was hazy, but she woke up tied to a chair in another of Rudy's rentals a few blocks away. This complex was vacant and in an even shadier part of Hollywood. The room had nothing in it, not even electricity.

Denise was defiled repeatedly throughout the day and night, beaten with the man's fists, burned with the butt of a cigar and sliced with a butcher's knife. Even on the bottoms of her feet.

The next morning when Rudy returned to his post at the apartment building, he tightened Denise's bindings and told her, "I'm not through with you yet."

Denise had hours to work on her escape. And she succeeded. She broke a window and, half-naked, she climbed out and ran to the nearest home. She knocked on several doors. No one would let her in. But someone called the police and when they first picked her up they assumed she was a drunk and disorderly. Though hysterical, she explained who she was and who had abducted her and killed Torey. There was skepticism since she herself had been questioned the morning before, but there was no faking those injuries.

Rudy was easily apprehended and as it turned out, he was a serial killer. Police found three fresh bodies underneath the newly-poured courtyard concrete in the vacant complex.

Natasha straddled Denise and brought the point of the knife to her taut trapezius muscle. "What were you thinking when Bonfiglio was raping you?"

"I... um... left my body," whispered Denise.

"Did it feel different from, say, rough sex? Did you cry? Did you say anything?"

Denise remained stoic.

Natasha put pressure on the knife, just enough to break the skin.

There was a flicker of fear in Denise's eyes. Shit just got real. "Yes, it was different. No, I didn't cry. I said I wouldn't tell if he'd just let me go." Denise swallowed hard. She met Natasha's eyes. "I won't tell if you just let me go."

Natasha got back on her feet and took a step back. She looked at the crimson stain on the end of the knife. She had done that. And it was so easy. Even easier than drugging Denise. *Am I a sociopath?* she wondered. Natasha had never hurt anyone before, never even thought about it. But this was important.

"I'll untie you once you give me some answers. The right answers. Good ones. I need details. I need to know what you know, to feel what you felt. Tell me. What does it feel like to be punched in the face?"

Denise looked like she wanted to show Natasha exactly what it felt like. "It actually doesn't hurt that bad at first. I was dazed, my ears rang and I was disoriented. Like my brain couldn't quite compute the physical part of it yet. But the next morning. Oh, my skin was too tight and it was hot and there was a constant dull throbbing. Sometimes there'd be a jolt of pain out of nowhere."

Natasha set the knife down on the table. She balled up her fist and punched Denise just under her right eye. She had never even slapped another person before. She blinked in surprise at herself.

Denise stayed quiet and righted herself as the chair wobbled.

"So that didn't hurt?" Natasha asked, stepping close and peering into Denise's face. She would need to be able to mimic that exact expression.

"What did you say when he was raping you?" Natasha demanded.

Denise repeated that she'd promised to not tell anyone, then revealed that she'd talked about Torey and she'd asked Bonfiglio why he did it. She revealed things he'd said and done.

Things she had never told anyone, not even her therapist.

Thirteen months later, Natasha was back at her cabin for the first time since the interrogation. Or as she remembered it, preparation and rehearsal.

It was March and quite chilly, so she had built a roaring fire and was sitting in her favorite easy chair. A bottle of Dom Pérignon she'd been given at one of the awards show gifting suites was set in a silver art deco ice bucket beside her. In her hand was a nearly-empty glass. Her third.

On the mantle sat her Golden Globe, SAG Award, Critics' Choice Award and yes: The Oscar—all for her tour de force performance as Denise Martin in *At Knifepoint*.

Finally, Natasha could be alone to savor her hard-won victory. She was exhausted, body, brain and soul.

She'd kept her promise to Denise: Natasha untied her after learning all that she needed to learn. The fact that Denise was dead at the time was a mere technicality.

Natasha shuddered at the memory of burning the woman's body in the firepit. It smelled like roasted pork and had taken so much longer than she anticipated. After the cremation she shoveled the chunky ashes into a paper grocery bag and walked to her pre-dug hole twenty-minutes into the woods. She buried the bag and jumped up and down on the dirt to ensure a tight pack. Then she put snow over it.

When she returned to L.A. she'd used Denise's phone to send out a few vaguely-distressed social media posts. She then smashed the screen, went to skid row and surreptitiously placed the device under the reeking blanket of a sleeping homeless man.

After a few days Denise's friends and family grew concerned—but nothing came of it. It was assumed that she was upset by the impending film and had gone into hiding. She was an adult, and if you were an adult you could choose to go off the grid at any time.

Natasha poured herself another flute of champagne and jutted it toward the gold, glimmering trophies. "Here's to me!" she slurred.

Half a mile away, Dan and Marta Cristal had finally finished unpacking for the long weekend. They loved their cabin but only made it out a few times a year. As a consequence, getting it dusted, aired out and stocked had taken the better part of the evening. Now it was time to relax.

Dan was stir-frying a frozen dinner-for-two premixed meal in the kitchenette and Marta had just turned on the TV. She tuned in to her favorite entertainment show and watched as the awards season recap played. *At Knifepoint* had swept and everyone was talking about it. Marta wanted to see it but hadn't gotten around to it yet.

There was a thump and a scratch at the sliding glass back door. Dan glanced up from his stirring.

"Hey, hon," he said. "Champ's at the door. Would you let him in, please?"

As she half-listened to the TV—"And Denise Martin is still missing," said the host almost gleefully—Marta got up to let the dog in. There were dried leaves in the plume of his tail and he had a grungy stick in his mouth.

She knelt. "What's that you got, Champ? Give it."

Marta took his prize as the shaggy golden retriever whined in protest.

It was not a stick.

Marta gasped. It was a charred human jawbone.

Ankle Biters

Missing pet posters were not unusual. Especially not in dog parks. I saw them every day when I was teaching my Puppy Boot Camp classes.

No matter how commonplace it was—they were tacked to telephone poles, fastened to corkboards, placed under the windshield wipers of parked cars—it was still sad. That's someone's heartbreak; it meant a four-legged family member was gone.

Those notices usually featured a full-color picture of the pet. In my area, Bel Air, the photo was almost always a professionally-taken, signed headshot of a purebred, papered pet. Since the folks around there had money, most of the dogs were microchipped. Hell, even some *kids* were microchipped—I remember reading an article that Prince William was electronically tagged for security reasons when he entered Eton College. This was back in the early 90s and because it was costly, it wasn't as common as it is now. There were some kinks to be worked out, but the emerging technology did help to find them. Most of the time they were just lost. Sometimes stolen. Or casualties of coyotes or careless drivers.

What was unusual about the spate of missing pet posters was that most of the gone-astray pets were Chihuahuas. Don't get me wrong—Chihuahuas were popular around there.

Celebrities have always loved the Mexican spitfires. Jayne Mansfield had several. So did Britney Spears. Paris Hilton had one named Tinkerbell that was almost as famous as her. Mickey Rourke insisted on taking his little Loki everywhere with him whether dogs were allowed or not. Then there was the movie *Beverly Hills Chihuahua*, which came out some years after the incident.

But to see *so many* "missing dog" posters featuring Chihuahuas… well, I should have realized something was off.

This is the first time I've actually talked about what happened. What *really* happened. What's now known in conspiracy circles as "The Taking of Bel Air" has been blamed on everything from terrorists to extra-terrestrials. Maybe you already know that. Or maybe you're some future reader, catching up on your history. It doesn't matter. What matters is that I tell the true story.

May 2, 1993

When I got home from my Puppy Boot Camp class that Sunday morning at 10 a.m., there were several messages on my answering machine. I got a lot of messages—I was, after all, known as the "dog trainer to the stars" and I had my own occasional segment on *Entertainment Today* —but not usually so early, nor so many. I saw the LED flashing: 6, 6, 6 over and over.

I poured myself a cup of coffee from the half-full carafe, put it in the microwave for a minute, then went to the machine and pressed Play.

The six messages were all from Enrique Goldberg, Geneva Hughes' personal manager. It was urgent, he insisted. He couldn't say over the phone what was wrong, but it involved her Chihuahua, Boo-Boo. Apparently, Boo-Boo was under Geneva's bed and wouldn't come out. I'd been the dog's trainer when he was a puppy, but I hadn't heard from his socialite "mom" in over a year, so I figured my services were no longer needed.

"Guess I'm back on the payroll," I said to myself.

I got my pager and looked up Geneva's phone number. I dialed it. Got a rude beep in my ear and a canned message saying, "All circuits are busy now, please try your call again later."

While a teacup-sized pooch hiding under his mistresses' bed hardly seemed like an emergency to me, I must admit the opportunity to see Geneva in the flesh again was too tempting to pass up. There had been a spark between us. Even though it never did ignite, I still had hope.

In addition to my group classes, I also gave private lessons. There were so many bored and beautiful Bel Air and Beverly Hills trophy wives—and I was a young, good-looking man then—that I seldom lacked female company. But it's always the ones that got away you remember best, isn't it?

Geneva was only twenty-five but thanks to her family's fortune, she was rich beyond the dreams of most people twice her age. She had blonde hair, blue eyes, cotton-candy lips and a statuesque figure bought and paid for by her daddy as her Sweet Sixteen birthday present.

Her voice was helium, her heels were just as high. The press called her "Baby Angelyne" after the famous billboard queen of the Sunset Strip. But Angelyne's star was fading, while Geneva's was just getting fired up.

The celebrity socialite may have looked like a walking cliché, but she was actually pretty bright. She had goals. She had a touch of talent. And she loved animals, which was a major plus in my book. The press took her to task for dying Boo-Boo pink, but the tint was organic and, in my opinion at the time, harmless… except to the animal's pride.

I lived in Santa Monica, not far from Geneva. In case you're not familiar, the toniest zip codes in the area include four main guard-gated communities: Bel Air Crest, Beverly Park, The Summit and Mulholland Estates. For those who desire access to the Bel Air Country Club, the Crest is the first choice. That's where she lived, all by herself in a three-story Gothic-Tudor mansion. I'd heard the place was fully automated—a "smart home" long before the term was in casual conversation—and rigged with cameras, intercoms and touch pads throughout. I'd been there before, when I was one of Geneva's hired hands, but I never saw beyond the foyer. We did our puppy training outdoors, on the gorgeously-manicured, bright green front lawn.

As I pulled up to the guard gate, I felt confident enough in my '92 BMW. It was no Lambo, but I fit in well enough.

The guard stepped to the edge of his shack and gave me the once-over.

"Stiles Whitaker," I said, handing him my driver's license as proof.

He checked his list, saw I was on it, gave me a curt nod and opened the gate.

As I drove through, I saw two loose Chihuahuas scoot in after me. I stopped my car, looking for their owner so I could chide them for disobeying the leash law. But there was no one to be seen. Even the dogs had disappeared.

I continued up the immaculate avenue, until I came to Geneva's private drive. I edged up to the intercom and hit the buzzer.

"Mr. Whitaker?" It was her manager, Enrique.

Odd. Shouldn't a servant be answering the page? I shrugged it off and rolled through the slow-opening wrought iron gate. The road to the top was long and winding, but it was very pretty, so I didn't mind. The place looked like a woodland forest, complete with pine trees, peppertrees, jacarandas, birds of paradise, wild rose bushes and the occasional wandering peacock.

I parked in the circular driveway. On my previous visits, a valet had come for my car and a doorman let me into the mansion. This time, there was no one. I saw three other cars parked: A candy-apple red Corvette, a classic Rolls from the 50s and a white Mercedes panel van bearing a personalized license plate reading: Z-E-R-O-K-E-L.

Oh, great. That meant Geneva's hip-hop star boyfriend, Zero Kelvin, was here too. So much for the spark.

Then I chuckled to myself. Two grown men couldn't get one pampered pooch to come out from under his mistresses' bed? Ridiculous. And where was Geneva, anyway? I'd begun to suspect she was out of town and didn't even know I'd been called in for reinforcement. Then I wondered who'd be paying for my time. I hate say it, but I was strapped.

No sooner had my TucciPolo handmade Italian shoe soles hit the pavement than the huge front door opened. Just a crack. No one came out. Again: Odd.

Mildly alarmed now, I made my way to the front door. I pushed it open slowly, staying put on the sisal-fiber porch mat.

"Come in," said Enrique. "And close the door behind you."

I did so.

The house was cool, drafty even. It had an empty, lifeless feel to it even though, once I entered, I saw people inside.

Enrique was standing, wringing his hands. He looked stricken, though immaculate in his trademark off-white suit. Standing at the foot of the left side of the sweeping double staircase—reminiscent of Tony Montana's in the movie *Scarface*—was Zero Kelvin. He was wiping tears. And then, seated on the massive leather sofa just a bit further inside, was an attractive woman and two older men. I'd soon learn that they were Jackson the gardener, Willis the vegan chef and Sheila, Geneva's personal yoga instructor.

"What's going on here?" I demanded, instinctively keeping my voice down. "Where's Geneva?"

"Come with me," replied Enrique, turning toward the staircase. He passed Kelvin, who in turn followed. So did I.

"And where's Boo-Boo? Is he still hiding?" I asked.

There was no reply.

As we walked up the magnificent staircase, I glanced at the framed photos and painted portraits hung on the adjacent wall. They were almost all of Geneva—and Boo-Boo. Plus a couple of her parents, since they did pay for the place, after all. Token acknowledgment.

I followed the men from the slick mottled marble steps to the Macassar ebony wood flooring and into a chamber carpeted in pink sheep's wool. Geneva's bedroom.

Sure, I'd seen pictures of it in magazine spreads—and her famous sex tape, *Kama Sutra Barbi*—but up close and personal, it really was quite something. It would have been perfectly lovely, had it not been for the dead body lying on the floor beside the bed.

Geneva was wearing pink velour yoga pants and a sports bra and she was barefoot. It looked as though she'd been interrupted while getting dressed for her class with Sheila. There was a lot of blood.

I'm no medical expert, but it looked as though her throat had been slashed while she was still alive, causing a spectacular spray of arterial blood. Crimson splashed the white goose down bedspread, the mirrored nightstand and the Tiffany lamp atop it. It soaked the carpet around her head like some kind of perverted halo.

"What happened?" I gasped, rooted to my spot in the doorway.

"That fucking mutt killed her!" Kelvin spat.

I almost laughed. *Boo-Boo?* The pink pooch weighed all of two-and-half pounds and probably couldn't stop shaking long enough to get a decent bite of anything, let alone tear out a human throat.

"We don't know that," Enrique said cautiously. "She could have been murdered by an intruder and then he... Boo-Boo... um, took a taste?"

Kelvin's expression grew stormier. "No way, Jose—"

"Enrique."

"Whatever. Look at her ankle. The little piece of crap bit her to bring her down and—"

I interrupted. "I couldn't help but notice, we're the only ones here. No cops, no ambulance. What's up?"

Enrique nodded. "We didn't call them. Look, she's beyond help. But her image isn't. The Hughes family doesn't need another scandal. I need to figure this out."

"I don't give a fuck. I'm out of here."

"Not so fast," Enrique said. "I know about your gambling problem, Stiles. I know you are hundreds of thousands in the hole. Keeping this quiet could be to your financial benefit."

I was listening. But wondering, too. Why call me at all? I had a feeling there was something they weren't telling me.

Or maybe Kelvin was right. Even so, why bring me into it?

Kelvin was crying again. Kneeling near his girlfriend, quietly sobbing.

Damn. Maybe he really did love her.

"I'm sure gonna miss boning you, babe," he whispered.

Kelvin hooked up with Geneva after seeing her sex tape. He didn't have one, himself—he purposely avoided the possibility by making his Mercedes van into a rolling sex shack. I'd read an interview with him in *Rolling Stone* and he said the so-called Love Lounge was one way he could control his environment at all times. No cameras or recorders were allowed. Not that he cared about his image—in fact, he cultivated the bad boy thing—but he did care about his money. The last thing he wanted, he said, was to be paying royalties to disgruntled groupies and greedy lawyers for the rest of his life. "I'm ice cold," he'd said in the interview.

That was his mantra and his namesake. At the physically impossible-to-reach temperature of zero kelvin, or minus 459.67 degrees Fahrenheit, atoms would stop moving. Einstein or somebody proved that, I think.

Anyway, it seemed the bereaved boyfriend did have feelings after all. He sniffled and rose to his sneakered feet. He was dressed street chic. If you were around in the 90s, you know the clothes were loud and roomy. From his faux leopard fur bucket hat to his Pony Slam Dunks, Kelvin was a hip-hop cliché department store mannequin. But I had to admit, he wasn't as homely as he seemed in pictures or his music videos.

Enrique, on the other hand… total weasel.

The manager straightened his tie and cleared his throat.

I tore my gaze from the gore-fest.

"The dog is under the bed," he said flatly. "You have to get him out. And take him with you."

Yes, I remembered my purpose. *Piece of cake,* I thought. *Remove dog from premises, keep mouth shut, get paid.*

As if on cue, Boo-Boo started growling. A low, guttural, menacing and somehow *knowing* sound.

I didn't think for a moment he was the culprit. He was probably staying beside his mistress, trying to protect her. No wonder he wouldn't let Enrique or Kelvin get him. The poor thing was grieving.

I reached into my trouser pocket and removed a small bag of Whitaker Doggie Bites—my own brand, carried in chains across the nation. And not selling. Dogs didn't like them, generally. But I had a feeling Boo-Boo must be so stressed and hungry, he'd probably welcome any sort of snack. He'd be eating from my hand in no time and we'd be on our way.

I circumnavigated the crime scene, moving to the far side of the girly, canopied bed. I knelt down and lifted the duvet. Boo-Boo's growls turned to sharp, angry yips. He snarled.

It was dim in the room, despite the fact it was still morning on a sunny spring day. "Hey, could you catch the lights?" I asked.

"Not working," Enrique said. "The whole system's out."

I shrugged and ducked down, peering into the shadows. I saw a flash of white fangs and felt a stab of indescribable agony.

I came to, lying on the leather sofa. Sheila was holding a cold compress to my forehead. I struggled to sit up and she gently guided me. I felt woozy. The house was nearly dark. There were some candles burning on the coffee table and there was a blaze in the fireplace.

I blinked, then noticed I only felt it in one eye. I reached up and touched bandages over one side of my face. "What happened?" I stammered.

"You were bitten," Sheila said gently.

"That fucken mutt took your eye out!" It was Kelvin, coming into focus. "I told you! Some dog trainer you are," he sneered.

The insult barely registered as I processed the far more pressing, distressing news. Took my eye out? As in… *out?*

I pressed the bandage, in spite of my pain. There was a hollow where my eye should have been. I don't mind it now. In fact, even though I could have a state-of-the-art prosthetic, I prefer my cool eyepatch. Chicks dig it. It really adds to my mystique. But then, it was horrible. I could feel my good eye tearing up with the shock. Then I felt dizzy again and collapsed back onto the pillow.

Enrique stepped forward and flicked my forehead. "No," he said sternly. "Wake up. You've been coasting on Geneva's stash for long enough. It's almost dark."

"Nobody's called the cops yet?" I asked, my voice weak. "This is ridiculous. Enough is enough."

I half-sat, then slowly stood as Sheila steadied me. She looked at me with concern. She now wore a long coat, probably one of Geneva's, over her skimpy yoga outfit. Her sun-streaked hair shone in the candle-light and her pretty face held a grim expression.

"We can't," she said.

"She's right." It was Willis, the chef. "This here house is wired. Everything is automated. The dogs chewed through the phone wires. And the electricity. The generator worked for a while, till they peed in the diesel and chewed through the fuel line."

Dogs, plural?

"Now the doors and windows won't open," said Sheila.

"So, break a window!" I said.

I was able to stand on my own now.

"Look," said Kelvin, pointing toward the paned glass French doors on the far side of the room. They led to the garden. Slowly, *en masse*, we made our way to the wall of windows. I saw a shape lying beside the back garden. It was Jackson, the gardener. He'd been killed by what I guessed was a pack of vicious animals. Dogs? I didn't see any around.

"I tried to make a break for it earlier," said Kelvin. "They chewed through the tires of the Love Lounge… and all of our cars."

"So? We run!" I said.

Enrique shook his head. "I've still got a job to do here. And so do you."

"Yeah. Aren't you pissed?" Kelvin demanded. "That pipsqueak shit took your eye, dude! Let's go get him!"

"And he killed your girlfriend," I added, getting fired up.

"Oh, yeah," Kelvin muttered. "Yeah!" He jutted his weak chin up defiantly.

"Boo-Boo is still upstairs, as far as I know," Enrique said.

"Let's go!" I said, leading the charge. Such as it was.

Only Kelvin, Enrique and myself headed up the stairs. "Good luck," Sheila called after us.

"Wait a minute," said Willis.

We paused.

"I just got a brand-new Masahiro Butcher's knife, carbon steel." He turned and dashed off, disappearing into the darkness beyond the doorway to the hall that led, presumably, to the kitchen.

We heard a horrible commotion. Willis screamed. We heard his body thud to the marble floor. Nobody moved to help him. He shrieked and then we heard loud guttural, wolf-like growls… but they were high-pitched, coming from small bodies. There an awful gurgling sound and flailing.

"Oh, no," Sheila cried. "They're inside the house!"

This time she led the way upstairs. We blindly scurried, taking two and three stairs at a time. We huddled in the landing, shaking. There was still a chill in the air, but now there was a tang of blood and fear.

Finally, someone spoke. It was me. "If this *is* dogs," I said, "then they're in a pack. We need to take out their leader."

"Boo-Boo," Kelvin spat. "I always did hate that runty rat."

"Well, of course it's Boo-Boo," Enrique said. He looked at me with disdain. "If you'd done your job right in the first place, we'd all be home now. I'd have everything figured out for the press and you'd be looking at your big bank balance."

"Me, too," said Kelvin.

I turned to Enrique. "You were going to pay everyone off?"

Sheila nodded. "Look, I —" then she dipped her head. "I'm sorry, Stiles."

I touched the bandage over my throbbing eye socket. "It's OK. I'm gonna have to get used to people saying 'look, see here, watch it,' and all that stuff. Don't worry about it."

"I didn't even have to be here," Sheila said. "I got my dates mixed up." She sighed. Terrible time to be disorganized.

"Like I said, we've gotta take out the leader." I gathered myself and headed into Geneva's bedroom.

It was darker than before, but I was relieved to see—with my one good eye—that someone had draped a sheet over the dead body. Blood bloomed at the head, but it was an improvement at least.

The moment I stepped onto the expensive, plush carpet, I heard an ominous growl. There was vibrato behind it. It was a menacing sound, one that made cold sweat pop out on my brow. I paused, listening. An irate yip came from the walk-in closet. Slowly, I headed towards it.

The closet was even darker. But I noticed something: A flashlight lying helpfully on the floor at my feet. Perhaps *too* helpfully, though the thought didn't hit my bingo button at the time.

All was quiet now. I picked up the flashlight—pink and blingy, of course—and turned it on. The beam was weak, but I was able to see Geneva's abundant wardrobe, row upon row of designer shoes and several handbags hanging.

One of the handbags moved.

It was a Chanel, the Caviar Quilted Medallion Tote that Geneva always carried

Boo-Boo in. *Hmmm*, I thought. *The little guy slipped up.*

I tiptoed toward the bag, picking up a lethal-looking Jimmy Choo stiletto along the way. Its spike heel was like an icepick. I'd rip open the purse and brain the bastard before he knew what hit him. I stopped. Maybe I should just take the tote off its hook and smash it against the floor and walls until its killer cargo was dead meat. *Yes, that's a good idea.*

As I reached toward Boo-Boo's hiding place, he poked his head out. I froze. His eyes glowered a greenish red in the beam of light. He looked... evil. In fact, his eyes seemed to get redder by the nanosecond. But no, I told myself. All dogs' eyes glow. There's a reflective layer called the tapetum lucidum just behind the retina in animals and that's all this was.

But it scared me. And he knew it.

The teacup pup rose up out of the purse. I swore at the time he was levitating, but later I convinced myself it had to be my mind playing cruel tricks on me. My depth perception was off, after all. And no matter what the pooch may or may not have done to his mistress, he was still just a dog.

I held my light on him and clutched the stiletto.

Boo-Boo's camel-colored hackles rose, forming a stiff mohawk at the base of his neck. He was trembling with rage. He sneered, exposing a row of razor sharp teeth, punctuated with dagger-like fangs. His pink-tinted paws flexed. He was getting ready to jump.

As he flew at me, I was flung against the wall and into a row of soft fur coats. But it wasn't Boo-Boo that knocked me aside; it was Kelvin. He saved me.

As I scrambled to my feet, my hand connected with something moist and spongey on the floor. My eye. Squashed now. The dog had dropped it there and lured me inside to find it. The *asshole*!

Then I saw Boo-Boo tearing out the closet door and dashing across the room.

Kelvin turned to me and grinned. His gold grill twinkled, then he was off—after the dog.

I caught up with him at the bedroom door. I could hear the tic-tic of Boo-Boo's claws hitting the hardwood floor. I could hear the heavy breathing of Sheila and Enrique, somewhere still on the landing.

Suddenly, Boo-Boo was back. He seized Kelvin's ankle, gnashing his tiny but formidable teeth. The dog dashed off again, as if daring us to chase him. I grabbed Kelvin's shirt tail. "Don't—" I exclaimed. "Let him go." I gestured to my ruined face.

Kelvin stood tall and fixed me in his bloodshot gaze. "I am a ghost driving a meat coated skeleton made from stardust, riding a rock hurtling through space...*I fear nothing*!" And off he went into the void.

I peered around the doorjamb and saw Boo-Boo dart out from where he'd been hidden against the wall. As Kelvin neared the balustrade, his Pony Slam Dunks collided with the dainty dog's torso and he flew forward. He was propelled over the railing and without even a gasp, he was over the edge.

So much for his philosophical Buddhist ideology. Fearlessness had cost the hip-hop superstar his life. I heard a squelchy thud as his head met the marble floor.

"Oh, shit!" It was Enrique. I figured he was responding to Kelvin's sudden death, but no.

It was much, much worse than that.

We'd been trapped on the landing for over an hour, trying to figure out what to do. Boo-Boo blocked our egress farther into the house, while a pack of purebred Chihuahuas congregated on the stairs. Still more pampered pooches stayed in the foyer, dining on Kelvin's splattered brains and leaving bloody pawprints on Geneva's imported flooring. When I glanced down, I saw two puppies fighting over one of the rapper's severed fingers, pulling at it, one on each end, as if it were a stretchy toy. I choked down bile and didn't look again.

"Where did they all come from?" Enrique asked me, as if I had all the answers. I figured they had to come from the immediate area. Chihuahuas aren't known for their stamina.

Since I had plenty of time to contemplate our situation, I remembered all the "missing dog" posters I'd seen and more recently, the stray dogs entering the gated community.

"I don't know," I replied. "But I think Boo-Boo is the key to… whatever it is that's happening."

"Duh," spat Enrique. "You already said that."

"Hear him out," said Sheila, putting her hand on my arm. She turned to me, wan but still quite beautiful. "Go on."

I sighed, more shakily than I meant to. "OK. You know that old movie, *The Birds*?"

Sheila nodded. "I love Hitchcock."

Enrique stared blankly.

"Well," I continued. "Birds have a sort of telepathy that enables them to move as one. Flocking is just one kind of collective behavior. It's called murmuration. Computers can do it too, though it's only in the early stages of development…"

"You mean like how computers can play chess?" Sheila asked.

"Not exactly… but don't quote me on that. As a trainer, I've seen evidence of a form of ESP in dogs. I've been thinking—what if these microchips implanted in the dogs are somehow interconnected?"

I stole a glance at Boo-Boo, who was standing in the deepening shadows. He growled, low and menacing. *Did he actually understand what I was saying?*

"I've been wondering too, if all these things that are done to these animals—dying their fur, painting their toenails, drenching them in perfume—if it's not somehow embalming them alive and affecting their natural instincts."

Enrique scoffed. "Who cares why this is happening! These pissants have killed four people. *Four!* And they've got three of us trapped here. I say we grab Boo-Boo and throw him over the banister. Give him a taste of his own medicine."

Boo-Boo yipped and instantaneously charged Enrique, covering an astonishing amount of ground as he leapt into the air aiming at the man's throat. The Hollywood hotshot bleated like a baby lamb and scrambled backwards. Catching the scent of fear, the pack of dogs on the stairs advanced.

Somehow, I managed to grab Boo-Boo by the tip of his tail. I yanked him away from Enrique and he fell to the floor with an outraged yelp. Sheila sprang into action as well, tackling the raging canine and pinning him underneath her body.

With a preternatural strength, Boo-Boo wriggled free and darted down the stairs, joining his brethren. He stared up at us, murder in his eyes.

The three of us collected ourselves. This was a lucky break. Now that the landing and upper floor was unguarded, one of us could climb out a window and get help. Or hell, why not all of us?

I whispered my plan to my companions and we slowly moved toward Geneva's bedroom. The swarm of Chihuahuas shadowed us, moving up the stairs. Some of the dogs were so small, they couldn't just step up on their own. I stared in disbelief as the larger ones made stepping stones of themselves, helping the weaker links.

As we got closer to the bedroom door, the first wave of dogs cleared the top stair. Growling and snapping, they broke into a run and headed for us. Boo-Boo was in the lead, tongue lolling, running for all he was worth.

"Hurry!" I yelled, bringing up the rear. Enrique fell into the room; Sheila and I were on his heels. We tripped over him, but somehow, I managed to catch the door with my foot and slammed it shut just as Boo-Boo and crew reached it.

I heard howls of frustration and the frantic clawing of many small paws at the door.

"Ha! You bite-sized bastards! Got ya!" Enrique crowed, as if it were he who'd foiled them.

I was liking him less and less with each passing moment, but then again—I never liked him in the first place.

As we knelt on the plush floor, Sheila hugged me. "Thank you," she murmured.

I gave her a half-smile, then helped her to her feet. Not that she needed it. That yoga bod of hers had muscles on top of muscles.

We watched as Enrique stood, then swayed. "What. The. Fuck." He shook his head and put his hands to his untouched throat.

I looked around the room for means of escape. The sinews in my hollow socket automatically contracted and I winced at the sting.

I walked over to the poofy bed, trying not to look at the prone, shrouded figure beside it and tugged at the sheer canopy material. It came free easily.

Sheila went to the window and opened it.

Enrique just stood there. His eyes seemed a bit glassy.

I tied the canopy to one of the bedposts, only half-noticing the silence in the hallway. Were the dogs gone? If so, where were they?

"Oh no," Sheila cried, looking outside. "They're in the driveway."

I felt the figurative wind leave my sails. *Well, shit. Now what?*

"We've got to try," I said.

"What if I go downstairs to distract them, while you go out the window?" Sheila said.

"I like it. But it should be the other way around." After all, the person doing the distracting was more vulnerable. Plus, I worried that my lack of depth-perception would be an issue if I had to shimmy down a gossamer sheet. What if I misjudged the landing and broke my ankle? "Do you have your car keys?" I asked.

She shook her head. "They're downstairs, in the living room."

I reached into my pocket, got mine, then handed them to her. "BMW," I said.

I looked over at Geneva's manager, who seemed to be slipping rapidly into a state of shock. Or maybe it was just cappuccino and cocaine withdrawals. "Enrique?" I said gently.

He looked at me and through me. I walked over to him and guided him to Geneva's walk-in closet, which was the size of a North Hollywood apartment. He'd be comfortable enough in there for the time being. I placed him inside and shut the door, making sure I heard the latch catch.

Our plan almost worked.

The dogs got confused when we split up. Barking while wagging their tails—a sure sign of consternation—they let us get as far as the driveway. Although it was dark, there was enough moonlight to see that the tires of all the cars had been slashed and bitten until they were flatter than piss on a platter. Kelvin wasn't exaggerating.

"So what?" I said to Sheila. "I'll drive on the rims."

As we neared my sedan, I noticed the cabin light was on. It flickered then went out. The door had either been left open by me, or somehow the dogs had managed to do it. The battery was probably dead.

Probably. It was still worth a try. I flung the driver's door open, then propelled myself back as I was hit by a wave of sickening stench.

The dogs had not only defecated all over my car—on the seats and on the pedals—but they'd urinated and thrown up as well.

"Ugh," choked Sheila.

I banged the door shut.

Now that we were together, the dogs had their target lined up. They honed in.

Boo-Boo barked once, then led the onslaught. His ears were back, pinned to his head, making his bulging eyes that much more malevolent.

The entrance to the house was blocked. The window was too far to run to. And I'd rather die than get inside my car.

"Come on!" I hissed in Sheila's ear, pulling her by her wrist.

Luck had to be on our side. Just this once. *Please.*

We made a beeline for the Love Lounge, praying to the lords of hip-hop and all that was holy, that Kelvin had left it unlocked.

He did!

We leapt inside, slamming the door shut. I caught Boo-Boo's snapping muzzle, crushing it in the jaws of the heavy van. He screamed, backing off.

Sheila and I dove for the locks.

I saw Boo-Boo frantically licking at his bloodied chops as his posse circled him. They sensed his weakness and they liked it. I shuddered.

"Come on," I said to Sheila, guiding her into the rear of the van. It was indeed a love lounge complete with a bed, mirrored ceiling and a mini-fridge stocked with champagne and fresh strawberries.

As I popped the cork, we heard the sounds of Boo-Boo being torn limb from limb.

Sheila and I shared the bottle, then fell asleep in each other's arms on Kelvin's well-used mattress.

We woke up at dawn. Sore, stressed and hungover... but untouched and alive. I moved the curtains aside and looked out. It was a glorious morning. A peacock followed by two peahens waddled across the driveway.

The dogs were gone.

At least, we thought so. We waited at least another half an hour before venturing out.

I stepped onto the pavement, holding my breath.

Nothing.

Sheila exited the van and we looked all around us.

"Enrique," she said.

"Yeah, we'd better see if he's OK," I said grudgingly.

The front door to the house stood open.

We entered, the sight of Kelvin's desecrated corpse still lying on its back, head cracked open. Only now there was... I blinked. *Was that a gun in his hand?*

I noticed the lights were on and I could sense the hum of the house's central air and heat.

Then I heard a voice. It was Enrique. We stepped into the foyer and then the den. Enrique was sitting at a desk and he was on the phone. He was already spinning the story.

Thanks to a covert cleanup crew, fixers, threats and payoffs, the official tawdry tale was that Kelvin had killed everyone in the house, then himself. The Beverly Hills coroner never reported any details of an animal attack.

Still, stories got out. Whispers here and there. Something strange that happened behind the gates of Bel Air. Maybe our devil dogs weren't the only ones. The Weekly World News had accounts of alien invasions—there was actually a comet that night, they reported—while still others said it was a military takeover and several citizens were killed by friendly fire.

I never really understood why the truth wasn't told. But to tell *you* the truth, I didn't mind. My reputation would have been ruined. Some dog-whisperer, bested by a pack of pedigreed frou-frou fluffballs. As it was, no one was the wiser. The killer Chihuahuas inexplicably went back to normal. They wandered back to their homes, wagging their tails and begging for treats. Not Whitaker Doggie Bites, mind you—those never did catch on.

They say shared harrowing experiences can bring people closer together. Sheila and I took our hush money and went to Tahiti. We had a passionate fling, but it didn't last. The only thing that's lasted—she's gone, my money is gone—are my memories of that awful night. Even Enrique is dead. And buried with him is my annual payoff.

So, I have no reason to keep quiet anymore. I'm selling this statement to the highest bidder.

Yes, I still gamble. The dog races, if you can believe it. Crazy, I know. But sometimes, when I look at those greyhounds, I think I detect something... *knowing...* in their eyes.

Tasty Waves

Bjorn had never seen a prettier face: The girl's eyes were bluer than the ocean and a constellation of freckles was scattered artfully across her pert, slightly upturned nose. Her plump, naturally seashell pink lips were parted in a slight, sexy smile. She had light, long blonde hair kissed with streaks of honey. He wished he could see the rest of her, but her body was submerged. She poked through the opening of a life-preserver, holding herself aloft with petite but muscular arms.

Bjorn usually surfed Zuma in the winter, but he'd decided it was too crowded even in the off-season. Today, he wanted a break from the bros so he'd taken Pacific Coast Highway, passed Point Dume and watched for the small sign on the right for El Matador State Beach. El Matador was strewn with rocks and surrounded by craggy cliffsides—there was a rugged splendor to the place that appealed to Bjorn's rougher side. He was glad he'd come here this morning; otherwise he might not have seen the girl.

At first, he wasn't sure what he saw. Was it a seal? A cluster of seaweed? But as the pale October sun broke over the horizon, he was sure that the shape was human. Using his custom-painted Serena pintail as a paddleboard, Bjorn braved the colder depths and headed toward the person, who, he imagined, wasn't out there for fun. "Hey!" he shouted, as he approached. "Dude, are you OK?"

The shape, backlit by the rising sun, came into focus as Bjorn expertly guided his surfboard toward it. When he got close, about ten feet away, he saw that it was a beautiful young woman. Her gender didn't change Bjorn's greeting, though. "Dude," he repeated, "What are you doing out here? Do you need help?"

All of a sudden, the song *Survival* by Muse pushed its way into his mind. Why?! He hated that freaking song. Earworms always came along at the worst possible time. Just as the chorus of vexing voices was coming up, Bjorn was carried on the tide which brought him several feet closer to his goal.

The girl fixed her gaze on Bjorn, hinted at a smile, paused, then started flailing. She sank for a brief moment and came up sputtering seawater. She gasped but didn't shout.

"I'm coming," Bjorn reassured her. "Be cool." He was shivering now, wearing only his short johns and the shore was further away than he'd thought. He took in the life preserver, thinking her boat must have sunk. "Is there anyone else with you?"

The girl took a few awkward stabs at the surface of the water, as if trying to swim toward him.

As Bjorn closed the gap, he encouraged her, "Kick with your feet. Come on, I'm almost there!"

She didn't try, or maybe she didn't understand him. Bjorn noticed a glazed look in her unblinking eyes. The poor girl was probably going into shock, now that rescue was on the way and she could finally relax.

Now Bjorn could touch her hand. When he did, he was amazed, peripherally, at its warmth. His heart began to thump and he felt a blush rise to his cheeks. He looked at her upturned face again. Damn, she was gorgeous.

"I've got you," he said, panting. Bjorn was in excellent shape, but he felt unusually weak as he got closer to her. Lightheaded, even. Still holding the girl's wrist, Bjorn turned back toward the shore and half-paddled, half-rode the relentless tide, as he pulled his foundling closer and closer to safety.

They were almost able to touch sand underfoot when she shrieked and with a mighty yank, she pulled herself free of his grasp. Bjorn stopped and turned to face her. The girl's eyes were wide with terror at the sight of the shore. She shifted her gaze to one of the many outcroppings of sea caves. She pointed to it and whined like a seal pup.

Bjorn figured she was traumatized. But she had to get to shore. He reached for her wrist again. He swiped at air. She was gone. The life preserver popped on the surface, empty.

"Heyyy!" Bjorn shouted. He dipped his head underwater and though he was in the shallows it was too murky to see anything. Where could she have gone so quickly?

Panic seized him. His hackles rose. He looked for a telltale fin, but there was nothing. He let out a sigh of relief. The great whites usually only trolled the Malibu beaches in the summer and were cleared out by October. Everything was going to be fine.

Then he heard a piercing shriek and his eyes followed the sound. It was the girl. She had somehow managed to swim underwater to the caves and she bobbed at the opening, beckoning him. Meringue seafoam clung to her, but as she rose up, he caught a glimpse of her magnificent breasts. He whistled low and whispered to himself, "Nice rack."

Bjorn was shivering. He looked at the nearby shore, knowing that his warm clothes and his phone were in his El Camino. He could call 9-1-1 and somebody else would come and get the girl. There was still a good hour of surf left.

But there was something about her… she was so very beautiful. He just had to be close to her one more time, then he'd call for rescue.

Bjorn heaved himself onto his pin and paddled quickly toward the jagged, moss-coated caves. The waves got smaller and choppier the closer he got, and if possible, the water was even icier. Sea-spray needled his face and he dipped his head, beelining to where he'd just seen the girl. When he arrived, she was gone.

She must be inside, Bjorn thought, lowering his right leg to see if he could touch bottom and praying there was no coral. His bare foot touched soft, silty sand that was surprisingly warm and velvety to the touch. In the waist-high water, he walked into the dark, fetid cave. The smell of live moss and dead fish hit him like a backhand. He coughed and hesitated in the entrance. "Ummm…" he called out, "you in here?"

A splashing sound came in reply. Bjorn forged ahead through the ever-shallowing water. He turned a corner that took him deeper into the cave and led to a large alcove. The girl was there, huddled against the wall. She had her arms crossed, covering her chest. But she couldn't cover the glistening, iridescent fish tail from which her torso stemmed. She looked at him with wide eyes. It was then that Bjorn saw she could not look at him with anything other than wide eyes, for she had no eyelids.

"What the…?" Bjorn blurted, rooted to the spot. He took a step back. "No way, dude." Then he grinned. "Whoa, that is one killer costume. Damn, it looks real." She smiled and Bjorn saw that her teeth were in tiny, sharp rows. "Jeez, the teeth even." Bjorn wanted a closer look, but then he remembered how he'd found her. "Hey, are you OK? What happened?" He figured she must have been on her way to some kind of performance. "Where's the rest of your party?"

The girl remained silent, but she slapped her tail against a thin puddle twice—hard. Then she shook her head.

Since he'd only had one bong-load before leaving his bungalow that morning, Bjorn caught on quickly. "One for yes and two for no?"

The girl slapped her tail into the puddle once.

"There's no one but you?"

One decisive slap. Then the girl held out her arms.

Bjorn ducked under the ceiling of the alcove and knelt beside her. She whined, then took him into her arms. Bjorn had never felt such deep, abiding love in any embrace before—not even from his mother when he was a baby. Not that he would have remembered being a baby under ordinary circumstances, but a flood of recollection washed over him, of all the love he'd ever been given. And all those loves combined were nothing compared to this. When she loosened her grasp, tears sprang to his eyes. Bjorn wiped at them and drew back. *What just happened?* he wondered.

The girl took his hand in hers. There was delicate webbing between her fingers, Bjorn noticed, as she guided his callused palm to her body. Not to her hooters as he would have liked, but downward to her scaly tail. He felt a warm seepage and saw slimy blood oozing from a small but deep wound.

Bjorn blinked. The cut was in the scaled part of her costume. No… not her costume. Her *body*. He knew, instinctively, that this girl was a creature—when she'd held him, he felt many hearts beating. One was his own, of course. The others were… hers.

"You need help," Bjorn said.

The girl's expression tightened in fear.

Bjorn took one of her hands in his. "It's OK. I know you're special. I know I can't bring anyone here. But I can take care of you until you're healed."

She nodded, then flapped her glittering green tail against the flat rock floor once. She lay back against the cave wall, as if struck by an onset of weakness.

Bjorn turned to go, but he felt a strange and overwhelming urge to stay with her. He wanted to hold her again. His pulse quickened and he looked back at her. Her face was turned to the wall and her breaths were shallow. She whined sadly. That clinched it. Bjorn had to get some first aid and food to her ASAP.

"Later," he said in parting and he turned and waded back into the water.

His board was waiting for him just outside the cave. The instant the fresh sea breeze greeted him, Bjorn took a long pull. The chill braced him. Bjorn placed the board flat, hopped on and went back to shore.

He could see his car parked beyond the beach. It was still the only vehicle in the lot, he noted as it began to rain. Even in Malibu, an early and wet Wednesday morning meant a warm robe and hot coffee for most. The other diehard surfers were probably at Zuma. But it was odd to not spot anyone at all, not even a dog-walker or a vagrant. He shrugged the questions away and hurried toward his sun-bleached 1972 El Camino. Once there, he tossed his board in the back, shucked his johns and put on a pair of board shorts, a long-sleeved sweater and his favorite Vans.

His bungalow, more of a yurt really, wasn't far. He was set up in his Aunt Ebba's backyard just a few miles away and he knew she'd still be sleeping—maybe he could nab some food from her pantry. Bjorn only had some sardines and crackers at his place… and he wasn't sure if the girl would eat fish. She'd probably consider it cannibalism.

Once home, Bjorn decided to take a shower and relax. The girl seemed so far away now. Maybe he'd even dreamed the whole thing. He settled himself into his beanbag, packed the bowl of his bong and lit up. After a couple of long draws, he lay back and went to the news on his phone. He went to the local page, to see if any wrecks or accidents were reported from off the coast of El Matador. There wasn't anything, so he decided to look up mermaids. He didn't see anything about sightings but fell into a deep rabbit hole of wikis and videos.

Bjorn had always loved the mysteries of the ocean more than anything. When he was a boy, he wanted to grow up to be a marine biologist. He was fascinated by the otherworldly physiology of sea life. He'd been captivated by the fact that octopus and squid, both cephalopods, have three hearts. One systemic, and then two more pumps that force blood to the gills. He vaguely remembered feeling several heartbeats when the girl—if there even had been a girl; he wasn't so sure now—had embraced him.

He decided to see if there were any other sea dwellers with multiple hearts and found one, right away. It was a gruesome-looking eel-like thing called a hagfish. It had four hearts. He hadn't heard of that one before. Or had he? He read a lot every day and forgot even more.

Ironically it was Hagfish Day which, the article said, occurs every year on the third Wednesday of October. "There's a holiday for friggin' everything," Bjorn muttered, reaching for his bong. Then he decided to look up National Bong Day. It was on 4/20, of course. He'd have to wait for months to celebrate. "Oh wells," he chuckled to himself, "Every day is National Bong Day here in Bjorn's Beach Bungalow."

After some time, Bjorn decided he was hungry. So, he took the three steps over to his kitchen area and got himself a beer, the can of sardines and a tube of crackers. He returned to the beanbag and went back to Googling. He wanted to learn more about this hagfish thing.

He was amazed to see there were seventy-six species of hagfish, each uglier than the next and that they could go for months without food. That's because they absorbed most of their nutrients through their skin. "Hagfish have two rows of tooth-like structures made of keratin that they use to burrow deep into carcasses," the article read. They were scavengers of the sea, rarely hunting game. They did that only when starving. "While eating carrion or live prey, they tie their tails into knots to generate torque and increase the force of their bites." The article went on to say, "When harassed, glands lining their bodies secrete stringy proteins that, upon contact with seawater, expand into transparent, sticky slime that stuns any living thing that comes into contact with it."

Bjorn pressed the home button on his phone. "Gross," he muttered, setting the device onto his chest. It was siesta time.

The place was completely dark when Bjorn woke up.

He pawed around for his phone and brought the bright, glowing screen to his protesting eyes. Damn. It was nearly midnight. Had he really slept all day, evening and night? He glanced over at his bong. He'd only done a couple of bowls... hadn't he? He shook his head, stretched and yawned. He got up, figuring he'd have to take a monster piss by now even if he didn't feel it yet.

While he was in his tiny cubicle of a bathroom, Bjorn heard his phone chime. Who would be texting him at this hour? Not that it was too late—or too early—but it just seemed weird.

The message was an hours-old face time from Roddy, his friend since high school. Bjorn swiped the screen and his friend's face came up. "Bruh! You OK, man? Coast Guard called your moms and she called your aunt but no one can find you... what up?"

Puzzled, Bjorn touched the Call Back button. He pressed and pressed, but the phone wasn't responding. Cheap-ass old thing. It slipped from Bjorn's grasp and he didn't bother to pick it up. He went to his window and peered out. From across the backyard, he could see that Aunt Ebba's lights were on. That was suspicious. Ebba was always sound asleep by nine.

In just a few strides he covered the distance from his yurt to her back door. He turned the knob, but his hand kept slipping. He heard voices. His aunt was crying and someone was consoling her. It was Peter, her ex-husband, Bjorn was sure. Dang, they hadn't been in the same room together for years. Bjorn figured they thought he was missing, but jeez, hadn't anyone bothered to look for him right there at home?

"Aunt Ebba!" he called, knocking on the door. He saw his fist pounding at the weathered and cracked wood, but he heard nothing. He felt even less. The door was soft as cream cheese. He took a step forward and the next thing he knew he was inside the house. He saw puddles of slime at his feet. "Ugh," he uttered. He was feeling lightheaded. "Better lay off the cannabis bliss."

"Ebba!" he called out again. "Peter!" Bjorn ambled toward their voices.

The couple were sitting on the sofa, holding each other. "I just can't believe he's gone," Ebba was saying. "His mom gets in soon. Oh, gosh. What should I say?"

Bjorn didn't hear his ex-uncle's reply, but he knew it had to be serious if his mom was flying in. She hated planes.

Bjorn shivered, then rubbed his arms for warmth. His hands slid on a thin, slick slush that was cold and sticky to the touch. He glanced down and saw that he was dripping in a cloudy ooze. When he looked up, he saw the morning sky. The breaking sun blinded him and suddenly, he was thrashing in an angry, icy ocean.

What was he doing there? Oh, yes… it was all coming back to him. He'd been surfing on some unfamiliar beach. He couldn't remember where, but as he got further out he saw the remnants of a small sailboat. On the stern was stenciling that read: The Merry Mermaid.

There was a life-preserver floating toward him and he could have sworn he saw a hand come up from inside the ring. Had someone survived?

As that thought came to mind, a slew of songs about survival flooded his brain. From Gloria Gaynor's *I Will Survive* to Eminem's *Survivor* and everything in between, lyrics lanced his psyche and blurred his focus. Worst of all was Muse's *Survival*. That one took up residence and stayed. A wave pushed him under into an icy blackness.

Bjorn fought the riptide and moved toward the wreckage. Just then his surfboard came up, hitting him hard under the chin. His choppers snapped together. Blood filled his mouth and leaked from his chapped lips. His tongue felt the jagged edges of broken teeth. He reached for the surfboard, but it promptly sunk then sprang up several feet away as if taunting him.

Through eyes narrowed in distress, he saw watery gore spreading from him and he fought to gather his thoughts. He looked back toward the shore. It was awfully far away. If he could just get to the wreck, then maybe he could wait there for the Coast Guard. Or at least rest, so he could swim back to the beach.

Bjorn treaded water, gasping. This was one serious shit biscuit. Not only was he freezing, in piercing pain, far from the floating wreckage and farther still from the shore, but he had a really bad song stuck in his head. Just when it seemed things couldn't get any worse, he felt a strange, stinging warmth envelop him. It was like a wet blanket of clinging goo.

Something surfaced just in front of his face: A hideous hagfish.

The so-called "velvet worms" were the most disgusting, reviled organisms in the ocean, if not on earth. Bjorn remembered reading about them, but he couldn't recall when or why. But hagfish were only about twenty inches long. This thing had to be at least *twelve feet*!

The eel-like organism bared all four pairs of the thin sensory tentacles surrounding its toothy mouth, honed in with its nearly sightless and certainly soulless eyes, then lashed its long cylindrical body around Bjorn's legs.

Bjorn resisted the beast's viselike embrace, struggling to disentangle himself. Thanks to the slippery slime, he managed to free one leg. But then he felt his arms being pinned to his sides. His heart hammered in his eardrums but still, it didn't quiet his cruel inner concert. "Dammit!" Bjorn cursed.

Then he relaxed his body and mouthed the sappy lyrics about life being a race. A race to what? Death? As Bjorn's lips parted, he winced at the pain in his chin and jaw, but he figured his agony would be over soon. He felt himself being pulled toward one of the distant caves, where he knew he would be devoured in peace, away from other predators and scavengers.

As the poisonous mucus from the humongous hagfish filled his mouth and clogged his throat, Bjorn saw the most beautiful girl in the world. She smiled at him and took him into her sweet, loving embrace.

Richter Mortis

Vegan hybrid drivers, lawyers in sleek German sedans, teenagers in old beaters and midlife crisis guys in flashy muscle cars—they were all there on the 101 when The Big One hit.

All Angelinos knew it was coming someday. Someday. *But not today, please. We're busy. We have places to go, people to see.*

They were in a hurry but going nowhere fast when the earth began to shimmy and shudder. The first rumblings were met with mild alarm by some, but in most cases not an eyelash was batted. After all, earthquakes were a common occurrence. Especially along the San Andreas and Northridge faults in the sweltering summertime, which caused the natives to joke about the "shake and bake" effect.

It was twilight, just getting dark. On one side of the freeway there was a sea of white glow and on the other a wash of blood-red taillights. Some of the more philosophical survivors likened those images to their bisected lives: Before and after the earthquake.

Before

On the morning of the earthquake, twelve-year-old Cosmo Colombo was rehearsing his lines for a big audition. He was at home with his mom and his three siblings, eating cereal and running lines with his agent on speaker phone. No one at the breakfast table was annoyed, as they were all ensconced in their own online virtual realities.

Cosmo felt sure he would nail the lead in this sitcom. Well, it was just a pilot and he knew pilots seldom flew—but at least he'd get paid. Stick-in-the-mud Mom always insisted most of his money go into his trust fund, but he had his eye on a limited edition Black Panther action figure and he hoped he could get one before it was discontinued.

After breakfast, his siblings went off to catch the bus for school. Cosmo stayed home so he could rehearse, plus he had to get some new headshots. His mom would drive him to the photography studio in the afternoon, then they'd go to the audition at Universal in the early evening. After he'd won the role, Cosmo figured he could talk his mom into taking him to dinner—just the two of them. He knew he was her favorite and that she secretly, or maybe not so secretly, wished he was an only child. She'd joke, "Having all these kids is a blessing in disguise. No, really… I can't find the blessing."

On the morning of the earthquake, Patsy Eng was trying to sleep in. The ageing madam, who hated both of those words whenever she saw them in the gossip columns, considered herself a pioneer in the field of ethical escorts. She always made sure her employees—known as "girlfriends" in the parlance of the biz—were completely comfortable, so she vetted each and every client thoroughly. She gave the women the lion's share of what they earned. They made their own hours and could come, no pun intended, and go whenever they pleased.

She'd had a very late night, so the rapping at her door and the sound of the ringing doorbell were most unwelcome. Patsy shoved her black silk sleep mask up over her bangs and reached for her robe. She swung her thin yoga-toned legs over the bed and opened the drawer to her nightstand where her iPad slept. She touched the screen and went to her home security app. The camera showed a flower delivery guy balancing two bouquets of roses big enough to fill The Kentucky Derby winners' circle.

"I'll be right down," she said, transmitting her voice to the speaker on the porch.

It turned out the blooms were from one of Hollywood's A-listers—just another satisfied client. Patsy figured she'd take at least some of the flowers with her this evening when she went out to interview a potential new girlfriend in Studio City. The young woman had done some porn, but that wasn't always a deal-breaker. She had class and style, qualities Patsy admired and coveted.

On the morning of the earthquake, Presbyterian pastor and recreational paint-huffer Albie Welch was going over the coming Sunday's sermon. He had a cup of black coffee in one hand and a piece of buttered white toast in the other, only half-listening as his wife Kira yammered on about some sale or other. *I'm surprised that woman doesn't wear camo to go bargain-hunting,* he thought. Then he decided that would be a good quip to incorporate into his oration, since it would be about greed in society.

He put his coffee on the coaster and took the last bite of his toast. He reached for his glasses. The TV news was on, blaring about one blasphemy after another. Albie reached for his DayMinder to double-check the address for this evening's sunset ceremony—it was a same-sex marriage, which was something he specialized in. He was almost glad his parents were gone now; they never would have approved of his liberal beliefs. Still, he did miss them and hoped they were looking down at him with pride.

Well, maybe not right at this moment. Albie and Kira were at an all-time low, struggling to survive as the rent was raised and their salaries lowered. Money was ever on his mind, which was why he was so aggravated by Kira's spending and why he could not help but escape into the euphoric haze of the occasional inhalant.

After

When the violent shaking stopped, the panic began.

The megaquake decimated huge chunks of the freeway creating chasms and collapsing steel-and-concrete bridges that crushed anything unfortunate enough to be below. Powerlines snapped, swinging crackling cables to the ground where dry brush ignited and raging fires multiplied. Sparks flew, detonating flammable liquids gushing from the crashed and disabled cars strewn like so many toys across the pulverized pavement. The neighboring hillsides crumbled as if made of sand and huge boulders came to rest on the 101. Felled trees blocked offramps and the birds they once housed flew around in dazed disarray. Lizards, rabbits, mice and spiders once concealed safely in the brush alongside the freeway slithered and scurried to the cars, seeking shelter. Semi-trailer trucks overturned, dumping loads of freight. Everything from slaughter-bound goats to steel rods and snack cakes to baby-clothes, littered the highway.

All was eerily quiet. Except for the screams.

Some devastated drivers found themselves pinned inside accordion-like wreckage, while others teetered at the edges of deep craters. Some were stunned and bleeding, while others were horrified to see their passengers hadn't survived. A few lost control of their bladders or vomited and several were annoyed by the volume of the keening and crying—only to realize the noises were coming from themselves.

There was no warning. The system of accelerometers, seismometers, cellular communication, computers and alarms devised for regional notification of a substantial earthquake only works while the event is in progress. Unlike other natural disasters such as tornadoes, hurricanes, ice storms and volcanic eruptions, no one had time to evacuate much less kiss their asses goodbye.

Cosmo Colombo came to woozily. His head had been slammed into the glovebox of his mom's Lexus as the airbag deployed and flung him backward into unconsciousness. It was darker outside, he noticed. The sun was retreating and thick, black smoke filled the air. The smell of raw electricity coming from under the hood was bitter and his throat felt scratchy. His eyes stung and watered. He reached for his mother's hand and squeezed it. She did not squeeze back. Wincing in pain at the stiffness of his neck, Cosmo turned to his left and saw that his mother had been harpooned by a steel rod. She had a gash on her forehead. The deflated airbag was soaked with her blood but not too much—a dead heart doesn't pump and so Cosmo assumed and hoped, she hadn't even seen it coming.

Patsy Eng fiddled frantically at the radio dial in her pummeled Porsche. Static greeted her. The satellite radio wasn't working either and her iPhone lay in pieces at her feet. She looked around at the Bosch-like horror swirling all around her. She didn't want to get out of the car. She huddled there, staring with wide-eyed wonder as a singed and smoking crow fell from the sky onto her hood, twitched twice, then went forever still. A glance in the askew rearview mirror showed a sea of scattered wreckage behind her. The smoking Lexus fused to the back of her Porsche had a windshield pierced by a steel rod.

Pastor Albie's wrist was broken but that didn't stop him from pushing the dented driver's door of his Toyota as hard as he could. It would only open so far. His heart was pounding in his chest, demanding freedom. Claustrophobia seized him, forcing him to ignore his pain in order to get out. The passenger side of his car was right up against another vehicle, so he had only one choice. He forced it again, this time using his shoulder. Metal hit metal. He got his face close to the window and peered down into the darkness. A hub cap was up against the door, held in place by a mass of asphalt. The window would not roll down, so his only choice was to break it and crawl through. But how? Pastor Albie prayed for guidance.

When he opened his eyes, he saw a shadowy figure in the backseat. The first thought that sprang to mind was that it was a fellow victim, looking for refuge. But if he himself couldn't get out, how did the passenger get in? Albie strained to make out the man's features, but the air was choked with debris and ash and it was nearly dark. Then, with a gasp of distress, Albie saw his face and body were formed by swirling black dust-devils. A hint of eyes glittered from the head.

Albie heard a voice but couldn't be sure if it was out-loud or in his mind.

"Son," it said. "Satan called. He wants his throne back."

Albie's eyebrows knit in a deep frown. "What?!" he sputtered. "Dad… is that you?"

"This is your fault," said the father-like thing. "You were on your way to do the Devil's folly. Faggots are an abomination against God! You are burning in HELL!"

"If that's true, then why are *you* here?" Albie asked.

Poof! The apparition disappeared.

"Holy guacamole," muttered Albie. "All this carbon monoxide is getting to me."

He looked in the rearview mirror and saw his empty backseat and beyond that, where there was a white Porsche shoved so far up the backend of his car that its front tires were visible to him. He saw someone inside—a flesh and blood woman—curled into a ball of despair. He had to help her.

Galvanized, Albie opened his glovebox and ransacked it until he found a lug-wrench and a tin of breath-mints. Using the tin as a hammer, he placed the end of the wrench so it was positioned as a tool to crack and break the driver's side window. With the final strike, the thick glass splintered into tiny squares and fell away.

Careful of his broken bone, the pastor leaned back against the passenger seat and guided his feet through the opening. Gripping the emergency brake lever with his good hand, he pulled himself forward then pushed off, propelling himself as gently as possible outside.

The air felt heavy. And hot. Several fires, large and small, lit the night along with weak beams from battered headlights. Ash floated on a lazy breeze. Albie heard some noises now, apart from the wailing and calls for help. There was radio static, the crackle of electricity, the crunch of broken glass underfoot and sirens screamed somewhere in the distance. The roar of a helicopter came from overhead. Then another. He saw them shine floodlights down, but it was still dim in his immediate vicinity. No matter. He had to help as many people as he possibly could, even if it was only delivering last rites and blessing the dead.

Albie, skimming the side of his Toyota for support on the uneven, rocky terrain, made his way to the driver of the white sports car. He went to her window. Even in her terror, she was beautiful. Her shiny black hair was cut into a short bob and she had bangs going straight across, landing just above her arched, laser-bladed eyebrows. Her makeup was still immaculate, in spite of her tears. She wore an expensive outfit. Albie saw at least a dozen roses strewn about the cabin. She watched his approach with stunned curiosity, then opened her door.

Albie took the handle and opened it for her, like some strange and beleaguered valet.

"Thank you," she said softly, reaching back inside for her purse. Then, without hesitation, she hugged her savior.

As she did, an aftershock came, bringing them to their knees. It was slow and rolling, but weak and brief.

"There's a little boy in that car," she said, pointing to the mangled Lexus with the windshield speared by rebar from… where? It seemed to have sailed out of nowhere, a target-seeking missile with only one victim in its sights.

Albie and Patsy righted themselves and made their way to Cosmo. They had to go around the back of the car and circle around to the passenger side. A huge dent jammed the door and Albie had the strength of only one hand. Patsy's yoga came in handy and with her strong grip she was able to get the door to move. Cosmo kicked it from the inside and it opened with an almost-human groan. As he squirmed out from the narrow gap, he took one last look at his mother. He saw four fat black spiders crawling on the steering wheel, trudging through her sticky blood.

"Oh," said the Asian woman, embracing him. "You poor child!"

"I'm Cosmo," he said, extricating himself. "Who are you?"

"My name is Patsy," said the woman who, Cosmo surmised, was almost as old as his fifty-something grandma. But still, she was reasonably hot. His older friends would have called her a GILF.

He turned his attention to the man, who had bland, thinning hair and somehow still had on his wirerimmed eyeglasses. The pale, skinny fellow was dressed like a schoolteacher. Cosmo noticed he was holding one arm against his chest and the wrist was red and puffy. That reminded him of his own injury. He felt tenderly along the back of his neck and checked his skull for cracks. There was only the laceration near his left temple.

He heard the man introduce himself as Pastor Albie, then ask Cosmo's mother's name so he could pray for her. But it all seemed to be coming from the surface, a faraway surface... Cosmo felt like he was drowning on dry land. It was all just so horrible. Strange thoughts pinged his mind, like, *Well, I guess I won't be getting that Black Panther action figure now.*

The ground felt slushy. Cosmo reeled as he felt himself being grabbed. "Come on!" someone shouted. "Move!" Cosmo couldn't be sure if it was Albie or Patsy, but the urgency of the command prodded him to action. As he dashed after them, his peripheral vision caught sight of the Lexus—his mother's coffin—being swallowed by a sudden sinkhole.

An instinctive devotion kicked in and Cosmo turned back. "Mom!" he cried. Three long strides took him to the edge of the void. Bubbling brackish water swirled around the rear of the car, leaving the windshield exposed. A helicopter's merciless spotlight gave Cosmo one last view of his mom. Her hands came up, pleading. The boy heard a faint cry, "Help..."

Just then, rough hands pulled him back. Cosmo fought. "She's alive! No, let me go! Mom needs me."

The next thing he knew, Cosmo was slumped against Patsy's small, comforting bosom. She was holding him in her arms. She and Albie stood several feet from the sinkhole, leaning against a car along with some other people. Cosmo listened to the voices before moving or saying anything.

"I saw things too," Pastor Albie was saying. "It's the chemicals in the air."

"Poor baby," Patsy sighed. "He's severely traumatized. We have to get him, and ourselves, to a hospital."

Voices projected through loud megaphones. Cosmo guessed it was the helicopter pilots, but he couldn't be sure. They were telling everyone to stay put and to wait for air-lifts.

"Screw that," Patsy said. "We can't wait. This is a deathtrap."

"I can walk," Albie replied, then gestured toward the shivering boy. "Can he?"

Patsy gave the child a gentle shake. "Cosmo? Come on, kiddo. Wake up. It's time to go."

Cosmo opened his eyes. They stung and burned. He let cleansing tears come, then blinked and looked again. "I'm OK..." he whispered.

Then he saw her: His mom was crawling from the sinkhole, somehow still carrying the spear in her chest. He could just make out the red of her manicured fingernails as she clawed her way to the pavement surface.

Cosmo broke free from his new friends and ran to his mother. But when he got there, she was gone. Within seconds, Albie and Patsy were at his side.

Patsy wedged herself between the boy and the danger, shooing him away. "Cosmo, your mother is gone. She's dead," she stated sternly, hoping to shock him into action.

"But I saw…" Cosmo choked, "saw her."

Patsy maintained her hard stance. "She's dead. You were hallucinating." From behind her, the sinkhole gurgled. Steam shot upward, then from the hole several small animal-things emerged.

Cosmo pointed toward Patsy's feet. Amazingly, she still wore both of her four-inch pumps. There was something slithering near the pointed leather toes. It wasn't quite a snake. The boy squinted, trying to get a better look. His brain had no answer.

Albie was looking, too. "Patsy," he said shakily, "Come over here. Step very carefully." The tiny creature coiled itself then levitated about an inch off the ground, taking on the form of something strange and misshapen.

Patsy looked down. Then she trained her eyes on Cosmo. "Hallucinations."

Cosmo didn't think different people could see the same illusions, but what did he know? He was only twelve and he had to admit he didn't know everything.

"Look," Patsy said with a forced smile, "I'll come over to you. There's nothing here."

As she took her first step, the thing made a crunching sound and coiled itself around her ankle. Patsy stumbled and fear flooded her eyes. *This is real.*

The pastor went to her and reached for her hand. A plump spider crawled from inside her jacket sleeve and sprang onto his broken wrist. Albie let go of her and slapped frantically at the eight-legged invader. He staggered backwards.

Patsy looked down. An inky, roiling wave lapped over the side of the sinkhole, bringing with it a cargo of bizarre beings that looked sort of like snakes but flopped more like fish out of water. Voices rose in unison from the mass of organisms: "Patsy… Come down with us, Patsy… Be with us. Be us."

Within a flash she was crawling with the things as they swam from the ground up. Breaking into millions of molecules, they covered Patsy like piranhas, consuming her alive as they dragged what was left of her into the smoking hole. A chorus of otherworldly laughter emerged from the depths.

Cosmo took Albie's hand and they ran as fast as they could through the slalom of fire and debris. They moved blindly through the night, crisscrossing the tumbledown freeway and dashing across the shoulder. They scrambled up the safest-looking hillside, stopping only when they reached the top. The pair looked down at the 101 from their perch, then took in what they could see of Universal and Studio City.

Just when it seemed things couldn't get any worse, a sleeper storm kicked up and dumped a steady stream of tepid drizzle onto the land.

Pastor Albie plopped to the ground. His wrist was swelling and the dull throb demanded his attention. He let out a long, ragged breath. "Dear Lord," he said, "is this Armageddon?"

Sirens droned and alarms rang in the distance but Cosmo couldn't see much, if any movement, in the streets below. Cars clogged the roadways and none seemed to be moving. Even if a person's vehicle wasn't damaged, it would be next to impossible to drive. People milled about as far as the eye could see and from somewhere on the 101 Cosmo heard goats bleating. The smells floating on the damp air were sharp and unfamiliar.

"Pastor Albie," Cosmo asked, "are we going to die?"

The man didn't answer. He seemed lost in his own thoughts, or maybe he was praying.

Cosmo wondered if his brother and sisters had made it through OK. He didn't worry about his dad. His dad was a bad guy, from what he'd gathered.

The boy remembered overhearing something his mom had said about the divorce and Dad's new girlfriend. "He buried me up to my neck in the sand and she kicked me in the face," she'd snapped, followed by a bitter laugh. "He didn't even ask for partial custody of the kids." She was drinking wine in the kitchen with a couple of her friends when she said that, not knowing he was listening. Well, he wasn't spying—he just happened to overhear. Cosmo, then eight, had been crushed to learn that his dad did not even want to see him or his siblings ever again. If he survived, where would he live? Who would take care of him? He pictured himself thrown into an orphanage like the one in a movie he saw once, called *Oliver Twist.*

He saw Pastor Albie stir, then rise. "Come on, Cosmo," he said. "Let's keep going." As the man got to his feet, a tiny spider leapt onto his shoulder. Cosmo watched in silent horror as the arachnid scuttled into Albie's ear. Albie caught the boy's expression. "What?" he asked.

"Um… nothing," Cosmo replied. It was too late to do anything anyway. "Your wrist is looking pretty bad." Cosmo pointed toward the Universal Studios complex, huge and sprawling, less than a mile away. "I was on my way to an audition there," he said. "It's somewhere in the backlot. The producer's office is near the soundstages."

The minister shrugged. "It's as good a place as any. And I'll bet there's a first-aid kit. I need to wrap this." He held his ruined wrist aloft.

As they began their slow and careful descent from the crest of the hill, Albie took Cosmo's hand. Continuing his pace and not looking at him, he finally answered the boy's question. "We might die. But I'll do everything in my power to make sure we don't. Heaven is a beautiful garden of light and love, Cosmo, but the Lord says it's not our time."

"Do you have kids?" Cosmo asked.

"Not yet. But I have a wonderful wife and we want children very much." In his mind he added, "If we can ever afford them." Then he realized money would be the least of their worries—if Kira had even survived—for a long time to come. His mind flitted back to stories on the news he'd seen in recent years about devastating earthquakes, floods, fires and a myriad of other disasters ravaging the globe. Acts of God. The newscasters covered the tragedies but seldom followed up. Albie had no idea how long it would take the City of Angels to bounce back from this blow, let alone the people in it.

They made their way to Barham Boulevard. There was more of the same destruction here. Crashed cars, fires, chasms, loose and lost animals, people in disarray. Albie shielded Cosmo's eyes as they passed by a man diligently and determinedly cutting his own hand off with a small pocketknife. The hand was nothing but crushed pulp pinned beneath the hood of an overturned car, but still it seemed an oddly drastic measure to Albie. Couldn't the man have waited for help to arrive? The earthquake was only an hour old; rescue teams were bound to be out soon. At least, he thought it was about that long. Time was passing in disjointed shifts between slow-motion and warp-speed.

As they got closer to the studio and theme park, they saw corpses and disembodied limbs beneath the collapsed Metro pedestrian bridge that once hooked across Lankershim Boulevard and Universal Hollywood Drive. Armies of insects marched toward the bodies. A few yards from the carnage, a seemingly unharmed couple were sitting on a cracked curb, kissing. It was surreal.

Cosmo spotted a golf cart marked: Security. "Look!" he shouted, pointing to their salvation. The pair were so exhausted and aching so badly, their relief was beyond measure.

The small motorized vehicle took them up a steep hill to the entrance of City Walk. Once a bustling, neon-lit tourist attraction, the place was eerie and menacing in the dark. Most of the buildings were at least partially demolished but that didn't stop people from huddling inside them. Some folks had taken command and could be seen handing out café scones and bottled water, while others barked orders to shell-shocked casualties. Still others walked around holding their cell phones aloft, desperately seeking signals.

Albie stopped the cart, disappeared into one of the shops and returned with two candy bars and a water. They ate and drank savagely as they continued toward the backlot. Cosmo gave directions as Albie drove, but he felt disoriented. The giant, iconic King Kong cutout was face-down on the ground. Tour trams lay toppled off their tracks. The signposts were askew. Nothing was as Cosmo remembered.

As they forged on, they were baffled to find the backlots deserted. After some time moving almost blindly through the dark, the cart lost its charge and came to a slow, grinding halt.

Albie and Cosmo got out. They looked up and saw they were right next to the *Psycho* house. Somehow, it had withstood the quake and towered tall and imposing as ever. Of course, it really wasn't a house. It was more of a façade with a slapdash structure behind it. There was the adjoining Bates Motel mockup too, but it was too dark to see the cabins.

"I need to rest," said the pastor. "And so do you. Let's stay here for a few minutes."

As they climbed the wending stairs leading to the house, Cosmo asked, "Is it safe to be in there? What about aftershocks?"

"We've survived so far. The Lord is looking out for us, son." He paused. "Besides, I'd risk death to get out of this rain."

The pastor had a point. Cosmo, having been born and raised in L.A., didn't have much experience with rain but this felt different. There was a humid heaviness to it and it clung to one's clothes and hair like sticky slush.

Cosmo tilted his head upward. The foreboding Victorian-style monstrosity loomed.

He saw the figure of Mother Bates in the uppermost window and shivered in spite of himself. He gestured toward her. "Ever seen the movie?"

Albie shook his head. "No. Too scary for me." They entered the structure, which seemed to be empty. "But didn't you say you were supposed to have an audition here today? I guess you're an actor, huh? You probably see all the movies."

"I see a lot," replied Cosmo. "Mom lets... um, Mom used to let me watch the scary ones, too."

They waded deeper into the room. As their eyes adjusted, they looked around for sources of light. Candles, flashlights, forgotten phones... anything. Cosmo went to the wall, feeling his way to the switch. It was worth a try. He found it and flicked it. A weak glow illuminated the sparse space. "Whoa," he exclaimed.

"Must be on a generator," Albie concluded.

They saw a modest setup. A utilitarian table, some chairs. Rough stairs leading to an upper level. "This must be where the performers hang out," Cosmo said. "On the tour, they have a guy who looks like Norman Bates come outside to scare the people riding the tram. I was never scared, though," he added.

"You took the tour? Isn't that a bit pedestrian for an actor of your rank?"

Cosmo couldn't tell if he was being teased or not. But he guessed his residual checks were more than a pastor's pay. Then again, what did he know? This Albie fellow might be one of those rich TV preachers. Cosmo didn't answer the question. Instead, he made his way to the table and opened the drawer. Inside was a handy first-aid kit complete with an Ace bandage and aspirin, plus a small flashlight and a few protein bars.

They took a seat and Cosmo wrapped Albie's wrist while the man chewed on a half-dozen painkillers.

"Pastor Albie," said the boy, his voice quavering, "Do… Do you think that lady Patsy was killed by… by demons?" His heart fluttered when he said the words aloud. He'd been wondering ever since it happened exactly what had killed her. The sight of his mother had been bad enough but he'd never seen anything like those things, not even in a horror movie.

"Demons!" Albie scoffed. "No, son. Those weren't demons. But they *were* from Hell."

Cosmo squeaked, "Really?" He wasn't sure he believed in a God who lived in the sky and a Devil who plotted from below the ground, but

Cosmo had to admit his opinions on things were being thrown into question by the minute. Maybe Heaven and Hell weren't so farfetched after all.

Albie put his sloppily-bandaged hand gently on Cosmo's shoulder. "Those were minions. The misbegotten, vermin, by-blows, whelps, mere errand boys." The preacher tried to spit on the ground for emphasis, but his mouth was too dry.

"Well, they seemed pretty dangerous to me," Cosmo said.

"Not to the righteous. Not to those who have accepted the Lord into their lives." He fixed the boy with a stare that was so intense Cosmo thought the lenses in the man's glasses might crack. "Are you saved?"

"Umm…" Cosmo hemmed.

A crash from above came, interrupting the conversation.

"Holy guacamole, what now?" Albie sighed.

Their eyes swung to the source: The darkness at the top of the stairs. They held their breaths. Then they saw something. A skeletal foot on the top stair, followed by the hem of a long gray skirt. It was the dummy of Mrs. Bates. But it was walking. Was it animatronic? As the figure landed on the third step down, its withered head came into view. With a wasted hand, it reached for its face.

Albie and Cosmo were rooted to their chairs. That is, until they felt something scurry across their shoes. Giggles emitted from under their seats and from the shadowy corners.

"Jesus," Albie exclaimed as the monster on the stairs removed its mask. It was Kira.

"He can't help you now," the Kira-thing said, its uncanny grin just a bit too large.

Albie propelled himself from his chair and dashed for the front door in such a panic he didn't even think about Cosmo.

Cosmo stared at the open door, stunned that Albie had left him alone. He looked up at the animated dummy, but it had stopped moving. He brought his feet up onto the chair and scanned the ground for minions. He saw dozens of tiny feet- and pawprints in the silt. He heard squeaks and chitters coming from the far corners cloaked in shadow. But he saw nothing.

What would The Black Panther do? he wondered. Then he realized he was not a superhero. He was just a twelve-year-old boy in a horrible and unprecedented situation. He took stock of the room. He was crouched on a rather rickety chair with the stairs to his right and escape to his left. In between stood the table containing some things he might need. Cosmo decided to make a break for the table.

He ran to the still-open drawer and grabbed blindly at its contents, feeling the flashlight and a protein bar in his hand. He also felt something slithering across his shoe, across his ankle and up his pantleg. Cosmo waited an eternity until he felt it clear his shin, then he raised his leg, smooshing the squishy bug between his kneecap and the tightened denim. He saw a brownish stain appear.

"Cosmo…" something whispered. "Join us… Be us…"

"No thanks!" Cosmo shouted as he sprinted toward the open door.

A puddle of tadpole-like squiggles spread onto the floor from behind the open door, flooding the threshold in a black, wriggling mass. Cosmo sprang over it and felt immense joy when his sneakers hit the dry boards of the porch.

The boy ran down the stairs so fast he was afraid they might collapse, but he didn't care. Breaking his neck was preferable to being eaten alive by Satan's piranhas.

Once he got to the bottom, he stopped, heaving for breath. He felt the sludgy, ash-laden rain and saw Albie's footprints in the mud. After glancing up at the house to make sure there was nothing coming after him, Cosmo turned his attention to the pastor's path. It seemed to be leading to the motel. Cosmo followed, his desire to be with another person overriding his anger at being left behind.

At first the footsteps were deep and distinct, not those of someone running in a panic. As they got closer to the cabins, they started to smear and the marks got smaller. Then they took on their well-defined shape again, only they weren't shoeprints anymore. They were animal tracks of some kind: two large teardrops side-by-side. Cosmo wasn't sure what kind of an animal would leave that impression, but he guessed they were hooves. They led to the first cabin and inside. The door was standing slightly ajar and an inviting warm glow seeped from the crack.

"Cosmo? Is that you?" It was a woman's voice.

It sounded like his mom, but as if she was far away. He knew this was some kind of trick.

"I'm here with Pastor Albie. Come in," said the muffled female voice.

Cosmo heard soft, ominous chortles coming from behind him. What if some woman and the pastor really were inside? There was safety in numbers. He racked his brain for the right answer but there wasn't one. A bony tap on his shoulder sent him running for the open door of the cabin.

Once inside the bare muggy room, Cosmo saw a large blue-gray billy goat standing on top of a pile of garbage that was soaked in a pasty sludge. The goat had a massive set of curling horns and a lush, yellowing white beard. It fixed its jaded gaze on Cosmo while placidly chewing its cud. With light topaz orbs and those unsettling rectangular pupils, the eyes seemed demonic.

But it was what came from the animal's mouth that was truly terrifying.

Cosmo stood rigid with fear as he watched ruby-red polished fingernails poke out from the corners of the creature's cud-filled mouth. The bolus of semi-digested hay dropped to the dusty floor with a muted thud, then a startling crack was heard as the goat's jaw broke. A woman's hand could be seen, then another. The goat's head peeled back, revealing Cosmo's mother's face. The ruined body of the goat fell away and she stood before him dripping in otherworldly afterbirth.

The first thing Cosmo thought was: "I'm seeing my mom naked!" which was almost as disturbing to him as the manner of her reappearance. The next was, "Is she real?" He'd seen so much that evening—more than all that he'd seen in his entire life combined—that it seemed anything was possible.

His mom looked brand-new. Her skin was perfect, her complexion dewy. Her hair was thicker, fuller and more luxurious than it ever had been. Her once-gashed forehead was smooth and unblemished and there wasn't a hole in her chest. She wore no makeup, no jewelry and no embellishment aside from her crimson finger- and toenails.

"Close your eyes, Cosmo," she said, smiling.

He was afraid to, but he never disobeyed his mother. Cosmo closed his eyes and waited for death to come.

Her voice came again. "OK, you can open now."

Cosmo took a cautious peek. They were alone in the room. The goat was gone and there was no trace of him left behind. Mother was all dry and dressed as she had been earlier that evening. She knelt and held her arms out to him.

Cosmo felt his lips tremble and tears sprang to his eyes. "Mom…" He went to her and embraced her. She was warm and soft.

"I love you, Cosmo," she whispered. "I love you more than anything."

They cried together for a moment, but the spell of their reunion was broken when they heard a voice coming over a loudspeaker and the sound of an engine outside.

"Any survivors?" the loud, distorted voice called.

Cosmo and his mom went to the door of the cabin. On the wide, warped cement road outside was a military tank flashing lights.

"Holy guacamole, it's rescue!" Cosmo's mom exclaimed, taking the boy's hand and leading him out. "We're here! We're here!"

Recovery was slow. Thousands of lives were lost and many more devastated. It took years for Los Angeles to get back to normal, but it did. And then it came back even stronger.

The same could be said of Cosmo Colombo. After being rescued on the night of the earthquake, he and his mother went home. There was structural damage to the house, but it was fixable. Cosmo's siblings had all disappeared and were presumed dead, but Dad started coming around to visit him on the occasional weekend and they grew close, forging a new bond in their shared grief.

In the early days following the quake Cosmo scoured the news sites for accounts of supernatural happenings. He looked for an obituary on a pastor called Albie. He found nothing.

Cosmo's mom never spoke of her resurrection and he didn't ask. Unanswered questions plagued him at first. Was it really and truly her? She'd always said there was nothing stronger than a mother's love… perhaps it was even stronger than death. Or had she not died on the freeway in the first place? Was the whole thing a hallucination? Maybe demons hadn't actually come to earth at all. Or maybe they had and Cosmo's mom was now one of them, playing the long game.

Finally, Cosmo decided not to look a gift-goat in the mouth. He was safe and happy, and that's all that mattered.

Free Admission

HERE ON THE PIER SINCE 1906!
proclaimed the flashing red, white and blue
neon sign in the dusky window. The blatant
lighting didn't make the Venice Beach Curio
Shoppe & Museum of the Odd seem very old
or authentic, but Ethel decided to give it a
whirl anyway. She was a tourist after all and
that's what day-trippers perusing the Pier did.
Plus, admission was free.

Ethel had traveled from her native London
many times, but this was her first trip to
America. She was pushing seventy and figured
it was now or never. She'd been in the
picturesque enclave for just a few days, but she
felt she'd pretty much seen everything it had to
offer. It was smaller than she'd thought and
colder than she'd hoped.

Next on her itinerary was San Francisco,
then home. She knew her trio of tabbies would

miss her terribly by then, but she also knew they were in good hands with Sandra, her neighbor and fellow spinster.

As a bon voyage gift, Sandra had given her a book to read on the plane. It was called "Tourist Traps and How to Avoid Them." But the book's author wasn't referring to wee shops filled with overpriced trinkets; no, the tome was packed with page after page of cautionary tales and had a long list of places to dodge after dark.

Ethel was almost afraid to disembark when the plane landed. She followed the rules to the letter. As soon as she picked up her rental car, she removed the license plate frame bearing the company's name. There'd been a perfectly horrid story in the book about a serial killer targeting tourists, who found his prey by spotting their telltale vehicles. After murdering them, he stuffed their dismembered bodies into the boot and under the seats.

She always made sure her purse was zipped closed and that she had mace tucked into her bra. Her phone had a quick-touch emergency number programmed into it.

One evening, she mistakenly wandered east of Main in Downtown L.A. and found herself being followed by a belligerent and drunken bum. His jaundiced eyes almost blended with his dark, pockmarked skin and his head was heavy with filthy, matted dreadlocks. She glanced over her shoulder and was horrified to see a small but nonetheless menacing pocketknife in his withered hand.

When she quickened her pace, he bellowed, "What's wrong, Becky? You scared?" Then he cackled with derisive laughter. "Ooh, Becky's running! Watch out, you might break a hip!" Ethel decided the best defense was a strong offense, so she stopped and turned to face him. He stopped too. She reached for her phone. "Don't come any closer," she said in a smaller and shakier voice than intended. "I'll call the police." His expression turned sardonic. He gave a crocodilian grin, revealing a mouthful of decay. "Oh, *really*? You think I'm scared of the blue-klux-klan? Bitch, they done killed me years ago." But the tactic worked. With a dismissive wave of his free hand, he turned and wandered off crookedly, leaving her alone.

That was last week. Since then there had been no incidents and actually, Ethel was getting bored of L.A.

She opened the narrow door to the curio shop and walked inside, an off-key bell announcing her arrival. It was dark and the shop would be closing soon.

The first thing she noticed was the smell—the odor of dust and mold, fighting to overpower the numerous potpourri sachets and sickly-sweet cinnamon-scented candles. The shop was cram-packed full of totally disparate trinkets—from "I Heart Venice Beach" commuter mugs, to perky stuffed toys, to tiny burlap sacks stuffed with gourmet coffee beans, to holy Madonna relics made in Mexico. An anemic muzak version of Randy Newman's *I Love L.A.* stuttered intermittently through tinny speakers.

What Ethel really wanted to see was the Museum of the Odd. It sounded intriguing and after seeing nothing but Starbucks after Starbucks all day in neighboring Santa Monica, she could use a brain tickle.

The displays were at the rear of the shop. Ethel wended her way through the maze of overcrowded, overpacked aisles and peered through the mini-mob of people checking out the oddities.

"Eeeewww!" screeched a tow-headed kid of about seven. "That's gross!"

"Not as gross as you," sneered what could only be his older sister.

Their mother shepherded them away and Ethel quickly stepped into their spot.

It *was* gross.

It was a shrunken head, "All the way from the darkest heart of Africa." It was buoyed in a jar of formaldehyde, its wispy black hair floating like spider legs in the viscous liquid. The tiny mouth was partially opened in a grimace and the eyelids looked squishy and loose, as though there weren't any orbs behind them to offer support.

Ethel shuddered, then moved on to the next display. A live, two-headed rattlesnake in a glass tank. And the next, a stuffed and mounted piglet with three tails. Another shrunken head. And then, the *piece de resistance*: A full-sized mummy propped upright in a battered Plexiglas display case. Behind her was an amazingly ornate sarcophagus.

Ethel stopped to read the plaque. "The Malibu Mummy, Mary Lou, was found in 1901 during excavations to build this boardwalk, which was erected in 1905. That part of the property and the roller coaster has since eroded and washed out to sea, so it is not known if other mummified beach bunnies rest beneath the sand. It is assumed that Mary Lou and her cat"—Ethel noticed the swaddled feline-shape at the mummy's feet—"are the genuine article from Egypt; but perhaps they're 19th century fakes."

Ethel figured they had to be counterfeit, or some kind of carbon-dating or testing would have been done and the results touted. It was more fun and mysterious for the shop owner to keep people guessing. She looked at the casing—the Egyptian version of a headstone, with its hieroglyphics giving the particulars. The plaque didn't say whether or not it had been found with the body.

She wondered how the curio proprietor had acquired them. She looked up at the mummy's head and let her gaze travel downward. Mary Lou was obviously female. She had an ample bosom, a nipped-in waist and full hips—she probably was a 19th century woman, wrapped while still wearing her corset. She was enveloped in what was once white gauze, now yellowed and stained with age. Unlike the mummies Ethel had seen in books and on TV, Mary Lou was not continuously wound from head to toe. Each of her arms and each of her legs, were individually wrapped. It was the same with the cat—even his little ears were sticking up! It was certainly one of the oddest oddities Ethel had ever seen. The stop had been worth her while.

It was funny, but she felt sorry for the pair. A civilized woman and her pet kitty on display in a tacky tourist retreat. They should be resting in peace somewhere, under the ground in a real cemetery. Then she stole a glance at the nearest shrunken head. *At least Mary Lou isn't resting in pieces like that poor sod*, she thought.

Ethel caught herself stifling a yawn for the third time and decided maybe she wouldn't mind seeing another coffee place before heading out into the night, back to her hotel.

Hours later, well into the void of deep sleep, Ethel was awakened by a muffled knock at her door. Who would be knocking at that hour? She didn't know anyone in the city. She sat up in bed and turned on her nightstand light. She listened intently. All was quiet. Shadows darkened the corners of the cheerless hotel room.

Just as she was about to relax, she heard a quiet meow.

Probably just a stray cat looking for a scrap. Poor thing. Ethel knew that itinerant animals were just as abundant on the streets of L.A. as were the homeless humans. It was a real problem and one the city councils didn't advertise in their travel brochures. Ethel, remembering roaming alone the other night, was a tad apprehensive about taking a peek. But what harm could a hungry kitten do?

Ethel walked to the door and opened it a crack. She looked out and down.

"Meow," repeated the cat.

"Oh, my gosh!" Ethel exclaimed. "You poor, poor pussycat!"

The critter was riddled with mange, so much so that its whiskers were completely gone. It was skin and bones. Ethel had never seen a more pathetic creature. She couldn't turn her back on it. She had a bit of scone left and there was some milk in the fridge of her minibar. She opened the door wider.

The door opened wider still—and quite suddenly—knocking Ethel flat on her considerable backside. She could only stare up in open-mouthed wonder as Mary Lou, the famous Malibu Mummy, walked into her room.

The fiend, still swaddled from head to toe, stood there with her arms crossed over her chest, apparently looking down at Ethel. "Are you going to invite me in, or what?"

The soprano voice was muffled and the words were barely audible, but Ethel heard them, all right. She sat up, then struggled to her feet. What was *in* that espresso? She shut her eyes and shook her head. She opened her eyes. The mummy was still there.

Ethel walked to the door and closed it. She looked at Mary Lou and the cat. "Uh, hello," she said. "What can I do for you?"

"Well, first of all," deadpanned the mummy, "You can unwrap me. I'm suffocating in here."

Ethel, hoping against hope that this was just a dream, stepped closer to the stinking stiff. She saw a lead on the gauze at the top of the head and began to unravel. As each new layer was revealed, the stench grew stronger. Finally, Ethel saw a bit of moldy hair and a patch of bald scalp. She glanced down at the cat—apparently Mary Lou had been able to free him of his wrappings, but not herself— who watched through calm and calculating golden slits.

"How did you find me?" Ethel gulped.

"Guinefort followed your scent," the mummy replied, shifting from foot to foot impatiently.

Ethel assumed that Guinefort was the cat. She continued unwrapping. Finally, she was to the forehead, then the eyes, which were mercifully shut. Or, as shut as they could be with the rotted, lacelike eyelids. Mary Lou's nose was ravaged and so was her mouth. Ashen teeth poked through lips that didn't quite meet. "I think I'd better stop here," Ethel said.

The mummy exhaled, grinning. Ethel almost asphyxiated on the putrid breath.

"It feels so good to breathe. Thank you, thank you, thank you!"

"Don't mention it," Ethel muttered, hoping the being would take that as a hint not to open its foul mouth to speak again. But then curiosity got the better of her. "What are you doing here?"

"You broke my curse," said Mary Lou simply, as if that explained everything.

"What curse?"

"My death curse, silly," the dead woman tried to roll her eyes, but she nearly lost one in the process. She giggled. "Oops, mustn't do that again." Mary Lou made her way to the small sofa and sat down. Her bones rubbed together like dry kindling. She sighed with deep satisfaction. "I've been standing in that damn display case for more decades than I can count."

"What happened to you?"

"Well," Mary Lou began, then paused. "Hey, you got anything to drink? I'm parched!" Then, to demonstrate, she patted her thighs and plumes of dust came up.

Ethel, still holding out hope for the bad dream theory, went to the sink and filled a glass with water. She handed it to the stinking corpse, staying as far out of smell-range as possible. The cat, Guinefort, rubbed his cheek against her leg and left a piece of flesh behind. Ethel stamped it loose and choked back a foamy heave.

Mary Lou didn't seem to notice her new-found friend's distress. She gulped down her water and then looked down at the spreading stain coming through the bandages at her midriff. "Hmmm... I guess I'm not too watertight anymore." She twittered.

"So, you want to know what a death curse is," the mummy rasped. "Well, you see, that's the problem: I can't really die. Guiney and I were in Massachusetts when we met our end then somehow, we got mummified and moved to Malibu and finally Venice Beach. Don't ask me how. Then we were underground for years and years, kind of in a dreamlike state, then they dug us up and stuck us in that case.

"I could hear everything going on around me, but I couldn't do anything about it till someone felt sorry for me. That was you. You're the only person in all these years who cared about me, the *person*. Everyone else was either grossed out or just took one look and bounced. I don't even have my own hashtag on Instagram."

"I hear you picked up on the modern lingo," noted Ethel, warming up a bit to the stinky specter. Poor Mary Lou couldn't help the way she smelled. "When did you… er, die?"

"I was burned at the stake in 1692 and so was my dear Guiney. As the Reverend Mather lit the pyre, he said that no one would mourn us. Nobody would ever care that we were dead, except maybe the Devil. With my last conscious thought, I vowed I'd prove him wrong someday, even if it took all eternity."

"So, you cursed yourself?"

Mary Lou said nothing for a long time. Finally, her eyelids struggled to open. Her moldering lips moved. "I guess you're right. I never thought of it that way. It was I who made the vow. I did curse myself. Well, how do you like that? How stupid of me!"

Guinefort growled, as if to say, "Thanks a lot."

"Well, that's all water under the bridge," Ethel soothed. "Er, pier. Spilt milk and all. But what are you going to do now? You can't go around like that, you know."

"I know," said Mary Lou sadly.

She got up from the sofa, amazingly agile, and before Ethel could even blink twice, the creature was on her. Ethel felt the bandaged hands around her throat, pulling her forward.

Towards that awful face. The mouth opened and the teeth ground back and forth—Ethel thought crazily of the maw of a garbage disposal with rotting, clotting food stuck in it—as the lips parted.

The sodden, mushy flesh, like the peel on a rotten banana, pressed against Ethel's gasping mouth. The hands at her neck tightened again, crushing her larynx. She could feel the vessels in her eyeballs bursting and hemorrhaging. Her eardrums popped, sending icepicks of pain into her brain. Her lungs were sucked dry, collapsing in on themselves.

Through the haze of her own blood, she saw Mary Lou's face become beautiful, full of life. *Her* life. As her heart exploded within her breast, she thought of a lyric from an old song, "Hello Mary Lou, good-bye heart." She would have chuckled at the irony, if she could have.

Ethel willed herself to die, making no final vow to return.

The Union Station Amtrak was a mess, as usual. Late nights were the worst; travelers were cranky, tired and in a hurry.

Ticket-taker Lenny Lancaster had put in for a shift change weeks ago but heard nothing from the higher-ups. So, here he was once again, when he should have been home watching porn. What a waste of time.

He called on the next customer in line and he took a moment to admire the sway of the woman's hips as she walked toward him. She carried a mangy cat under one arm—it was wearing an Emotional Support Animal vest—and her compact, wheeled suitcase trailed behind her. She pressed her I.D. into his moist palm, letting her fingers linger on his for just a moment too long.

He would be in big trouble if anyone ever found out what happened next. But Lenny's dumbstick made all the really big decisions for him. The voluptuous brunet named Ethel White didn't match the photo or the age on her British driver's license, but she did have a first-class ticket to San Francisco and a sinful smile.

That was good enough for Lenny. He gave a short nod and said, "Safe travels, Miss White."

"Bye, now," said the woman with a wink as she sashayed away, blending into the crowd.

Depraved Indifference

Stage One: *Shock*

When I heard Kurt Cobain had committed suicide, I was surprised. This was in '94. I was in middle school.

Yeah, sure, he was a dark, twisted mofo. No doubt about that. Just listen to some Nirvana lyrics. Look at who he married. He had to have been pretty damn depressed.

But why would someone so young, with so much talent and a new daughter, kill himself?

At first, I thought maybe he just wanted to be in the "27 Club"—so many musicians have died at the age of twenty-seven. Morrison, Hendrix and Joplin being the big three. But there's also bluesman Robert Johnson and punker Mia Zapata of The Gits. Both of them were murdered. Even Andy Warhol's protégé

Jean-Michel Basquiat kicked off at two-seven. Though Basquiat is way better-known as a painter, he was in a band too.

Some people think Kurt's junkie wife, Courtney Love, talked him into putting that shotgun to his head. Her detractors say she plied him with drugs, including heroin, that she goaded him into it.

But can you really talk someone into suicide? I mean, that's *real* power.

The note he wrote, found underneath a flower pot in the greenhouse room above his garage—the same place where his body lay for three days before being discovered—quotes a Neil Young song, "It's better to burn out than fade away." He was listening to the *Automatic for the People* album by R.E.M. sometime before he ended it all. At least, that was the CD found in the player.

Right now, I'm listening to Nirvana's *Come as You Are*, in which he sings, *"...And I swear that I don't have a gun."*

Actually, he was a collector. He even had guns as a kid growing up in Washington. Several. People say he hoarded them, people say the police took them away. Whatever the case, I guess he had one too many on damp April 5th.

I've seen the photos of the scene. There are some fakes out there—for one thing, he didn't blow his face off. If anything, he looked peaceful there on the floor, as if resting. The shotgun, a Remington Model 11 20-gauge given to him by his best friend Dylan Carson, lay on his chest. Just a slight trickle of blood could be seen coming from one ear, his features in serene repose. The last words he wrote were, "I love you."

Time to turn the music off and get to work.

I work at a very exclusive museum.

Speaking of Basquiat, we got *Hannibal* back. That's one of his paintings which was stolen, spirited away to Brazil, then recovered. And stolen again. I think it's kind of ugly myself, but Basquiat is one of those painters I admire more than I actually like. I pass the canvas every night on my way to my undersized office. I'm the one who arranges the private tours. Well, they're all private, actually. Our museum is not open to the public.

The sun is at its most intense now, glowing like an orange coal before trading shifts with the moon. I like this part of the day. It's a good time to start.

Taking my last swallow of Thanksgiving blend, I put my mug in the sink and head for the door.

The driver is waiting for me, as usual. He and I are not allowed to speak to one another but we do say hello and goodbye, twice a day.

The car's windows are tinted darker than is legal, but it's otherwise nondescript. Attention mustn't be drawn to me, or to anyone else who works at the museum.

I slide into the backseat, playing with my iPhone and answering emails during the relatively short ride to LACMA.

We turn right onto Wilshire Boulevard, from Fairfax. The Petersen Automotive Museum is there, its newly unveiled exterior design by Kohn Pedersen Fox Associates commanding my attention. I still haven't gotten used to the flashy, almost Gehry-like façade. It used to be kind of charming—a touch tacky, even—like the overpriced tourist magnet it is. Now it's got these ribbons of stainless steel around three sides and over the top of the deep red building, meant to mimic the streaking speed of a vehicle in full throttle.

Aside from that, the Miracle Mile and L.A.'s Museum Row haven't changed in years. I've been here all my life. My dad held the same position before he retired, died, and I took over; our work is traditional, familial and fraternal. Not unlike Yale's Skull & Bones

Society or even the Freemasons, if I had to draw comparisons.

Traffic is terrible. Crawling along Wilshire, I glance up only occasionally. Mini museums, coffee shops, office buildings. The usual. Only a few people are out and walking about. The sun's gone down and a half moon now hangs casually in the sky, nestled amongst a few wisps of smoggy clouds.

Finally, I'm dropped off. "Goodbye," says the driver. It's the same one, every day I work. I don't know his name and I never will.

Even in the museum, we have… codenames. Nicknames are more like it. Somebody must know who I really am, though: every Friday, my cover paycheck shows up electronically wired into my bank account. My real paycheck, the much heftier one, shows up in the numbered Swiss account of my family (essentially me) every three months without fail.

Still above ground, I head for the LACMA campus, step onto the Resnick North Lawn and pass beneath the Levitated Mass. It's a silly structure passing itself off as art. Not unlike the pyramid in front of The Louvres in Paris—it's just piling stuff on top of stuff. The Levitated Mass is a big rock straddling two high walls and people walk underneath it, thinking it's something special because someone calling himself an artist put it there.

I walk to the front of the museum, where the Urban Lamps are illuminated like soft beacons. I like this installation. Several lampposts, all in neat rows and forming a square, make for excellent cover and camouflage as I hide in plain sight, entering the dense forest of metal, glass and light. I stand where I'm supposed to. I flick that familiar, flush switch. Without a sound I'm lowered quickly underground via high-tech trapdoor.

This is the real museum, as far as I'm concerned. The Los Angeles County Museum of Art is just a cover for us. We're windowless of course, but there's an airiness about the place. It smells nice and it's spacious.

I nod and smile at our receptionist, Lefty. She smiles curtly back. She's an older woman, upper-crust and librarian-like with her blonde bun and her 60s-era Chanel dress suit—not a hair out of place, not a wrinkle in her skirt. She's looking into her monitor as I pass by, headed for my office.

I pass *Hannibal*. I go through the Dutch corridor on my way, as I do every day. I pause to admire Vermeer's *The Concert*. It was stolen in 1990 from the Isabella Stewart

Gardner Museum in Boston. News reports say it's from the largest, most catastrophic art theft in world history… I don't know about that. I would say the Vikings, the Romans and the Nazis did some pretty substantial five-finger discounting back in their times.

Basically, the same players and setting as Vermeer's *The Music Lesson*, the painting depicts three figures—two women and a man—lit by sunny windowpanes, a black and white marble floor at their feet. A big instrument, a cello I guess, sits in the foreground. It's been reframed, of course. It was cut out of the original. No way around that. We keep our frames simple here, anyway. Almost everything is in plain, thin, straight ebony wood.

Occasionally there's a "break in the case" reported on that particular heist. I always chuckle to myself when I read that—I've got it plugged into my Google notifications. Sometimes, for karma's sake, we give stuff back. But that's only to maintain a cosmic balance of sorts, so we can take something else. We're a superstitious lot.

I was still a kid when this heist took place, but Dad knew all about it before it happened. Hell, for all I know he pulled the strings.

On March 18, 1990, two thieves dressed as police officers tied up the security guards, smashed frames, tore canvases and made off with thirteen masterpieces, including *The Concert*. There was also a Manet, five drawings by Degas and three Rembrandts, including his only known seascape, *Storm on the Sea of Galilee*.

That's my favorite. I just glance at most of the other stuff, but there's something so violent and palpably... I don't know... *visceral* about *Storm on the Sea of Galilee*. I have to stop and look at it.

It's such a dynamic piece. There's the delicate ship on the crest of a wicked wave, the dark sky, the determined terror on the faces of the few fighting the mast. There's a man soaked in sea-spray. The others are sitting in quiet resignation on the deck.

I think of it every time I go fishing. (Which isn't as often as I'd like these days.)

I remember once reading about what it's like to drown. I think it was in Sebastian Junger's book, *The Perfect Storm*. It seems horrible and beautiful all at once... it's like the seven stages of grief are playing out within seconds in the mind of the doomed. Up until the time of death when the brain—playing tricks of kindness in the form of hallucinations—reaches acceptance. I think about that whenever I gaze at the painting.

Sometimes I feel sorry that only the privileged few will see this incredible Rembrandt from now on. It's exclusively on display for the eyes of those with cash and connections.

"Hey, Hawkeye." It's my supervisor. "What's up today?"

"Two viewings and a dinner viewing," I say.

In addition to our underground labyrinth of chambers—containing bottles of oils to ancient sculptures, Egyptian sarcophagi to Hollywood movie costumes—we have an incredible private restaurant which seats only two at a time. We employ the best, and most discrete, French chef and wait staff. While our clientele consists mostly of political figures, religious leaders and men so rich their billions cannot be counted, on occasion we do have in the odd actor or musician. I'm told John and Yoko had dinner here, back in my dad's day.

My supervisor nods and bids me a farewell.

Like most, I find my job boring. It's an important job—one I don't take lightly—but I watch the clock, just like anyone else. I play around on Facebook, I see what's up on TMZ. I Tweet. I've got 856 followers on Twitter, under yet another pseudonym. Or would that be a nom de guerre? After all, I am a writer of fiction on Twitter.

I may be bored most of the time but at least my office is nice. It's small, but neat as the proverbial pin and is decorated retro-style with streamlined Art Deco pieces swiped from various homes and antique shops in Paris. I have no art on the walls—there's enough of that everywhere else in my life.

I've wasted enough time, had some more coffee. I guess now I should get to work. I need to let the chef—we call him Frenchie and he doesn't seem to mind—know what tonight's anonymous art appreciator and her date will be having for dinner. We don't offer a menu. The client tells us what they want and we get it. Or more rightly, we steal it.

Nothing here is bought. We have the lowest overhead and maximum profits. That's all I know, though. In the scheme of things, I'm a peon. I am well aware there will be consequences if I ever stray and I am well-paid, so I don't ask questions. I have a whole other life outside these walls.

I press the button on my intercom. "Frenchie, it's Hawkeye."

He answers instantly. His heavily accented, deep voice sounds obsequious, but I detect disdain. I've never actually seen his face but I picture it sharp, hatchet-like.

"Tonight, we'll have two guests at 11:30 p.m. They want Kobe-beef burgers, medium-rare. Please be sure and put all of the condiments on the side. Buns should be lightly toasted. Extra well-done sweet potato fries for him, fresh fruit for her. Please be sure it's not too ripe. No pith. They want two bottles of Krug Clos d'Ambonnay and for dessert—champagne cupcakes made from the same."

"Got eet," he says. "Bonsoir." He clicks off before I can say goodbye.

I tweet: *Some people think just because they have a French accent, they're better than everyone else.* Then I delete it.

I click a few keys on my computer and before long it's time for my first client of the night. This gentleman—I call him "Shoes" in my mind because I don't know his real name and he always wears chichi leather loafers with tassels—has been a regular patron for years.

Shoes likes to look at the Medieval artifacts room. There are illuminated manuscripts, suits of armor, jewelry, weaponry, and several panes of stained glass filched from various cathedrals and mausoleums. My favorite Medieval relics are the skeletons, taken by grave-robbers. One of the disembodied skulls is rumored to be the remains of Matilda of Flanders.

Shoes arrives on the dot, his blindfold recently removed, a world-weary smile on his wan, pale face. We nod to each other, but don't speak. I lead him to his favorite chamber, opening the steel pocket door with my eye. The scanner does its thing and in we go. The armed guards are already inside, of course.

In spite of their presence, I'm not to leave Shoes alone. Not that we don't trust him— quite the contrary. I'm here to be at his beck and call. He sits on the hard, unyielding throne of swords and stares for a long time at a painting I consider quite amateurish. I stand silently by the door, waiting until he is finished.

Finally, I am done for the day. Nothing special happened and I'm eager to get back to my personal life.

Stage Two: *Denial*

Badfinger has to be one of the most depressing, and depressed, bands of all time. They were hailed as the "next Beatles" back in the early 1970s but thanks to sad romances, bad breaks, and even worse management, they wound up penniless and not one, but two of them dead by their own hands. Hands that once wrote lyrics and played the most beautiful, poignant music did the devil's work and ended their lives.

Badfinger had some plucky pop tunes, such as *Come and Get It* and *No Matter What,* but my favorites are the ones about their doomed relationships. *Baby Blue* is a song the lead singer Pete Ham wrote about the love of his life, Dixie Armstrong. It's about how the roving rocker's neglect brought about their breakup and how he "got what he deserved" when she wouldn't take him back.

Without You is the saddest song, ever. *"I can't give... I can't live anymore... without you."*

Badfinger seemed poised for success from the start. They opened for top acts like The Yardbirds and The Moody Blues before being signed to The Beatles' Apple Records in 1968. Paul McCartney himself wrote their biggest hit.

But Apple Records was mismanaged, at best.

In 1975, just three days before his twenty-eighth birthday, lead singer Pete Ham hanged himself in the garage of his new home in Surrey. On his arms, he left cigarette burns. In his pocket, he left a note blaming Badfinger's manager Stan Polley, calling him a "soulless bastard."

He assured his pregnant girlfriend Anne Herriott he loved her, but "It's better this way." Alone, Anne gave birth to their daughter one month later.

Eight years after that, in 1983, Ham's main songwriting partner Pete Evans also committed suicide by hanging. He used a willow tree in his backyard. This was following disputes over Badfinger's royalties. Too bad he couldn't have… if my gallows humor can be pardoned… hung on until 1994. Mariah Carey had a huge hit with *Without You* and Evans would have made bank.

Maybe money is the root of all evil, I think as I hand the cashier a crisp twenty and get only six bucks back. Parking is highway robbery at the Hollywood & Highland complex. I was there longer than I meant to be, but still.

I now have a mere forty-five minutes to get over the hill into the Valley. Highland Avenue crawls, until I finally get to the Cahuenga Pass. I avoid the freeway at this hour… Hell, at almost any hour.

I crank *Suicide Solution*, one of my favorite songs. It's by Ozzy Osbourne and it was released before I was born. "Suicide is slow with alcohol…"

I hope I won't be late for my group.

We meet in Toluca Lake every Wednesday. As with nearly everything else in my life, it's anonymous. Until it gets personal… but that's another story.

I pull my new, paper-plated Mercedes-Benz SLS AMG Black Series over to a side street and walk a few blocks to the modest, nondescript community center. I don't want anyone in my group to feel bad, don't want them to think I'm better off than them. Don't want to be resented. I'm one of them, after all. Just a human being, with all the failings and foibles that go along with it.

Some of us have been in the group long enough to be considered OK to be sponsors. I'm a sponsor, but not all the time. For months on end, I just listen and sometimes I share my story. There's no pressure.

Our group is called "Above the Influence." ATI for short.

We have eight right now. James, a real sad sack if ever I saw one, joined about three weeks ago. He hasn't said much and I'm eager to know more.

One of our newest members is Donna. At least, that's what she calls herself. Whether it's true or not is anybody's guess. Donna suits her, though. She's pretty and I think that's what the name means, though it translates as 'lady' in Italian.

In some ways, she reminds me of my sister.

When Jessie and me were kids, it was us against the world.

Dad worked all night, every night. He was in the museum of course, though we didn't know it then. We imagined all kinds of cool, clandestine careers for him. Was he an international spy? Maybe he was a pimp-slash-mortician like in our favorite movie, *Night Shift*.

Mom was an alcoholic. That was a full-time job for her and she took it seriously.

One morning when she was in her room behind a closed door, blackout shades over the windows, I got Jessie ready for school. Same as always, I got the mini stepladder from the side of the fridge and got the cereal down from its dusty top. We liked Life. The cereal, I mean. Life in general was... well, it was all we knew. I was eight, Jessie was six. She was a sweet kid, curious and a bit wistful. Unlike mine, her hair was blonde. Her eyes were pale blue. Later they'd remind me of a song by The Velvet

Underground. *"Linger on, your pale blue eyes…"*

She was a good girl, always did what I told her. I rather liked my position of authority. "Drink your juice," I'd command, even as she was doing just that.

We were still in our PJs that morning. She wore a Cabbage Patch nightie, as I recall. It was early, but our daddy would be home soon. He'd ruffle our hair, then go into the den and turn the news on. Though he slept most of it away anyhow, he liked to be informed what the day's weather would bring. Who knows what he did after Jessie and I went to school.

But Dad wasn't home yet. It was just us.

And Mom.

We had to be very quiet in the mornings. Even at our tender ages, we knew what a hangover was. To us, she was like a sleeping lion. A mane of matted blonde hair (she usually hit the pillow with spray-saturated strands), a nude-colored slip (I could see right through it and she never wore panties), and a nasty temper (don't even think it). That was Mom.

I say "was"—though I assume she's still alive out there somewhere.

Jessie's not alive anymore. But she was that morning. She probably wished she wasn't, or at least wished she were invisible. That's what I excelled at: keeping under the radar. Maybe that's why I'm so good at my job today.

Jessie was bouncing around in her chair a bit, as six-year-old girls will. I'd finished my breakfast and I was in our room, getting dressed. I picked out a blue unicorn tee-shirt and some jeans and flip-flops for my sister to wear, and I was just about to look at the clock when I heard an awful clatter.

Mom and I made it to the kitchen right around the same time, but she got to Jessie first. Jessie had dropped her dish and it lay broken on the floor. A few soggy pieces of cereal lay amongst chips and shards of ceramic.

I stood in the open arch between the kitchen and the den. My bare feet straddled the carpeting and linoleum. I said nothing, but I looked at my little sister in mute sympathy.

Mom's stiff Aqua Net coif conflicted texturally with her soft pink peignoir, just as her smooth, fleshy fingertips clashed with her long, sharp nails. She grabbed Jessie by her left upper-arm and I could picture the bruises and crescent-shaped marks that would be left. If we got to school at all, Jessie would be wearing long sleeves.

Her small body was flung to the floor, her head narrowly missing a table-leg.

Mom pushed the back of Jessie's head to the floor by her broken bowl. "See what you did?"

Jessie was silent, but tears flowed down her reddening cheeks.

"Do you think we're made of money? Do you think we can just break dishes and waste food?" She paused, as if waiting for an answer. "Eat it."

Jessie shot me a look. I was helpless. Motionless. Eight years old.

She cast a watery glance up at our mother. *Really?*

Mom nodded, her face set, features fixed in fury.

Jessie picked at a lump of sodden Life, one without any ceramic dust and did as she was told. There were about five or six pieces in all, some with shards and those had to be eaten too. How she survived that incident relatively unscathed, I'll never know. She didn't have to eat much glass, but even not much is more than enough. I guess stomach acid really is that strong.

She was forced to mop the floor and then piece together the bowl with Krazy Glue. For at least a week, that was Jessie's bowl. After that, Dad must've thrown it away because it just disappeared. I don't know if he ever knew what happened that morning and I never asked. Such was the way of our household. Don't ask. Don't tell. Be quiet. Keep secrets.

I was fine with that.

But Jessie didn't fare so well. She was always happy, playful, boisterous and bouncy as a baby and a youngster, but over the years she changed. She became bookish, lonesome and desperate for affection. She stayed with friends as much as she could, proposing slumber parties at their houses, inviting herself over for dinners, to movies, and even church on Sundays. Anything to get away.

Maybe that's why Donna reminds me of Jessie. She's talking to another woman in the group. Though she obviously doesn't know this person, she's proposing coffee after the meeting. As if she doesn't want to go home.

Since most of us are regulars, we don't rehash our life stories. This isn't A.A., where everyone's labeled an "addict" and made to stand before all those eyes and say, "My name is so-and-so and I'm an alcoholic."

I did go to Al-Anon for a minute, back when I was twenty or so, but it wasn't for me. I'm not the one with a problem.

I'm above the influence.

Stage Three: *Anger*

I wasn't born yet when Sid Vicious of The Sex Pistols OD'ed on heroin while he awaited trial for the murder of his girlfriend, Nancy Spungen. He killed her in Manhattan's Chelsea Hotel—the same place Leonard Cohen and Bob Dylan wrote poignant love songs to Janis Joplin and Sara Lownds.

On the morning of October 12th in 1978, Sid claimed to have awoken from a drug-dream to find Nancy's lifeless body on the bathroom floor of their room.

She was a junk-whore and an ex-hooker, so I guess it's not surprising she came to a bad end. And it's not surprising Courtney Love wanted to play Nancy in the film version… Both were toxic sirens, as far as I'm concerned.

Nancy suffered a single stab wound to her belly and bled out. The fancy blade had recently been bought by Sid on 42nd Street and was identical to a collector's knife given to his friend Stiv Bators of the Dead Boys by Dee Ramone.

Upon his arrest Sid admitted he'd fought with Nancy, but that she fell on the knife by accident. Then he said, "I stabbed her, but I didn't mean to kill her."

Ten days later, he tried to slit his wrist with a broken light-bulb. After that he went to Riker's, made bail and went home with his new girlfriend.

But he never forgot Nancy.

Sid succeeded in his second attempt, this time with powerful heroin supplied by his own mother. Seems like not a bad way to go. Better than a bullet to the brain or hanging yourself, anyway. I've never tried heroin, but I hear it's like the afterglow of an orgasm multiplied by ten. No wonder it's so addictive.

Sid's mom later found a note referencing his slain love, saying, "We had a death pact and I have to keep my half of the bargain. Please bury me next to my baby. Bury me in my leather jacket, jeans and motorcycle boots. Goodbye."

Adding insult to the ultimate injury, he was cremated and since Nancy was laid to rest in a consecrated Jewish cemetery, Sid's remains could be left nowhere near her.

Right now, I'm near Donna. She's in week two of recovery. She seems fine to everyone else, I'm sure—but I see the fragility. I'm close enough to see the slight blue tint of the vein in her temple, to smell the faint sweetness of her herbal shampoo. Her nails are filed short and rounded (but I see some rough edges), and she wears a faded black sundress.

I'm still curious about James, too. I watch him as he shares his story.

"Afterward, I felt like such a failure," he's saying. His thinning beige hair is slicked back, the length tucked behind his ears. He wears an Ed Hardy tee-shirt—*There's your failure right there*, I think—and whiskered dark wash denim jeans. Cowboy boots, too new.

"I couldn't tell anyone about it, of course. I had to carry on, to present a face to the world of happiness and calm. Of being in control." According to him, it affected his work, his social life. It was all he could think about. Not an uncommon story. His wife, now an ex, knew about it and she made sure he was never alone. She tried to keep him distracted, tried to tell him he was better than that. She got rid of all the bottles.

It didn't work. He wound up in the hospital and then an asylum of sorts. Rock bottom, but not the end. And here he was, trying to sort it all out. We all offer words of encouragement, pats on the back and clichés. *It's always darkest before the dawn, don't worry it gets better, tough times never last but tough people do.* And so on.

After our meeting, Donna and I go for coffee. She's not ready to talk yet about what's brought her to us and that's fine. She admires my ring and I tell her it belonged to my little sister Jessie. I wear it on a chain around my neck. It's my only jewelry, apart from my wedding band. I allude to the fact that Jessie's dead, but Donna doesn't pry.

We talk about mundane things.

"Where are you from?" she asks me. She's enjoying a Grande quad nonfat one-pump no-whip mocha, while I stir at my flavorless, colorless green tea. I'm trying to get on the antioxidant bandwagon, but it's a hard row to hoe. At least tea is gluten-free, so I've got that.

"Here," I say. "I know, I know. Nobody's born and raised in L.A."

"Meet your match," she says.

"No shit? Where from?"

"Temecula. You've probably never heard of it. Maybe that's what drove me to drink," she chuckles.

So, she doesn't want to talk, but she wants to hint. I just nod and sip.

"You don't look like… er…" she falters.

"Oh, I'm not," I say a bit too quickly. "I mean, yeah. I get it. Been there. But nowadays, I counsel. I'm a sponsor. You know, people call me when they're feeling weak." I change the subject. "What's your line of work?"

"I'm not working now. I lost my job."

Oops. I should have known better than to have asked that. I'll avoid romance, family and pets while I'm at it. "Do you like art?" I ask.

She nods. Who's going to say no to that question? Nobody wants to think of themselves a philistine.

"There's a great exhibit at LACMA," I say. "It's a retrospective of Llyn Foulkes. Portraiture, narrative tableaux. Existential landscapes, his postwar abstractions."

She blinks, blank.

Tone it down. "His later works focus mainly on Disney. There's some freaky stuff, like Mickey Mouse clawing his way out of Walt's eye."

Donna's right eyebrow shoots up. I just can't seem to get it together, conversationally, today. I smile and shrug.

"So, you're an expert, are you?" she asks. "Really, all I know is what's popular."

"I know a lot about art. My dad worked in a museum. But I'm no expert. I'd really rather get a mani-pedi and binge-watch Netflix than go to LACMA."

Donna chuckles. "Same here!" Then the smile disappears. "But I can't afford it these days." She holds out her hands, so I can see her ragged, unpolished fingernails.

"Come on, then. It's on me," I say, trashing my tea in the nearby wastebasket.

"Oh, I don't know," she demurs. I can tell she doesn't want to owe me anything, or maybe doesn't consider herself worthy of a treat on someone she barely knows.

"I insist," I say.

She nods and stands. She's malleable.

There's a chic salon nearby, but I don't want to overwhelm her. I want her to trust me. After all, it's why I do what I do. It's why I've been going to group for so many months. I want to help.

There's a place I know a few blocks down the road. I say I'll meet her there and after parking my car out of sight and changing into the pair of flip-flops I keep in the trunk, I walk over. She's there, having just arrived. Her fingernails are chewed to the nubs, so she opts for the pedi only.

I get scrubbed and buffed. No polish for me, not even clear—though it's offered. No one who works at the museum is allowed to wear anything that might damage a painting or a statue... the swipe of a red fingernail, or a keychain hanging from one's hip, could do disaster. I'm surprised we're not obliged to wear hairnets.

Donna and I chat a little more. I find out she was an only child. That her dad was an alcoholic. That she's never been married. That she used to be a bookkeeper. She likes classic literature.

Afterwards, we part ways. We'll see each other in group next week. Maybe I'll tell my story. It's been awhile. What should I say? The possibilities gallop through my mind like so many roughshod horses.

But now it's time to go home and await my chariot to work.

Stage Four: *Bargaining*

WOW. Or Wendy O. Williams as she was better known, was the lead singer of the seminal heavy punk band, The Plasmatics. They reigned from 1978 to '88.

The brash blonde was known for destruction. She reveled in it. Onstage, she would use sledgehammers or chainsaws to wreak havoc on TV sets, guitars and Cadillac Coupe de Villes. When she was dressed, she favored nurse outfits, leopard print and black electrical tape over her nipples. Her hair was usually worn in a Mohawk and when she pranced onstage, she channeled a Roman warhorse with a roached mane and fire flowing from its flared nostrils.

She would have liked that analogy, I think. Wendy loved animals. She lived in a dome in the forest and she spent her final days nursing injured baby squirrels back to life. She was a vegetarian. And an advocate of healthy living...

...That is, when she wasn't trying to kill herself.

In 1993, she stabbed herself in the chest. Actually, she used a hammer to lodge a chef's knife into her sternum. In 1997 she overdosed on ephedrine. But it wasn't until she took a shotgun into the woods, put it to her head and pulled the trigger, that she succeeded in her grim goal.

Wendy was a thoughtful suicide. She set aside presents for her longtime love, Rod Swenson, including his favorite noodles, seeds for salad greens and oriental massage balm. She left a note: "My feelings about what I am doing ring loud and clear to an inner ear and a place where there is no self, only calm."

She wanted to die. Maybe that's why she sings with such fierce conviction on *It's My Life*, a song written by Gene Simmons and Paul Stanley of KISS and first released on her

1984 album WOW. It was her life. Hers to live, hers to take.

If someone decides they want to die, they should be allowed to make it happen.

That's how I've always felt, even before Jessie died.

After Jessie died, I learned what the legal terms were for acts which arose from those feelings. Depraved-heart murder. Reckless endangerment. Culpable negligence. Did you know suicide is illegal? Well, no one attempting suicide has ever been prosecuted, but it's construed as a crime nonetheless, because it allows the state to lawfully detain you for treatment without your consent. But people have been prosecuted for encouraging suicide in others... Say, during a friendly game of Russian Roulette. The winner is really a loser, in the eyes of the law.

But that's a pretty clumsy way of doing it. Getting someone to kill themselves, I mean.

Putting a pistol in a depressed person's quivering hand, that's easy. Or plying the bereaved with booze and downers, putting them in front of the TV and sticking in a DVD of *Angela's Ashes*. That's child's play.

But tipping someone over the edge who doesn't really want to die? That's the rabbit from the hat.

I shouldn't be dwelling on the past. I'll get back to Jessie again, I promise. Right now, I need to think about… now.

It's a big day at work. I have three showings, which is going to show up big on my paycheck.

First, I have a very famous reality TV producer coming in to see—but not touch. No touching allowed. It's the magnificent Davidoff-Morini Stradivarius violin. What a beauty it is! In October 1995, the three-million-dollar 1727 instrument was stolen from renowned violinist Erica Morini's New York apartment. Poor Morini, who was ninety-one years old, died shortly after the robbery. Perhaps its loss was just too much for her frail soul to bear. But the melody-maker lives on, cloistered within the walls of our magnificent museum.

After that, I have a client flying all the way in from Jordan to see one our Picassos. It's *The Pigeon With Green Peas* (AKA, *Le Pigeon Aux Petits Pois*) and it was snatched from the Musée d'Art Moderne de la Ville de Paris in 2010. The lone thief was later convicted, though he was found empty-handed. The guy said he threw it in the trash, but the framed canvas was never found. And it never will be.

Lastly, I'm showing one of my personal favorites, a religious piece by Jan van Eyck's called *The Just Judges*. (Though some folks suspect his brother, Hubert, might be the actual painter.)

Before my dad was even a gleam in his dad's eye, this trinket was taken from its display at Saint Bavon's Cathedral in Ghent, Belgium, where it served as part of the *Adoration of the Lamb* altarpiece created in the mid-1400s. There were some ransom notes swirling around in the 1930s shortly after it was swiped and the self-proclaimed thief—a flamboyant politician, artist and lover of detective novels, named Arsène Goedertier—revealed with his dying breath that only he knew where the painting was hidden and that he would take the secret with him to his grave.

The Just Judges is the lower left panel of the Ghent Altarpiece and it shows portraits of several contemporary figures such as Philip the Good and possibly the artists Hubert and Jan van Eyck themselves. In the forefront is a serene-faced young man astride a magnificent white stallion, its mane—perhaps a bit like Wendy O. Williams' bleached blonde hair—flowing in the winds of change.

I've done lots of research on this one. I must admit, I'm fascinated with what drives people to steal. I'm not talking about Jean Valjean style stealing, a loaf of bread to survive. We can all understand that. Then there's the thrill of taking something of value, something you don't actually need. The plotting, the planning, the devising and the deft skill.

To steal a thing is a tangible act. People notice. But to steal a life, without detection, now that's real talent.

"If you'd just stay here and help out, I'll buy you a car," Mom pleaded. "How about a classic Mustang?"

She was always doing that. Bribing us. Making bargains. "If you do this, I'll do that." She made it seem so easy. It never was, of course.

Dad had left us by then. It was just me, Jessie and our mother. I was eighteen and I could have gone out on my own.

But I couldn't leave Jessie with her. Being with Mom felt like being choked from the inside. I figured being *alone* with Mom must've been infinitely worse.

Jessie was almost sixteen. She'd talked to Dad about it and he said, "It's up to your mother."

My sister wanted to go away to study. In Paris. She would rather spend her time with brooding, espresso-sipping French intellectuals who seem to do nothing for a living and have all the time in the world to ponder deep philosophical things in Left Bank cafés.

That would not do. She couldn't leave me. I wouldn't allow it.

The idea came to me one night while I was in my bedroom, listening to music. I put on Bad Company's *Shooting Star*. Although Paul Rodgers didn't kill himself (at least, not yet. He's still alive and well as I write this), the lyrics portray an alternate reality the singer envisioned for himself, had he succumbed to the deepest depths of rock 'n roll decadence. *"Johnny died one night, died in his bed. Bottle of whiskey, sleeping tablets by his head."*

Although she'd cauterized her emotions to the point of nonexistence around others, Jessie was always honest with me. I knew her pain. I knew how to bring it out.

A few years before, I'd talked Jessie into keeping a journal. I told her I kept one too, to hold our secrets and to keep a record of our pain. I didn't, though. Not then. I simply read hers, which soothed my soul with words. She wrote about the solace of suicide. Sylvia Plath poetry mixed with rock lyrics was vomited onto the thin, cheap pages over and over again, along with the occasional teenager frivolity about cute boys and sexy shoes.

One phrase in Jessie's journal always stuck with me: "Unexpected death is an abduction." I don't know if they were her own words or not, but they made sense.

In the end, there was no bargain. Mom simply said, "No, Jessie. You can't go." And that was the beginning of the end.

Stage Five: *Guilt*

When I think of suicide by shotgun, I think of men. Hard-drinking, hard-riding, hard-handed men. Ernest Hemingway. Hunter S. Thompson. Calluses against metal as they squeezed the grip.

Women usually go for the soft embrace of drugs and alcohol. *Usually.*

Mindy McCready couldn't have been any more different, musically, from fellow trigger-puller Wendy O. Williams. She was an angel-faced country chick, with a sweet smile and a touch of sass. She had a handful of hits, but all too quickly fell from fame's fleeting graces. She spiraled into the usual depression and addictions.

Ironically, just days before she shot herself on her front porch, she was working on a suicide prevention video. Presumably, it was to assuage her own grief and guilt after the front porch shotgun suicide of her boyfriend a month earlier. But later, friends speculated Mindy was actually warning them that she was next.

Too bad nobody warned the family dog. Yep, that's right. The singer popped the pooch just before doing herself in. I always thought that was a strange touch. I mean, what for—to ensure she'd feel bad enough about herself to be able to put the gun to her own head? To test how quick and hopefully painless it would be?

There was some speculation that Mindy actually killed her boyfriend, that his wasn't a suicide at all.

The couple had a baby son. Talk about tragedy.

In fact, I'm talking about it tonight. It's Wednesday again and time for another A.T.I. meeting.

I'm going to offer to sponsor Donna. She needs me. I can tell. I want to help her, like I helped Jessie. And Rose.

(I'll get to Rose, later.)

I stand at the podium, looking out over the wan, deeply shadowed faces, hard-edged in the cheap fluorescent tube-lighting and years of pain, anguish and self-doubt. These are my people. A black-haired, dark-eyed messiah, my nails buffed, teeth gleaming and dressed in a dark eggplant silk shirt, classic slacks and sandals, I knew I had the admiration—and envy—of them all.

James has just finished sharing. Again. At first, he didn't say much. Now he won't shut the fuck up about his one measly suicide attempt. Of course, I'm all grace and compassion. I beam at him. "James. That was beautiful. And you are so right. There's no time like the present. And there's no present like time. We mustn't waste it."

James, still wearing egregious Ed Hardy, clasps his hands together and juts them out, mouthing, "Thank you."

I glance over at Donna. She catches my eye, then smiles and dips her gaze. She likes me. I can tell.

While everyone else is slurping caffeinated swill from white Styrofoam cups, I've got my Starbucks Thanksgiving blend. (Yeah, I just couldn't do the green tea.) I take a small sip, before beginning. I clear my throat, pretending I'm nervous. I pull Jessie's ring to-and-fro along the string of platinum chain around my neck. I give a half-smile, a faint chuckle.

"I haven't told my story in a long time. But there are enough new faces here, to warrant a re-telling. It's not easy, even after all these years..."

The sheets are damp, steamy and rumpled from our first time together. Donna and me. Her fingertips trace my jawline. The corners of my mouth rise in a smile that follows the smooth, sensuous tickle.

She tilts her head and looks at me. Somewhere nearby, a weak streetlamp shines stubbornly through the slats of her cheap, white plastic blinds. Her bittersweet chocolate eyes are so dark, they're nearly black.

"Where'd you get that scar?" she asks, touching the thin white line on my chin.

"Handlebars of my Huffy."

"A bike?"

"Yes. But not just any bike. I was a very discerning nine-year-old. I had a genuine vintage Slingshot model with a sixteen-inch front dragster wheel and twenty-inch rear. I pimped it out with a Flaming Stack chain guard, which was designed to look just like the side exhaust pipe covers of a Corvette."

"Sounds like you were a bit of a daredevil," she smiles.

She takes my left hand in hers. I slipped the wedding band off before getting into bed with her, though of course she's seen it before.

"Yeah. The bike was totaled," I sigh. "But that's nothing compared to this," I say, lowering the sheet a touch so she could get a good look at the long, wavy scar just under my right pec.

"Botched boob job?" she jokes.

"Funny. I like that. You're a real card, you know that? An ace." I scruff her hair playfully, then go on. "This is from the bill of a marlin. I was fishing off the coast —"

"Which is way better than fishing on the coast."

"You're a regular comedian, aren't you?" I grin. But really, I am getting a bit miffed at all these interruptions.

"—off the coast in the northern Atlantic. I had the bastard hooked and it was like something out of a Hemingway novel —"

"*The Old Man and the Sea*?"

"Right. Anyway, the slick bastard comes flying right at me and grazed me with his nose, which is like a swordfish's. I was bleeding like I'd been gored by a bull —"

"*Death in the Afternoon*."

I sigh. "You know your Hemingway. Good. OK, so anyway, I'm gushing blood and this

S.O.B. is flopping all over the deck. That sword of his is like an out of control chainsaw and I'm dancing around, trying to avoid getting hamstrung. Finally, I grab a folding chair and start beating this thing over the head until it stops moving."

"Oh, my God. That must have been terrifying!"

"Not really. At the end of the day, he was delicious. I sautéed him in a butter and garlic sauce, with a touch of port. He fed me for a week. All's well that ends well."

She shakes her head.

"I have some scars, too." Donna's gaze dips. She's pensive, now.

She's so pretty. Not a very good lay, but lovely to look at. Besides, it's only our first time. I'll get her to come around. To want and need me and only me. This is a very important stage in our relationship. It's about earning trust. She already likes me. I can tell that one day soon, she might even love me. But that's not what I'm after. She has to trust me more than she trusts herself. More than she trusts her own instincts. Like that marlin, I have to hook her before I can cook her. So to speak. I'm no Jeffrey Dahmer, if that's what you're thinking.

Anyway, I know the routine. It never fails. Charm and disarm. Tell her she's gorgeous, smart, funny, great in bed. Whatever it takes. Then, I start chipping away.

As Michelangelo once said, "It's my job to free the human form trapped inside the block." Donna is like a precious work of art. She's like one of the Elgin Marbles. My work begins with the selection of a perfect, yet unformed shape. After I find my stone, one that speaks to me, I begin chiseling. Getting rid of the parts I don't want: Self-esteem, the ability to make unilateral decisions, and confidence. Especially confidence. Then I'll place the tapered point of my chisel against a selected part of the stone, swinging the mallet at it with precisely controlled strokes, careful to strike accurately. The smallest miscalculation could damage the stone, not to mention the sculptor's hand.

I take her hands. Gently turn them palms-up. "I know about those scars. Show me another one."

Donna smiles again. Shyly. I can smell the faint mint residue on her teeth and the musk of my kisses. She moves her right leg out from under the crisp, crumpled sheet. She brings it up, so her knee is held aloft. There's a scar in the folds of flesh.

"My knees are so ugly, you probably can't even see it. But right there," she points, "is where I fell while getting out of the limo at my high school prom."

"Oh, man. Seriously? You fell in front of everyone at your prom?"

"The story of my life," she says, sighing. Then she shrugs.

I can tell the memory still haunts her. She feels things very deeply. They affect her. She doesn't let go.

This is good for me.

My one regret is that I wasn't there when Jessie killed herself.

I was there for Rose. Oh, yes. I made sure of that.

But like I said, the first time isn't always the best. You know you want to do it again, you vow to hone your technique and sure enough— it gets better.

Rose was my fiancée. Ten days before our wedding, she overdosed on pills. I held her in my arms, made sure she kept everything down… I knew she wouldn't want to be found in a puddle of vomit. Besides, what if she'd tossed the lethal cocktail? That would not do.

Now, you might be wondering, if you're fan of morbid primetime true crime, *Why didn't I wait a while? Why not get married, insure her life and then pull the curtains?* I find that vulgar. Money as a motive. I can make money. Anyone can make money. But to be a honed, undetectable killing machine that never once lays a finger on his prey? To make them think it's their idea? That, my friend, is pure talent.

You have to be willing to change things up, shake them up. Not follow any pattern. I like to think I have a jazz brain and rock 'n roll soul.

I'm like the David Bowie song, *Rock 'n Roll Suicide.* If only the world knew about me, I'd have fist-pumping lighter waving hordes in my wake, wherever I go. *"So natural, religiously unkind..."*

I learned a lot about Rose in the few months she was my patient. Not officially. I'm not a PhD., or a certified therapist or anything like that. But I told Rose I was. Told her lots of things. She believed them all. When I told her I loved her and that I would be there for her until the end, she believed me.

One of my favorite ways in—and women love this; they dig psychology—is a little litmus test that goes like this. I take her out to dinner. A nice, but not too nice, romantic hideaway where we have a light dinner and lots of wine. She's loose and feeling pretty in the candlelight. I hold her hand, placing it in my lap. Nothing too overt, merely suggestive. If she doesn't pull away… and mind you, this is on the third or fourth date… I know I can start chiseling.

I tell a story, asking questions along the way. "You are walking in the woods. It's a lush, idyllic place. Who are you walking with?" Whomever she says, that's the most important person in her life. If she says, "No one. I'm alone," that's a great sign for me to move ahead. Next, I'll ask, "You see an animal in these woods. What kind of animal is it?" The animal is representative of her perception of the size of her problems. So if she says it's a bunny, then that's not as good for me as if she were to say a grizzly bear or a mountain lion. (Now, if she says "a penguin" or something like that, then I know she's either bat-scat crazy or has no idea what kinds of animals live in the forest.)

Then I tell her she comes to a house and I ask her to describe it to me. I can get a lot from that, but what I really want to know is, "Is there a fence around this house?" If not, then she hasn't got many walls up and I can get in easier. Then I say she goes in and she sees a table in the kitchen. I ask her to describe the table. If her reply does not include food, people, or flowers, then I know she's secretly miserable. This is good news. Overtly unhappy people aren't very likely to off themselves. It's the quiet ones you have to watch for.

The test goes on. There's a huge tree felled in the forest and I find out how she gets around it. These represent her problems; so, does she climb over the tree? Dig under it? Go around? The best one is about the body of water she comes to. This is how she views love and sex. Is the surface glassy? Can she see clearly into the water? Is it murky? Is it cold, or warm? Does she want to take a swim, or not?

Rose answered all these questions just about the same way Jessie did. It's not foolproof, but damn near close.

Jessie was pretty distraught when I gave her the test. She loved answering my questions, though. She thought I was asking because I really cared about her and wanted to help her. Well, maybe I did. I was younger, then. Idealistic.

I loved Jessie, but I also loved my power over her.

Jessie was almost seventeen by now. She was becoming a woman in some ways; physically, anyway. She had that burgeoning bloom of youth, curves appearing where before there were only angles, elbows and knees. Her eyes were clear and bright, but usually downcast either in thought or worry. Mom was a constant source of worry. We both still lived with her in our palace of eggshells and glass.

I didn't tell anyone (not even my sweet sis), but I'd opened up a line of communication with Dad. I knew someday soon, I'd be joining him in his very special line of work. Instead of Jessie leaving me, I'd be leaving her.

Or maybe I could have my marlin and eat it too.

When Jessie was gone, I'd read her diary. Then I'd carefully put it away, seemingly undisturbed. When we'd later have casual conversations, heart-to-hearts, or even just joking around, I'd throw in tidbits about her I'd learned from reading the journal. She was amazed at the depth of my perception. How well I knew her. How I was the only one who really, really knew her. Or I'd pose a thought similar to something she'd been thinking. "We are so much alike," she'd marvel. I'd nod in mutual amazement, the picture of perspicuity.

So much alike. After a few months, I began to suggest to her that we were just the same as our mother. No good. Unlovable. We'd never be worthy of a soul-mate. Who in their right minds could ever really care about us? There was something wrong with us. We were fucked up and that would never change. It was in our blood.

So why bother going on living?

I told Jessie I wanted to kill myself.

She nodded, hugging herself as if wrapped in a placenta of grief and self-loathing. "Me, too."

The last words she wrote in her journal were, "I love you."

Stage Six: *Depression*

Sometimes, you have to find the good in goodbye. And it seems the rakishly handsome, ringlet-haired lothario-like lead singer of the Australian pop band INXS did just that.

Michael Hutchence went out erotically asphyxiated, so maybe he died with a smile on his face. I like to think so. The poor guy deserved that, at least.

In death as in life, his story was front and center of a media circus. Before his nude body was found on the morning of November 22, 1997 by a maid in his Ritz-Carlton Sydney hotel room—#524, booked to a Mr. Murray Rivers—Michael's messy life was splashed across all the rags. He was in torment not only over extreme drug addiction, but because it would be a Christmas without his beloved sixteen-month-old daughter, Heavenly Hiraani Tiger Lily. Lily's mother, a bottle-blonde TV personality named Paula Yates, was in a bitter custody battle with the father of her other children, Bob Geldof. It was a nightmare all around.

Michael was terribly depressed by most accounts, especially after a freak accident a few years earlier had robbed him of most of his senses of taste and smell. A cocktail of alcohol, cocaine and Prozac was later noted by the coroner.

Michael hung out with friends, then phoned a few people before meeting his maker. One of his ex-girlfriends was so worried she actually went to his hotel room and knocked on the door on the morning of his death, but he didn't answer. Maybe he was already gone. The last time his voice, that voice which was on so many hit records, was recorded was on his personal manager Martha Troup's voice-mail. He said, "Marth, Michael here. I've fucking had enough."

Far from "Elegantly Wasted," Michael was pathetic in the end. He didn't die pretty. There was evidence he'd scrounged through wastebaskets, searching for even a crumb of leftover cocaine and there was a week-old cigarette burn on one of his fingers that had gone down to the bone, indicating he'd passed out and didn't even feel the pain. In the same trash can he'd dumpster-dived for drugs, police later found lyrics to the last song he wrote—which have never been published.

His death was ruled a suicide by auto-erotic asphyxia.

Apparently, this form of sex-play is not uncommon amongst more adventurous paramours. When it's done with a partner, the act is called Breath Control Play. But what it really is, is strangulation without death (hopefully). The carotid arteries on the sides of the neck flow the most oxygen-rich blood to the brain and so restricting that stream produces lightheadedness and even giddiness, which surges the sensations during sex. When pressure is released, the rush of that elemental necessity to the brain is a *zing!* of pure euphoria.

When engaged in a little hand-to-gland combat, the soloist can use a plastic bag over the head, or a belt or scarf around his neck.

Michael Hutchence opted for a snakeskin belt. Three years later, Paula Yates opted for heroin, leaving Lily to grow up without her parents.

Jessie and I grew up without parents. Real, normal, present ones, anyway. I only got close to my dad later, after Jessie's suicide. And following her funeral, Mom disappeared altogether. Good riddance, I say.

I'd told Rose about most of this, tailored to fit my needs of course, shortly after we met. I think it made her trust me that much more as her therapist and her confidant. She thought I got it. Got *her*. Poor, trusting Rose.

We never did live together or exchange house keys. My work schedule wasn't known to her, only my limited availability. At first, she assumed I was married and not hiding it too well. I talked her out of that nonsense, leaving out the fact I was divorced. From a man. Does that make me a widow, or a widower? I always get the two mixed up. In any case, I'm far too evolved to be defined by something as base as gender. I'm beyond all that. Divine.

No, I'm not delusional. I know I'm just a little-ol' flesh and bone human being. Some might say I'm like a surgeon with a God complex. Nothing could be further from the truth. Just because I've used psychological sleights on others doesn't mean I'm blind to my own… Well, I wouldn't call them *faults*. More like, peculiarities. Yes, I like that: I'm "peculiar."

In case you're wondering why no-one's connected all these deadly dots, it's because I'm a well-kept secret. All of us who work within the walls of the museum are provided with a brand-new identity every six months, like Swiss clockwork.

Anyway, it was a moonless Wednesday night when Rose faded from this world. I'll never forget it. It was truly transcendental.

I told her it was the right thing to do. Everyone would, indeed, be better off without her. "No one will miss you, Rose," I said softly. Her entire existence was nothing but a cacophony of monotony. Pointless. Futile. *End it now, before it gets too painful.* I put on some soothing music, poured her a glass of rich red wine and gave her a handful of pills, which she accepted gratefully. She really did. "Thank you," she said breathily between swallows.

The room was candle-lit, the aroma was of warm sandalwood.

I held her until she was no more. I watched her blue eyes, nearly the same shade as Jessie's, close for the last time. There was no violence. No sickness. No fight.

Nothing but ragdoll limbs and a lolling head as I dragged her slight form off the bed and slipped her inside the waiting bath. With her final, shallow breath, she inhaled oil-slick, soapy water and clinched the coroner's report of accidental suicide by drowning.

I've just been dropped off at the museum. I walk to the front entrance of LACMA, where the Urban Lamps light my way. Standing in the middle of the metallic forest, I flick that familiar, flush switch. Without a sound I'm lowered underground by the high-tech trapdoor.

I nod and smile at Lefty. She smiles curtly back, mouth-corners raised, no teeth showing. Tonight, she's in a Chinese dress—a cheongsam. It's red, with gold dragons on it. We're sort of in synch. Even though I'm in slate grey, my scarf is scarlet with flecks of gilt.

I pass *Hannibal*. I go through the Dutch corridor and I pause to admire Vermeer's *The Concert*. I linger at *Storm on the Sea of Galilee*.

And now, I'm in my office looking over the night's assignments. One of my favorites—a client we call "The Encyclopedia" because he reels off facts at the speed of light (which is approximately 186,000 miles per second, he once told me)—will be here in an hour (3,600 seconds).

Encyclopedia wants to see the famous Ruby Slippers from the classic 1939 film, *The Wizard of Oz*. Mind you, these aren't the only pair ever made. And they're not even worth all that much—only about two million. But we have lots of movie memorabilia. It's a popular display in this town.

This particular pair of kicks disappeared on August 27, 2005, from the Judy Garland Museum in Grand Rapids, Minnesota. No one's tried clicking the heels together three times to see if they'll find their way home, but I can't say I haven't been tempted.

They sparkle prettily under the spotlight. So small and delicate. Not many people know this, but Dorothy's supernatural shoes were actually described as silver slippers in the 1900 novel written by L. Frank Baum. MGM's costume designer Gilbert Adrian decided to switch the hue in order to take advantage of the gorgeous glitter effect on the sequined slippers when it was decided the movie would be shot using the brand-new three-strip Technicolor film process.

The bell dings and I head for the door to the vault. Lefty is there, with Encyclopedia. His blindfold has been removed and his hair is a bit mussed. Otherwise, he's the picture of perfection: shined shoes, creased slacks, starched shirt, silk tie.

"Thank you," I nod a dismissal to Lefty. She disappears down the corridor.

I move forward, shake Encyclopedia's hand heartily and smile big. "Welcome back! It is so good to see you again, sir."

"Likewise," he replies, stepping into the room. His eyes go immediately to the gleaming ruby slippers.

I lead the way and we stop at the Plexiglas podium on which they sit.

"Gorgeous! Just magnificent," he says reverently.

"Indeed."

Still staring at the shoes, he asks, "How many times have you seen *The Wizard of Oz*?"

I shrug. "A dozen? It was on TV every Easter when I was young. I guess nowadays a kid can see it anytime."

He sighs. "Yes. Instant gratification. No anticipation." He pauses, glances at me. "Ever watch it again, as an adult?"

"Only if you count the whole 'Dark Side of the Rainbow' thing," I say with an impish grin.

His brows raise. "Hm?"

I tilt my head. "You mean… you don't know…?"

He shrugs.

"Well, if you start playing the movie at the third MGM lion-roar and begin Pink Floyd's *Dark Side of the Moon* album at precisely that moment, here's what happens: When you hear the lyrics 'The lunatic is on the grass' you'll see the Scarecrow dancing on a lawn. Then when the Scarecrow and Dorothy start skipping down the yellow brick road, you'll hear 'Got to keep the loonies on the path.' And when the lyrics 'Don't give me that do goody-goody bull' come on, that's when Glenda the Good Witch ascends in her magic bubble. When the song *Brain Damage* starts? Well, that's when the Scarecrow launches into his 'If I only had a brain' lament. And so on."

"Wow," Encyclopedia says. "I'm impressed."

"Oh, there's more. You should try it sometime. Cannabis helps."

He chuckles. Not to be outdone, he quizzes me. "Did you know that Toto the dog was actually a girl? Her name was Terry and she was a Cairn Terrier. Before costarring with Judy Garland, she was in a movie with Shirley Temple called 'Bright Eyes.' She went on to have puppies who were also in pictures."

I nod, already formulating my response. We have this little one-upmanship thing going on. He loves it. I am sure of this, otherwise I'd never do it. Our clients and their satisfaction is our utmost priority. "Speaking of dogs," I say, "The Beatles song *A Day in the Life* has an extra high-pitched whistle in it, audible only to canines. It was slipped in there by Paul McCartney especially for his Shetland Sheepdog."

"Really? What was the dog's name?"

Uh-oh. "I don't know."

He smiles, smug. "Martha. In fact, he wrote a song about her, called *Martha, My Dear.*"

"Hm." I think for a moment. "OK, well, did you know Robert Plant, the lead singer of Led Zeppelin, wrote a song for his favorite dog, too?"

"Yes. *Black Dog.*"

"Nope." I had him now.

Encyclopedia was stumped.

"The song is called *Bron-Y-Aur Stomp*," I say, praying I'm pronouncing the Welsh correctly, "and it's about his blue-eyed Merle, Strider."

"Named after the *Lord of the Rings* character?"

I nod. Hell's bells. I never can stay ahead of Encyclopedia for very long. I give up. "Would you like a glass of champagne, sir? Or perhaps an Australian sparkling red?"

He nods. "The red. Of course," a wink. "Thank you."

I shoot a text to Lefty, who in turn makes it happen. Moments later, a valet appears with a cut-crystal goblet of ruby-red wine on a silver tray.

I take a seat nearby, letting Encyclopedia roam the display on his own. I open my Twitter app and I post a quote by T.S. Eliot. "Only those who will risk going too far can possibly find out how far one can go."

My thoughts wander to Donna and my plans. I want to try something different this time. Up the stakes. Take a risk.

Stage Seven: *Acceptance*

"Joy Division" was a term coined by the Nazis. It's a euphemism for the sadistic, sexual assaults perpetrated by the SS on their female prisoners.

Then there's the British post-punk, new wave electronica band called Joy Division. Lead singer and lyricist Ian Curtis and his bandmates Stephen Morris, Peter Hook and Bernard Sumner decided on that name because their fathers had all fought in World War II. That's the reason they called themselves Joy

Division, not the glorification of rape. Or so they say.

Ian had accepted for a long time that he would die. If not sooner, then later. But why prolong the inevitable? You see, he had terrible blackouts brought on by epilepsy. More than once, he'd had them onstage while performing. Some audience members thought it was part of the show, but Ian was mortified. He spiraled into depression. Although they were becoming ever more popular, the band never did make it overseas for their first-ever U.S. tour. Their single, *Love Will Tear Us Apart* was a hit and every hip kid in America wanted to see them.

On May 18, 1980, Ian was home alone. He watched the Werner Herzog film, *Stroszek*, released in 1977. I looked it up, because I've never seen it. One contemporary review says, "For all the supposed lightness, it is the film's core of despair which in the end devours everything." Apparently—spoiler alert—the hero of the story, a Berlin street performer who makes the trek to Middle America, dies of self-immolation on a ski-lift. I, of all people, believe in the power of suggestion. Seeing this must have pushed twenty-three-year-old Ian over the edge.

He didn't set himself ablaze, though. Ian opted, like so many others before him, for hanging. Why is it that singers, whose voice rises from their diaphragm, lungs and vocal chords, choose the method of strangulation in which to forever silence themselves?

While an Iggy Pop album played, Ian wrote a long letter to his estranged wife, Deborah. He knew she'd be home in a few hours, where she'd find it—and him. Romantic, or cruel? I can't decide.

The despondent singer got a laundry line, and in his kitchen, he ended it all. If he was like most home-hangers, then he didn't have a long enough drop to break his neck and go instantly. He probably felt instinctive panic for a few moments before losing consciousness, then finally slipped away.

Ian was, like the film character Bruno Stroszek, put to fire a few days later. Cremated. Deborah Curtis had the words "Love Will Tear Us Apart" inscribed on his tombstone.

In late June of 2008, someone stole the stone marker. It's never been recovered.

That's because it's at the museum, along with Jim Morrison's funereal bust and Edgar Allen Poe's bronze effigy which was swiped back in the 70s. We have a special place called The Chamber of Curses. You would not believe the wait list, but as with all of our exhibits, each client gets complete privacy. On only very rare occasions are plus ones allowed.

I'm especially fond of The Chamber of Curses, because I'm the curator. A morbid magpie, I've collected the best of the dead. In this room, which is painted a bright, buttery hue and boasts a mural of hand-painted bluebells, we have not only stolen stones and monuments, but famous murder weapons, burial clothes and yes, even body parts. Poet Percy Shelley's heart. Mad monk Rasputin's mummified, thirteen-inch member (the one floating in formaldehyde at the Russian Museum of Erotica ain't it). A lock of murderess Lizzie Borden's hair. Her ax. OJ Simpson's knife. And my personal favorite, the icepick used to lobotomize famous 40s actress Frances Farmer.

Sometimes, I fantasize about driving it up through my eye and into my brain. I once watched an old PBS documentary clip on YouTube, about Walter Jackson Freeman, the American physician who invented the transorbital lobotomy. He used icepicks from his own kitchen and the tap-tap of a mallet. It doesn't look painful and it erases all the bad memories.

But enough about me. Tonight, it's all about Donna. Not the end game, of course.

Not yet. That could take months, maybe even a year or more. But I am going to add the new ingredient. It's dangerous, but exciting.

I'm taking her out to a nice, but not intimidatingly expensive, restaurant. Pace (pronounced "pa-chey") on Laurel Canyon Boulevard, and just steps from the famous "Love Street" immortalized on an album by The Doors, is upscale but cozy. Brick and ivy, recessed dining room. They have the best pizza in L.A. and even better spirits. We'll sit out in the covered patio, just below ground level and whisper sweet everythings by candlelight.

I'll tell her more about me than anyone has ever known. Is forewarned forearmed, or will she be a self-fulfilling prophecy?

"I still think about it sometimes," Donna admits, matter-of-factly. "How I'll do it. When. Why." She nibbles at the dry crust of her pizza slice, as if to stop herself from saying more.

I nod. "Yes. It never goes away."

"That's not very positive, coming from you. My sponsor." She seems more curious, than anything. "Have you ever, um… lost someone in recovery?"

My sigh is weighty. It says yes without the word.

"Oh, my god. I'm sorry. I shouldn't have asked."

I hold up a hand. "No, no. Nothing is off-limits. Ask me anything." Inwardly, I'm beaming. She's playing right into it.

She's got her hair pulled back tonight, into a loose chignon. Her lips are tinted nude, bringing out the darkness of her eyes. Her eyes are almonds of depth and intellect and usually a bit sad. Right now, they're searching mine.

My eyes are dark, too. And piercing. That's why my codename at work is Hawkeye. It's really who I am. Like a bird of prey, I can spot fresh meat from the greatest of great distances. But I'm not ready to swoop in just yet.

Donna looks at the flickering flame, fragile as a life. One quick blow, or a slow burn to the wick—either way, it's inevitably extinguished. She chuckles nervously. "That's OK. I really don't want to talk about it tonight. Let's have a good time."

"We are," I say, reaching across the table to take her hand. Her fingertips are finely dusted with pizza crust flour.

She gives a gentle squeeze. "Yes. A good time." She pauses. "I have something to tell you."

"What?"

She looks down, then meets my gaze. "I love you."

I gasp. Not from surprise at her declaration. I expected that. It was her eyes. Her pale, blue eyes.

I blink and look at her again. Her eyes are brown as ever.

My surprise and long pause unsettle her.

"I'm sorry," she mutters, withdrawing her hand from mine. "I shouldn't have said that."

I collect my wits. "Donna. Please, it's not that. I love you, too."

"You're just saying that now. I'm so embarrassed."

But I do love her. Or at least, what she could be. Mine. Soul and body, mine. I take her hand again. "I'm not. Really. It's just," I grin, impishly. "You stole my thunder. That's why I brought you here tonight. Plied you with pizza and white wine…"

We laugh. But it's awkward.

And that's good. I have her a little off-balance. A little unsure of herself. Of me.

Problem is: I'm unsure of myself, too.

I refill her flute, then mine. Almost to the rim. I drink it in two long swallows, then pour more. I'm surreptitiously searching her eyes. Her dark *brown* eyes.

I shudder. *What just happened?*

We made love that night after dinner. I kept my eyes closed for most of it, telling myself it was merely to heighten my other senses. I slept, but fitfully. I dreamed in shades of cobalt.

It's a couple of days later and I'm better now. It must have been the wine. Fatigue. Mercury in retrograde. Could have been anything.

Donna and I are sitting in her kitchen sipping hot, black coffee. I've added a pinch of cinnamon to mine. It's still powdery laying on the surface and its dryness makes me cough a bit. But it tastes sweet.

Now is as good a time as any. "Donna," I begin. "I haven't been telling the whole truth at the ATI meetings."

She nods, once. "I'm sure everyone holds something back. It's just too painful. And private..."

"No. I mean: I've never tried to kill myself."

Her eyes widen. Her mouth doesn't exactly fall open, but her lips part. "What are you saying?" She leaps to the worst possible conclusion immediately. "Are you some kind of grief groupie? I've heard about people who –"

I hold my hands up. Defensive. "It's not like that."

She puts her mug down on the tile counter. I see age-old dirt in the grout and wonder why grout is always white. She's waiting for my reply.

I take my time. I want her to get a little angry, work it up, so she will feel that much more guilty about thinking so poorly of me.

I let out an audible breath. "My little sister killed herself."

"Go on…" she prompts, probably wondering why I'm not in the appropriate support group. Seeking closure, commiserating, crying, the whole bit.

"I'm not in ATI to trick anyone…"

"But you lied to us! To *me*. I thought you really understood me…" She shrinks and hugs herself.

"I do. I understand you better than you understand yourself." Maintain the upper hand. Keep sowing the seeds of self-doubt. That I know more than she does. I shrug. "Oh, never mind. I don't know why I even thought I could confide in you. You're not special, you're just like all the rest."

This clearly stings. "No, I'm not. I want to hear. I'm sorry. I'm really sorry. Come on, honey. Tell me," she begs.

I make a show of relenting. I sit up straight at the breakfast nook and spread my arms out, owning the space.

"Her name was Jessie. She was two years younger than me. She was seventeen when she did it… and to this day, I have no idea why." I swallow. "I couldn't save her."

Donna sidles over to me. I can feel her warmth. "You were a kid yourself. It's not your fault."

"She hung herself," I say softly, pulling her ring to-and-fro across the chain around my neck. "I found her."

"Oh, no. You poor thing."

"We were so close, I felt like she was me and I was her. That's why I'm in group. Because in a way, I *did* succumb to suicide."

I squeeze out a tear.

That's not how it happened at all.

Well, not exactly. It was our mother who found her. I knew Jessie was there, suspended in the basement by the washer and drier. I told her that would be the best if, "You know, if you were really to do it. Which you won't."

"Of course not," she agreed. "But why there?"

"Because of the door that leads to the garage. The EMTs, or whoever it is that shows up in such cases, would just have to cut you down and take you discretely out back. No big scene out the front door, no neighbors standing around, gawking."

Though she'd once liked to be out with her friends to escape our mother's wrath, as her depression increased Jessie became a recluse. And shy. She hid her face behind veils of long, blonde hair, avoided eye contact and basically didn't want to be seen at all. That's how I knew the idea of discretely slipping out the back door would appeal to her.

"I know it's kind of mean," she said, "but I'd want her to find me. To see what she did to me. Maybe then she'd be sorry."

I nodded. "I bet she would."

"Do you think it hurts?" Jesse asked.

"No more than the day to day pain of our crappy existence," I mumbled, picking at my fingernails.

That night, I gave her some poetry to read. The Keats bit about easeful death, hemlock and dissolving. *Ode to a Nightingale*, it's called. "*Tender is the night*," and its undying question, "*Do I wake, or do I sleep?*"

As predicted, Jessie chose sleep.

She didn't say goodbye to me, but somehow when I woke the next morning—laundry day— I knew that she'd done it.

Mom's scream confirmed it.

I snuggled deeper into my bed, brought the covers over my ears and pretended to be still asleep when she came flying into my room, frantic.

Not long after that, I reconnected with my dad, left the nest, and never saw my mother again.

My coffee's grown cold. The cinnamon has left an oily film on top.

Donna is holding me. She begins to kiss me. Here it comes—the pity sex. She feels sorry for me. Everything is going as planned.

I return her kisses, gazing gratefully at her through my tears. Pretty soon, robes are opening and we're stumbling toward the bedroom.

I pin her down and am rougher than she's used to. It's all a blur, really. But it feels good and it's a physical manifestation of my power over her. Of my power in admitting that I have a sister who died by her own hand. Next, I'll tell Donna about Rose. And my ex-husband, Noah. He was so distraught after the divorce… It couldn't be helped.

Afterward, Donna gets up and goes to the kitchen to wash the breakfast dishes.

I head for the W.C. to freshen up. When I enter, I see the bathtub is full. There are bubbles on top, but I could swear I see a figure. I look a little closer.

No, there's no one in there.

"Donna?" I call out. "Do you want me to drain the tub?"

She comes to the doorway. "What do you mean?"

"Didn't you take a bath earlier?"

She looks into the room. "No. What are you talking about?"

I turn, following her gaze.

The tub is empty. And bone dry.

"Oh, sorry," I say, grinning sheepishly.

Donna shrugs. She turns and heads back into the kitchen.

I take a step closer to the tub. It *is* dry.

But there's steam on the window above. Written in the steam are the words, "Thank you."

I'll never forget those words. That was the last thing Rose ever said to me.

There's a great power in knowing someone's last words. Jessie's were "I love you," (written). Rose's were "Thank you" (spoken). Noah's were "I can't live without you" (written).

I wonder what Donna's will be?

It's a quiet night at work. We only had one client and she wasn't mine. So I'm here in my office, looking through some of the new acquisitions. I've put on a record by The Velvet Underground, I have my coffee percolating and I'm ready for the next several hours.

There are four crates on the floor. I'm opening them one by one. It's my job to catalogue and authenticate the treasures inside. It's going to take a week or so, but I don't mind.

This exhibit will be called *Spoils of War*. It's all the best stuff plundered from the biggest battles in history. One box contains various Viking pillage. Another one has armor from the War of the Roses. There're dolls from Dresden, and massive jewels from Iraq.

One object I can't stop staring at is Cleopatra's hand mirror. Made of thin bronze, so light and shiny it reflects almost as well as glass and silver, it's backed by enamel with an inlaid serpent design. The handle is made of wood and ivory. When the Romans sacked her palace, they took everything.

I look at my face in the mirror and imagine the Queen of the Nile herself looking into that exact same surface. Did she give herself a final once-over before taking her own life? I like to think that she did and was satisfied with her beauty.

Just as I'm about to set the mirror aside, I see a streak pass behind me.

I turn. "Hello?"

No reply. I'm alone in the office.

Of course. Silly me.

But just to be sure, I hold the mirror up again and search the periphery of its dark gleam. I think I see... No, *for sure* I see an indistinct figure huddled in the far corner of my office. I turn to look.

It's gone.

Tentatively, I raise the mirror again. There she is. It's Rose, nude and dripping wet. She sees that I see her. Rose's mouth moves, but I hear nothing.

I drop the mirror with a clang. Take a deep breath.

I should go home; I'm too tired.

But the night's work has only begun and I am no quitter.

I place the mirror back in its box and I pick up a doll from Dresden. She certainly looks authentic. She's a bit burnt on one hand and there's a reddish mark across her neck where the enamel was worn away—probably from a little girl carrying her around by the throat. But her shaped porcelain hair is perfect. Bright golden blonde, the color of sunflowers. She's got a slight, rosebud smile. Her eyes are dark blue.

No, wait. "Light blue," I write in my notations.

The record skips. I turn to look at the player, somewhat annoyed. Someone's been playing my records without permission. I take immense pride in my vinyl and there isn't a single scratch on any track. The needle jumps again, placing itself perfectly at the beginning of *Pale Blue Eyes.*

I shake my head, annoyed. I turn back to my notations, only to find that I didn't write "light blue," to describe the doll's painted eyes—I wrote, "pale blue."

I glance over at the doll. I stare. It looks an awful lot like my sister. But no. It's just a doll, handmade, burnt and stolen back in the blitzkrieg. Just a coincidence. Still, her face taunts me.

"Linger on…"

The doll's lips move.

No. It's just shadow-play.

I look for the source of the shadow and see it. *Just* the shadow. Nothing casting it.

But I know Noah's shape. There's a fluidness to the head, a… drippiness, from where he shot himself. I can't look away.

The volume on the record player suddenly increases. It's so loud. Then louder still. Somewhere, between Lou Reed's voice, the guitar and the bass, I hear whispers. "I love you. Thank you. I can't live without you."

Finally, I tear my gaze from the shadow.

I take a seat at my desk. A deep breath. A sip of cold coffee.

Then I see the icepick and the mallet.

"How did you get here?" I stupidly ask the inanimate objects. Then again, how inanimate can they be, if they somehow got themselves out of the Chamber of Curses and onto my desk?

That was a strange night. But things have gotten stranger still. The icepick and the mallet wait for me everywhere, now. At home. In my car. At restaurants and bars. On my nightstand.

I can't help but wonder... should I use them? I want to. There's an almost overwhelming need to see what would happen. Will the nightmares go away if I do? What if I do it wrong? What if I kill myself?

"Do I wake, or do I sleep?"

Remote Trigger

Wade, Bob and Helen fought their way to the front of the paparazzi pack using whatever means necessary. Sharp elbows and heavy boots were almost as important in their line of work as a good camera and a nose for news.

Someone from inside Potions, the hottest bistro in Beverly Hills, had leaked—for a price, of course—that Mommy would be brunching there at 11 a.m. and before long, word amongst the city's seamy shutterbugs had spread like a Topanga Canyon wildfire. The superstar singer seldom stepped out onto the street without her trademark drab-olive surgical mask and black pioneer-style bonnet, but today she would be eating… in public. Surely, she'd have to drop the mask and maybe even lose the hat.

While they waited, Wade looked around with leisurely disgust. "I can't believe this place is so popular. I hear they bought their A rating after they tried to pass mouse droppings off as capers."

"Yeah, it's basically a petri dish with menus," said Helen. "Gimme good old In-n-Out over this overpriced swill any day."

Bob was looking a little green around the gills all of a sudden. "I've got a friend who works here. I had breakfast in the kitchen earlier," he gulped. "But I only ate some scrambled eggs. I should be OK, right?"

Helen chuckled. "Can you spell salmonella?"

Suddenly, the assembly of photographers and fans stirred.

Mommy's unmistakable purple minivan came into view. In the back window was a yellow diamond-shaped sign reading: *Mommy Onboard.* It stopped in the valet area and the driver got out. He was well-dressed in an impeccable suit, but his neck tattoos were plainly visible and his steroid-enhanced physique strained the seams. He wore dark Ray Ban sunglasses. Stepping lightly but purposefully with his Bruno Mali black Nappa leather slip-ons, he opened the sliding door for his employer.

The four-foot-eleven-inch, twenty-two-year-old megastar exited the vehicle flanked by her usual posse: Granny DeShawna, and two of her backup singers, Flash and Cash. Nobody cared about them. It was Mommy's barely-visible phizzog in the crosshairs of all those camera lenses.

Shouts rang out. "Mommy!" "Hey, look over here!" "Take off the mask!" "What are you going to order?" "Where's your fiancé?" "Just one smile!"

The standard-issue, textbook response of all celebrities since the olden days when paparazzi were sketch-artists was to pick up the pace and duck the face. Mommy was no exception… usually. But today, she was in a rare mood.

She paused, turned to the throng of fans and opportunists and lowered her mask just long enough to say, "Fuck yourselves."

Her granny added, "And drop dead while you're at it."

Mommy's bodyguard then blocked the petite powerhouse from view, shielding her as they entered the bistro. Flash and Cash were already inside.

The photographers instantly checked their images. Fans with phones didn't get much, but the pros with super-shutters got the best pics of Mommy taken in months. They were better still, because her pretty pout was contorted in anger—unflattering shots always brought higher prices.

Bob showed Helen and Wade one of his shots. "Look, I think she's winking at me. She likes me."

Helen guffawed. "The only way you'll ever get laid is if you crawl up a chicken's ass and wait." She paused, then added, "Egg-boy."

Bob sighed and made a face. "I'm busy now. Can I ignore you some other time?"

"That's right, Bob. Keep rolling your eyes. Maybe you'll find a brain back there."

"Now-now, kiddies," Wade said as he began uploading the photos through the small device he always carried. "The longer you argue, the longer your outlets will have to wait."

The paparazzi stayed where they were, uploading the current batch of pics as they angled for a look inside the bistro. If they couldn't get a snap of Mommy feeding her face, then they'd still wait until she came out. Maybe they could catch another outburst.

They waited and waited, the relentless summer sun baking the backs of their necks. The more experienced sharp-shooters brought small folding chairs and flasks of water or booze. Most of them dispersed after about an hour.

"She must have ducked out the back," said Wade. "Let's split."

Helen swiped left on a dating profile, then pocketed her phone. "Good idea." She glanced over at Bob, who had apparently nodded off on the job. "Hey," she said, elbowing him.

Bob lolled to the side of his flimsy chair, which promptly fell over and spilled him out onto the blistering pavement. Bob didn't flinch. In fact, he didn't move at all.

The pair peered down at him. It was plain to see that their friend and colleague—and in Helen's case, ex-husband—was quite dead.

Bob's funeral was held two days later. The coroner chalked it up to a heart-attack, but Helen wasn't convinced. Regardless, that's what she said when she delivered the eulogy: His heart attacked him. She'd decided to take the humorous route because she knew that's what Bob would have wanted.

"Some of you may know me," said Helen, standing at the podium of a modest church Bob had never set foot in. The small crowd was chuckling already. They all knew her. Bob didn't have many friends and those he did have were all in the same celebrity-snap business.

"Right, right," she continued. The flowered dress she wore felt too loose and too light. She was used to her long-sleeved shirts, cargo pants and hiking boots. And her camera. As if on cue, she saw a flash go off—Wade was taking pictures.

Helen ran her hand through her short-cropped bright violet locks, then began. "Anyway, when I met Bob he wasn't a photographer. He was in a band called The Blank Checks. They were unsigned. We got married, but it didn't last. Bob was no quitter though, so he gave it a shot three more times. He didn't have any children; at least none that he knew of. So, when he wasn't working he had lots of free time. Bob loved basketball. In fact, he asked that the L.A. Lakers be his pallbearers so they could let him down one more time. Seriously, though. He did love this city, the Lakers, his work and all of us. We can take comfort in the fact that Bob died knowing *Star Wars* is the best movie ever and that chicks dig Camaros. And he lived a long life. In fact, he was so old his birth certificate was expired by the time his heart attacked him." She looked heavenward. Then straight down. "Rest in peace, Robert Weber." She returned her gaze outward toward the sparsely populated pews. "Oh, and if you want to chip in for his burial plot, we'll be passing a collection plate." Helen gave everyone a smile, then added, "I'm not kidding on that last bit."

After the services, half of the attendees headed for Hollywood and Highland. There was a movie premiere at the El Capitan. While the real money was in candid and unbecoming photos of the stars, posed red carpet pictures were in semi-demand.

Helen and Wade weren't in with Getty or Shutterstock, so their sales weren't guaranteed but the schlep was worthwhile. Especially since Mommy was still in town—her name was on the tip-sheet the studio had sent out and since she had a song on the movie's soundtrack, there was a good chance she'd show. Not her face of course. That mask-drop in front of Potions had been a rare exception. Fortunately, Helen was able to sell the photos Bob took that day to pay for most of his no-frills funeral.

Helen and Wade were front-and-center as usual. They were both big and bulky, and masters at channeling their inner boulders. No amount of elbowing, toe-stomping or gradual pushing could get them to budge.

As they waited—it was always a wait for the first celebrity to appear—Wade and Helen reminisced about Bob. Helen and Bob were long-divorced but still friends when they met Wade. They'd all just started out in the business of freelance photography. That was back in 2004. Their first premiere had been

Harry Potter and the Prisoner of Azkaban at the Chinese Theatre.

"Those kids are all grown up now," Helen mused. "And Bob's deceased. I don't believe it was a heart-attack," she added bluntly.

"Why not? He was getting up there. He was out of shape."

Helen couldn't put her finger on it. "It's just weird, isn't it, that Mommy said drop dead… and he did."

Wade guffawed out loud. "Oh, come on now. You've seen too many Harry Potter movies. There's no such thing as curses. Plus, it was Granny DeShawna who said that."

"But… in interviews she said her grandma raised her on Haitian Vodou."

"Please!" Wade scoffed. "Don't you know anything about the Hollywood mystique machine by now? I'll bet her parents aren't even dead. And her grandma's probably from Compton, not Port-au-Prince."

"Cynical much?" Helen asked.

"Gullible much?" Wade returned. "Hey, look: There's Paris."

Helen craned her neck, but she couldn't see anyone important in the throng of gowns, high heels and scowling publicists. "Jackson, or Hilton?"

Wade rolled his eyes. "Please. Would I waste pixels on Paris Hilton? She's yesterday's fish-wrap."

At once, Paris Jackson was on the carpet and chaos ensued. It was a long and tiring night and by the end of it Mommy hadn't shown.

"I'll bet she's at the afterparty," said Wade. "It's at Lure. Let's go."

Helen cracked her neck and sighed. "I'm so tired. I just can't take anymore. I'm going home."

"Your loss," replied Wade, rubbing his thumb across his fingers to indicate the dollars in hand if Mommy showed.

Helen really was exhausted. Sure, she and Bob had been divorced for ages, but it was still stressful. She'd handled all the burial and memorial arrangements and stayed up all night writing and memorizing her eulogy. It was time to hit the drive-thru, go home and take a bath with a nice glass of white wine. Maybe she'd even blaze up a fattie.

She refused to pay for premium parking, so Helen had to walk a few blocks to get to her car. As she trudged along the avenue of stars, stepping squarely on the likes of Viveien Leigh and Liberace, she remembered a bit of trivia: When the Hollywood Chamber of Commerce honored Muhammad Ali with a star, he insisted they raise his off the ground—floating like a butterfly. They acquiesced and mounted it on a wall by the Dolby Theater as a sign of respect. "I bear the name of our beloved prophet Mohammad and it is impossible that I allow people to trample over his name," Ali had said, as Helen recalled. She'd been there, shooting pictures of the ceremony. Apparently the G.O.A.T. didn't want to be walked on by "people who have no respect for me." Who could blame him?

As she sidestepped the stars' names, Helen saw a blinking neon sign in a shop window she hadn't noticed before. It read: "Gypsy Tarot Reading $10." Only ten bucks? She could certainly afford that, and she did have questions.

She shambled into the shop, her trusty Nikon D5 still hanging from her neck. It was like a different world in there. It was dark and cool. It was quiet in contrast to the bustle of the boulevard, but ambient music could be heard. The air carried the soothing scent of vanilla and cinnamon and smoke from the incense wafted in gentle, diaphanous clouds. There was a miniscule lobby in front of a pair of heavy red drapes.

Hands parted the drapes and a youthful, curvaceous female stepped through as Helen was stuffing her camera back into its bag.

"Hello." The gypsy's voice was suitably sultry. "May I be of assistance?"

Helen zipped the bag closed, cringing at the abrupt sound. "Oh, yeah. Hey," she replied. "Um… is the reading still ten dollars?" Helen dipped her head, embarrassed. She was a cow compared to this delicate damsel.

The self-proclaimed gypsy was petite yet pulchritudinous and she had long, dark hair that cascaded in perfect waves to her waist. Her dark, smoky eyes smoldered in contrast to her bright red lips. She smiled, revealing a row of perfectly straight, very white teeth. "Yes," she answered. "Come in." She stepped back, parting the velvet curtains.

Helen entered the sanctum. The area was even darker, lit only by flickering candles. Helen's heart raced. She wondered if this was a good idea, but she stepped deeper into the room. On the floor were four crimson satin cushions, arranged in a semi-circle around a legless tabletop.

The proprietor gathered her skirts daintily and sat. Her bare knees poked through the multilayered indigo sari. She picked up a deck of tarot cards and indicated that Helen should take a seat on the cushion opposite her. Helen plunked herself down.

The gypsy held out her left hand and said, "Cross my palm."

Helen looked blankly at her.

"Pay me."

"Oh. Sorry." Helen dug at one of the many pockets in her cargo pants. She extracted three fives and plunked them on the table, cursing her inelegance. "Here," she said needlessly.

The gypsy smiled sweetly. "Don't be nervous."

She swept the money away discreetly, then laid the cards out in the form of a Celtic cross. She explained the significance of the complicated formation, then she turned over the first card. It was the Death card.

"Oh, shit," Helen mumbled. "That can't be good."

The gypsy looked at her with kind eyes. "It's an indication of rebirth. It actually *is* good."

Helen eyed the grinning skeleton on the face of the card. It didn't look so hunky-dory to her. "But my ex-husband just died. I was at his funeral today."

"Hmmm," said the woman, her perfect brows knitting. "Let's see what the next card is." She turned it over and it showed The

Devil. The drawing looked like something out of the Old Testament. Lucifer had one hand in the air as if swearing to cause doom and destruction, while at his hoofed feet were a man and woman shackled together. Was that supposed to be her and Bob? Would she die too?

Then Helen got the Ten of Swords, depicting a man lying face-down and with ten blades buried in his back. "This is an indicator that you are likely going to suffer some unwelcome surprise in the near future," the gypsy said blithely.

"Ya think?!" Helen retorted. She cackled out a brittle laugh, but inside she was shaken to her core. What a horrible impulse this had been!

"Don't panic," said the beautiful soothsayer. "This is only the beginning. I am sure your future holds better things."

Helen didn't wait to see what the next card revealed. She scrambled to her feet, groped the curtains open and exited the shop. She took a deep and grateful breath of the exhaust-infused air outside and half-ran to her waiting car.

Helen stuck to the rest of her plan: McDonald's, bath, fattie and wine. Then she fell into a deep and dreamless sleep.

The next morning, she was awakened by the insistent chime of her cell-phone. It was set to play Mommy's latest Top 40 hit, *Ho, You Don't Know*. Helen swam slowly to the surface of wakefulness, wondering why on earth she would have chosen that ringtone. Instinctively, she brought the potentially-explosive Samsung to her ear. "…llo," she muttered.

"Helen! Helen, it's Judith. You awake?"

It was one of her colleagues. She didn't know Judith very well. How'd Judith get her number? She didn't ask. Instead she replied, "Um… yeah?"

"You won't believe this! Wade is dead."

Helen sat up with a start. Then she remembered: Judith was crazy. "Listen, Judith. Keep the circus in your own tent. I don't find this funny at all."

She pressed the red button at the bottom of her phone and ended the call. Then she blanched. There were dozens of text messages stacked up on the display.

It was true. Wade had been murdered by a mugger—or so police guessed—on his way home from the after-party at Lure.

Helen called Judith back, apologizing.

"No problemo. Hey, at least he got some pictures of Mommy," said Judith brightly. She sighed. "But then again, the thief took the camera."

"Maybe that's the way to catch the killer," Helen replied. "Those pictures are worth more than the camera. I'm gonna call the cops and let them know."

"Good thinking," Judith enthused. "Want me to call them…?" She always did like to take credit.

Helen hung up. She was about to dial 9-1-1, but then she figured Wade was dead anyway and she could really use a cup of coffee and some of those raspberry-filled powdered sugar donuts she had in the fridge.

She swung her legs over the side of the bed and stepped into her slippers. She padded toward the kitchen.

She stopped dead in her tracks. There was a man in her apartment. Not just any man; it was Mommy's bull-sized bodyguard. He was dressed the same as he had been the other day at Potions, from his Bruno Mali shoes to his Ray Ban sunglasses.

Helen stepped forward and stood tall. "How did you get here? Did someone leave your cage open?"

A huge butcher knife, taken from the block in her own kitchen came up. With his other meaty paw, the bodyguard took his sunglasses off.

Helen's heart trembled. The bodyguard's eyes were pure white. He groaned. "Brrrrrains…."

"A zombie?" Helen sputtered. "Seriously?"

From behind the hulking mass stepped Mommy's nana, DeShawna. The small, powerfully-built woman wore a traditional Haitian quadrille dress and a colorful turban. She smiled slow and sinister.

"He's just backup." From a slit-pocket in her dress, the young grandmother produced a voodoo doll. A chubby one, with short purple hair like Helen's. Around its neck was a small camera.

DeShawna twisted the camera strap tight around the puppet's neck.

Helen began to choke. She clawed at her throat, trying in vain to loosen the phantom ligature. She fell to her knees and tears flowed from her eyes.

The zombie peered at her through seemingly sightless sockets. As if from very far away, Helen heard DeShawna say, "No one steals my granddaughter's soul."

The world faded to black.

Sometime later, Helen surfaced back into consciousness. She opened her eyes, expecting to be laid out on the linoleum floor of her modest kitchen. But she wasn't. Where was she? Her head throbbed with an insistent headache and her blood boiled with fever. It took her a moment to orient herself. Not the kitchen. Not a hospital bed. Not a coffin.

She was on the press line.

Wade elbowed her. "Hey, what took you so long?" Blood flowed from his mouth as he spoke.

Bob was there too, pressed up against the metal stanchion. There was a weeping hole where his heart should have been.

Her brain spun to catch up. Helen felt the weight of her camera in her hands. Stunned, she looked around. Behind her was a sea of faceless photographers. In front of her on the red carpet was an endless parade of grinning nobodies.

"Take the picture, Helen!" A booming and omniscient voice commanded.

Helen raised her Nikon with shaking hands, but she couldn't get the shot. Every single image was wrong: Out of focus, overexposed, distorted, the subject's head cut off, lens cap on. Each time she checked the viewfinder and saw a mistake, she felt hot flames lick at her feet.

She wanted to ask Bob and Wade what to do, but the words died in her crushed throat.

Doom for Rent

You never know in advance when you're inviting the devil into your home. I was clueless as could be when I answered the door that fateful Sunday morning and said, "Come in."

I stepped back so she could enter.

Jane Johnson smiled. "Thanks for letting me come take a look on such short notice. I wasn't expecting to have to move so soon."

She was in her fifties or thereabouts—older than me and my roommate Chuck, by about twenty years. She wore boots, dark wash jeans, a sweater and little makeup. Her hair was pulled back into a messy bun and I noticed her fingernails were clean and cut short. Just a regular, everyday sort of person. She peered into the house from the entryway. "Looks nice. And you say a dog is OK?"

I nodded. "The room is small but there's a sliding glass door that leads to the backyard and pool… Let me show you. Your dog could hang out there, as long as he doesn't bark. I don't need any trouble with the neighbors."

I wasn't keen on taking another roommate, especially not one with a dog, but things were getting tight. Pilot season was still a few months away and I hadn't had an acting gig in a while. Not even an indie short.

Chuck was an aspiring ganjaprenuer with hopes of opening a dispensary within a few months. For the time being he made gluten-free meat-based edibles from a workshop he'd set up in the basement. He sold them to friends and friends of friends. He was doing OK, but only squeaking by on the rent.

So, with things looking uncertain I decided to advertise the room I'd been using for storage. Even though rents are beyond insane around here, especially in the Hollywood Hills, I'd had a helluva time finding someone suitable to split the load. When an interested party did bother to show up after making an appointment, they either wouldn't follow up or they'd miraculously find another place just before seeing mine.

Really, my house—which I bought on a short sale after my first (and last) big role—was great for a musician, an actor, or anyone just coasting on the L.A. vibe. The 2,000 square-foot casa was old-school Spanish art deco with hardwood floors, it was secluded yet close to the action and with rent being split three ways, there'd still be demo or headshot money left over. Not that Jane looked like an actor or a musician, but I had been expecting someone younger.

I led the way to the room, making small talk as I went. "Any trouble finding the place?"

"No," she said. "My Uber got me here with no problem." That told me she didn't have a car. Probably couldn't afford one. Not a good sign.

"What do you do?" I asked, opening the door to the unfurnished room.

"I'm studying law," she answered. She stepped into the room. "Hmm, it *is* pretty small."

She was right. It was more a cubicle than a room. I felt bad charging as much as I was but my mortgage wouldn't pay itself and besides, it was still cheaper than other ads I'd seen on the likes of Craigslist, Zillow and Rad Pad.

I walked to the sliding glass door which was in need of a cleaning, I noticed too late. "Yes, but you could keep this door open during the day. There's the pool right there and some grass for your dog. I do ask that you clean up every day, though."

She nodded and looked around again as if the room might somehow grow before her eyes.

Jane was the only female to answer my ad. I made it clear that the house was shared by two males in their 20s and that parties would happen from time to time. *She must really be desperate*, I thought.

"Well, I'm desperate," she said, as if reading my mind. "The place I'm renting now has been sold and I have to be out in two days."

"They didn't tell you?"

"Nope. Just found out," she said with a put-upon sigh.

"Do you have references?" I asked.

She reached into her jeans pocket and pulled out a folded piece of paper, along with a hefty chunk of cash in an envelope, which she handed to me. "My references, plus first and last month's rent. Do you need a security deposit?"

I separated the money out and said, "I'll need to check your references first."

Just then, Chuck, stoned as usual, shuffled in. "Hey, man. This the new roomie?"

Jane introduced herself. She turned back to me. "I really *am* desperate. I don't want to wait until I'm out on the street before finding a place. I can move in right now. I have more money, if that helps."

"Money talks, bullshit walks. Give the lady a break," Chuck muttered, ambling off from whence he came. (Probably the sofa in the den, his favorite spot in the house when he wasn't cooking up new edible recipes in his basement abode.)

I looked at the list of references, which were nicely printed out and organized by name, number and relationship. They looked legit and honestly, I was tired of the roommate runaround.

"You seem like nice boys," Jane offered. She sighed again. "I am so tired of the treatment I've been getting. Half the time someone will make an appointment to show me a room, then they aren't home. You know the adage: You can't spell 'flake' without 'LA.' That is, if you don't mind my saying."

"No, I get it," I answered. "I moved here from Philly."

"Are you an actor?" she asked.

I wasn't sure if I should take that as a compliment or not, so I nodded and added, "I'm also a screenwriter," though I hadn't completed, let alone sold, a single script.

She told me she'd lived in Philly briefly, but her house had burnt down. "Life is a chain of events and so here I am."

I figured I had a bird in the hand, so I tucked the list of references in my back pocket and asked, "When can you move in?"

"Now." Jane grinned. She headed through the living room and foyer and out the front door.

Less than a minute later she was back with a huge rolling suitcase, an even bigger dog and an animal carrier. Surely the dog wouldn't fit in there! My silent query was answered with a long, angry yowl.

"You have a cat too?"

"Yeah, is there a problem? My animals stay in my room, I promise. This cat is a rescue. I'll find her a home real soon."

Meanwhile, Sparky the dog was dashing around the living room, its massive tail wagging mightily and knocking things over from the tabletops.

Jane clicked her tongue and the dog went obediently to her side. "He's just a big ol' puppy. Oh, hey—can I get a receipt for my cash?"

I gave her one, she shut her pets in her room and went off to get the rest of her stuff.

I hoped the animals would stay quiet after she left them so abruptly. Not that Chuck would mind; he was pretty laid-back and when he was home he usually just watched TV with his earbuds in.

As I went into the shared kitchen to make myself a sandwich, I thought to myself, *I hope I'm not reduced to renting a room when I'm her age.* Then I admonished myself. Living in L.A., or any big city, wasn't easy and from what I gathered, Jane had caught some bad breaks.

She returned within the hour and the pets had stayed quiet. She had a few bottles of wine with her, so she put two in the cupboard designated for her and then opened the other. We shared it and talked.

I learned that Jane had divorced a couple of years before and took no settlement. "I'm just happy to be free," she said with regret hanging heavy in her voice. She told me she moved to L.A. to be closer to her brother but shortly after her move, he died. "So, I'm just trying to get a foothold here, you know, see what happens. I'm taking some pre-law, mostly it's an online curriculum, but UCLA's not far if I want to audit classes."

As we chatted and the red vino flowed, Jane spoke of her nomadic upbringing and how, with her father being in the military, she'd been educated in several different countries. It sounded pretty exotic to me. She was well-spoken and seemed quite educated. She asked me questions and kept the conversation going. She was the anti-Chuck. He was cool, but not the brightest bulb. I figured the three of us would strike a nice balance.

Within the first week of her living with us, Jane did all the laundry, folded it, made the beds, cleaned the windows—including the sliding door—and swept the floors. She was kindly, even motherly, toward us. She tended to her pets with care and concern. She spoke to Sparky exclusively in a series of tongue-clicks. "It's called Xhosa," she explained. "It's one of the official languages of South Africa. I learned it in Zimbabwe." Which was yet another stop in her amazing array of travels. In those first few days, she shared all kinds of fun stories with me. She was eccentric, to say the least.

Her love of animals, she said, came from when she was a child living in Amish Country and helping out with stable chores for pocket change. Sparky was fed organic kibble and freshly diced chicken outside by the pool, morning and night. The cat, who never did get placed into another home and was dubbed

Anna Bell, shared the feasts. Jane called her animals her "children."

Once when I was out in the backyard, I saw through the glass that Jane's room was an unholy mess. To look at her, you'd never peg her for the slovenly type. Her clothes were strewn all over the floor and there was a landfill-like pile of empty soda cans and assorted wine bottles. But mostly she kept the door closed and as the days went on, we saw less of her. She'd stopped cleaning up after us but as long as she didn't bother me or Chuck, it was all good. In fact, Chuck told me he barely noticed we had a roommate.

But all that was soon to change.

The trouble began just after Jane paid her second month's rent, again in cash and again with a receipt requested. It was a Friday evening, so I put the money in my sock drawer. When I went to retrieve it a few days later to take it to the bank, I noticed it was short. I could have sworn I counted it. Even though it was probably my fault, I decided to ask her about it.

Jane, in a now-rare social moment, was in the kitchen with Chuck. He was working on a new batch of edibles—gourmet jerky laced with just enough THC to produce a protein-packed high—and she was drinking her ever-present Pinot. As I mentioned, she was old enough to be his mother and she was speaking to him accordingly. "You know, you could get a small business loan and open a storefront now," she was saying. "I could read the contracts for you. You'll have to be careful, though. Opening a business is not easy, young man."

Chuck smiled. "Sweet," he said, "Thanks," and moseyed off toward the den.

"Hey, Jane," I said, blushing as I entered the small but open kitchen. "I think I miscounted when you paid your rent the other day. It's sixty dollars short."

"No," she replied, stepping up to me and standing quite close, chin jutted up so her eyes could meet mine. Jane was a buck-ten soaking wet and five-three at most to my 200-pound, 6-foot self. Inexplicably, I felt a prickle of sweat under my arms.

"You are charging me for utilities I don't use. I don't consume near as much as you and Chuck. You boys take twenty-minute showers, for heaven's sake. And part of that gas bill is from *before* I got here. Remember, those are sent every two months, not monthly."

"Oh, right," I muttered. But *was* she right? I'd have to double check.

She stepped back and took a delicate sip from her glass.

I left the room. *Well, that was awkward.*

The day and evening went by without further incident but that night as I lay in bed, nearly asleep, I heard light footsteps in the hall. Jane seldom left her room, but maybe it was all that wine and she had to pee. The steps stopped at my closed door. I felt, I don't know, a *presence* reeking of malice. Like someone—or something—was checking to see if I was sleeping. I stayed quiet and after a few long moments, the footsteps retreated.

The next morning when I woke up, I went to the bathroom and flicked the switch. Nothing. I moved it up and down, then looked up at the light fixture. The bulb was missing. Turns out Jane had "borrowed" it to replace the one in her room. When two dining chairs disappeared the next day, I found them in the corner opposite her twin mattress, fashioned into a desk with her ancient laptop on them. Sometime after I returned them to their rightful place, she put a lock on her door.

She quit associating with Chuck and I entirely, using the glass doors and side gate in the yard to come and go. Although I seldom saw her, her existence was known. One day I came home from an audition only to find the things on my shelf in the kitchen moved to another, less-convenient one. She started adding her novels to mine in the living room bookcase and sometimes I'd find hand-written post-it notes on the bathroom mirror or on the refrigerator admonishing me for one thing or another. "Please check expiration dates," read one. "Don't leave wet towels on the floor," scolded another.

When we did run into each other in the hallway, I'd try to talk with her about the problems. Suddenly her speech was sprinkled with legalese. When we argued about the state of affairs in the house, she'd accuse me of breaking "the covenant of quiet enjoyment." I had to look that one up and sure enough: It's a thing. When I found remnants of cat litter in the toilet bowl and confronted her about it, she said toilets are for shit and added that she would not be paying the next month's rent.

"Google the warranty of habitability," she snapped and retreated into her room, shutting and pointedly locking her door.

When I told Chuck about it, he shrugged. "Cut the lady some slack. She's old and has nowhere else to go."

I remembered she'd provided references. Too late, I know, I decided to check them. She had washed my jeans the day after I put them in the pocket and most of the writing was too faded to read. Most. I was able to read two names and numbers. Neither was valid.

I knocked on her door, knowing she was inside. "Jane, I just checked your references. Look, we need to talk." Almost instantly, I heard a chime coming from my phone. I took it out of my pocket and saw the words, all in caps: DO NOT COMMUNICATE WITH ME AGAIN UNLESS IT IS THROUGH YOUR ATTORNEY.

Whoa. I'd bumped into some assholes along the way, but never had to deal with anything like this.

I called the non-emergency line for the police. The officer who took my call said he could file a report, but there wasn't much he could do. Jane was right about the tenancy laws.

I tried looking her up online but didn't get far. Her name was just too common. If it was even hers. Then I stumbled upon a tip: Image lookup. But I didn't have a photo of Jane and it was beyond unlikely she'd pose for one. What's more, she didn't use social media so it was impossible to see if I could find a trail.

One morning when I woke up and went to the kitchen to make my coffee, I found a bullet in my favorite mug. She'd gone from post-it notes to ammunition.

Jane-the-bane, as I'd started calling her, continued to make my life difficult. I'd started to read up on tenancy laws and found many horror stories of so-called roommates from hell. There was an epidemic of serial squatters operating on shocking scales ranging from extreme nuisance to all-out war. The accounts often started with a desperate arrival; some made-up emergency pushes these people to a doorstep. For some it was the loss of a home due to fire or flood, or a sudden move due to a sickness in the family. Who could turn anyone down under those dire circumstances? For others, an alcoholic roommate or a sudden change in employment did the trick. For me, it was partially sympathy and partially my own dire straits.

As month three's rent came due I was behind on my house payments and while Chuck tried to help out with a little extra, it wasn't enough. I knew I'd have to pay a few bucks to formally evict Jane and maybe even sue her. But that would all take time and meanwhile she was still under my roof.

I'll admit, she scared me. She continued to wander the home at night after I was in bed. I could hear her gentle footfalls outside my door.

I'd get an unsettling sense that she was listening for the sound of heavy, even breaths of sound sleep.

Once when I saw her in the kitchen, I told her that if she didn't leave I would have to take legal measures. She confirmed my worst fears, telling me she'd beaten many a landlord in court. She actually laughed. "Oh, and I have a gun so don't even try thinking of getting physical with me."

Regardless of the fact I may lose, I decided to try my luck in small claims court. My plan was to file papers the next day. But I caught a bit of luck and landed a role—a walk on, really—on a network TV sitcom, so I was on the set for hours. It was as if a great weight had been lifted from my soul and I forgot all about my troubles. Plus, I was getting paid SAG minimum!

I was practically floating on air when I got home that evening and put my key in the lock of the front door and turned it. Turned it again. Then I jiggled it.

That crazy lady had changed the locks!

I grabbed my cell from my back pocket and called Chuck. When he answered, it sounded like he was in a wind-tunnel. "What's up, bro?"

Turns out, he was helping Jane look for her missing pets in the nearby canyons. "I think it was coyotes," he said.

"Did you know she changed the locks?" I seethed through clenched teeth.

"Yeah, man," he said nonchalantly. Chuck was always mellow. Nothing fazed him. "Don't worry, I was gonna copy my key for you."

Jane's voice blasted into my ear. "YOU BASTARD!" she shouted. "What did you do with Sparky and Anna Bell? Chuck says it was probably wild animals, BUT I KNOW IT WAS YOU! You are no longer welcome in my home!"

I called the police, who showed up right around the same time as Jane and Chuck.

The pair, a male and a female, looked at the whole thing as a domestic dispute and did nothing beyond making sure I was able to get inside my house. Chuck said nothing in my defense; he just shrugged, wanting to steer clear of the drama. Jane put on her sheepish face and apologized to the cops for any inconvenience. "Oh, officers, I was just so upset about Sparky and Anna Bell," she told them, "I plumb forgot to give him his new key."

Once they left, Jane went directly to her room, bolting the door with an audible flourish. Chuck said he had a batch of jerky going and he had to get it out of the oven before it got too dry. He disappeared into the basement, leaving me alone with my thoughts. There just had to be something I could do. I entertained all kinds of fantasies from poisoning her wine to hiring a hitman to shoot her with her own weapon.

Later, I heard Jane crying. She really did love her pets. I sincerely hoped they'd come back. But they didn't and within a few days, I'd know why.

It was a Sunday night. Late. Thanks to Jane I added insomnia to my mounting list of troubles, but I was just drifting off to sleep when I heard a loud, strangled cry.

"No, no, no…!" It was a woman's voice. *Jane's.*

I tried to ignore it, turning toward the wall and putting a pillow over my head.

Then there was a crash. It was coming from below. Chuck's workshop apartment.

I sat up. Another crash. Then a gunshot. This, I could not ignore.

Pivoting my legs over the side of the bed, I slid my feet into my slippers and went to my closed door. I listened for sounds in the hallway. There were none. I opened the door and made my way quickly to the entrance of the basement.

Chuck had had a heavy door installed above the stairs. It had good seals to keep the smell of meat and marijuana out of the common areas. I turned the knob, but it was locked.

I heard another cry, this one muffled. Again, it was Jane. Was she hurting Chuck? Did she have her gun aimed at him? I knocked at the door. "Hey!" I shouted.

I was met with sudden silence. I realized too late that I'd left my phone in my car. I listened for a long moment, then pounded again. "Let me in!" I cried. "This is *my fucking house*!"

I leaned in, knock-knock-knocking and not letting up. The door opened abruptly and I tumbled in.

Chuck fell back and I went with him. We found ourselves at the bottom of the stairs, dazed.

I blinked, clearing my head. I saw that Chuck was covered in blood. The fall couldn't have been that bad. No, Jane must have shot him.

I righted myself, scrambled to my feet and looked for a place to take cover from Jane's wrath. But I soon realized there was no need. She was dead.

Jane lay on the floor, her throat cut. Beside her were her pets, shaking and whimpering and stuffed into a cage. Anna Bell looked drugged and Sparky was muzzled. Oh, lord… Chuck was going to make edibles of Sparky and Anna Bell.

He was a monster.

The millisecond after I articulated that thought, I fell headlong into a blackhole of unconsciousness.

I don't know how long I was out, but it was long enough for Chuck to have put Jane up on a meat hook and to have dressed her carcass. Her guts lay in a bucket and thankfully he'd taken the head off so I wouldn't have to see her face. Sparky and Anna Bell were still alive in the crate, but I did see a skinned animal, possibly a rabbit or a cat, on another hanger. Then I saw a disembodied arm in the shadows… Jane had both of hers, so that could only mean she was not his first human filet.

"Oh, hey bro," I heard Chuck say amiably. "You're awake." He stood before me, wearing boot-foot rubber waders and a blood-smeared Bon Iver 2016 Tour tee-shirt. I saw he'd wrapped his upper arm in gauze—I figured his wound was from the gunshot I'd heard earlier.

I was handcuffed to the radiator and sitting in a wet puddle. The whole floor, which was cement and had a large drain in the center, was slick with gore.

Chuck, who'd never strung more than four or five words together in the two years he'd been renting my basement, said, "New recipes." He leaned forward, his pale and pudgy face close to mine.

I said nothing, unsure whether he wanted a reply.

Regardless, I was stunned and probably could not have spoken even if I wanted to. I had no clue the easygoing ganja go-to guy was anything other than a pacifist. Chuck and I were friends. Well, sort of. Aside from our epic Super Bowl parties and *Resident Evil: Biohazard* video game playoffs with our stoner friends, I realized we didn't hang much. I thought I knew him but of course this moment proved that I didn't. I kept to myself and so did he.

But now here we were—plunged deep into this hell together. Just the two of us. My life depended on this man I barely knew.

"I see you're surprised," Chuck said, stepping back and taking a seat on his bed. He chuckled softly. "Listen. I'm going to make you a deal. Jane-the-bane gave me an idea with all her, what-do-you call them... antics. You sign your house over to me and I don't kill you."

Could it really be that simple? I didn't think so. But what else could I do other than play along? I mumbled, "OK. The papers are in the safe in my bedroom closet."

He asked me for the combination and I gave it to him but with one wrong number. I figured it would keep him busy for at least a few extra minutes.

While he was gone I struggled mightily to free myself, but I was cuffed tight and the furnace was stronger than it looked.

Just when I thought I'd pass out from fear and the stench of blood and offal, Chuck returned. He grinned, looking embarrassed. "Dude, I am *so* baked. I can't get it. Come on, I'm gonna bring you with me. You open it." As he uncuffed me with one hand he produced Jane's .38 Special from his waistband with the other. "No funny stuff," he commanded. Then he laughed. "I've always wanted to say that."

I gave him a feeble smile and got to my feet. The no-tread soles of my slippers hit the blood-slick and I instinctively grabbed onto Chuck to right myself.

He skidded too and as God is my witness, this is true: The gun went off. A bullet entered Chuck's skull from under his chin and that was that.

The next few days blurred by in a nightmare montage of cops, paperwork, statements, animal welfare activists, reporters and journalists. Within weeks, my story was wrapped up and forgotten.

Forgotten by all but one important person. I've signed non-disclosure agreement but suffice to say, she is one of the biggest producers in Hollywood and she's got money. Her company optioned the rights to my story, and with the stipulation that I will star as myself, I am now writing the screenplay.

My mortgage is paid. I officially adopted Sparky and Anna Bell. Overall, I can't complain. But I do still have trouble sleeping; Jane haunts the hallway, while Chuck concocts ghostly recipes from the basement.

My Mother the Carcass

"Just close your eyes," said Dr. Dick Carlson slowly, soothingly. His voice was on par with the drone of almost-imperceptible room tone.

Two-hundred-and-twenty-eight pairs of eyes closed. The space was so quiet, you could hear a pin drop on shag carpet. Carlson prayed that no one's phone would buzz, despite his earlier admonitions. This was a very important time in the hypnotism. Everyone had to be completely at ease.

"Now, think of those lost loved ones… someone you cared about, who has crossed over to the other side…" He let his voice trail off, easing each person into a rock-a-bye lull. Their minds would be ready and ripe for any suggestion.

As two-hundred-and-twenty-eight brains focused on dead loved ones, Carlson's brain conjured up dead presidents. Lots and lots of them.

These mass-hypnosis deals always brought in the most money with the least effort on his part. But, he couldn't bring himself to do just that. He needed more. Carlson felt he had to take on some private clients as well; regulars who had more issues to work through than the usual crowd. It was his solemn (and lucrative) duty.

"The woman in the fifth row," came his assistant's tinny voice through the invisible earpiece, "she's wearing a red scarf over a green pantsuit." How could he miss her? He should have heard what she was wearing, even if he hadn't seen it. Christmas on crack.

Ingrid's voice continued and Carlson could hear her fingers clacking the keyboard of her iPad. "Her name is Sisely White. It was front-page news five years ago… her husband John was gunned down in front of their apartment—the LEVEL building in Downtown L.A.—and they never caught the murderer. They think it was supposed to be a mugging, but there was a witness who interrupted… Sorry Dick, there isn't much info here."

Carlson, pacing the stage, abruptly stopped. "I'm getting a name," he said, still soothing, but speaking loudly enough for everyone in the auditorium to perk up. He decided John was too common… he'd 'get' the wife's name first. "Sissy… Sisely?"

"That's me!" The woman raised a lime-green clad arm, waving it in the air.

"You may open your eyes, everyone," Carlson said.

He turned his attention back to the woman. "You lost someone very close to you some years back, but you're not over it yet." She nodded, gob smacked. "I'm feeling a male presence. Jack… no, John. Jonathan, right?" Again, the nod. Eyes brimming with tears. "I'm sensing violence. Unexpected violence. John wasn't ready to go, but he's accepted it, Sisely. He wants you to know he's at peace."

"Hey—no harm, no foul," Carlson stuffed another wedge of chicken cordon bleu into his mouth, while Ingrid picked at her skimpy salad in a chic beachfront bistro.

"I know… I just feel a little guilty, Dr. Carlson. These people really believe their loved ones are speaking to them. It just doesn't feel right."

Perhaps a pay raise would feel right. Carlson couldn't afford to lose Ingrid now. Not only was she a fantastic researcher, but she could hurt him if her conscience got the better of her. Carlson had just signed a book deal; his seminars were doing better than ever. There was no place else to go but up. If Ingrid quit, and if she decided to go public with what she knew, it would all be over. Nondisclosure agreements weren't worth the paper they were written on there days.

Of course, he could drag her down with him, but that was all useless worry. Nothing had happened yet; Ingrid hadn't even spoken of quitting. Then again, Carlson did have a doctorate in psychology and he knew human nature. It *could* happen.

"Now, now," he soothed her. What if he made a pass at her? Got her to feel something for him? Maybe she had daddy issues. Maybe if she had a few more glasses of wine.

No, too complicated. She was awfully pretty, though. "Ingrid, I know you don't think my powers are real. They *are*—it's just that I can't turn them on and off at will. That's why I need you."

It wasn't a complete lie. His powers had been real, once. Or at least, he thought so. He'd always been an imaginative child and had lots of invisible friends. Friends who told him they were ghosts. Then he'd been put on medication and the friends went away.

"I know," Ingrid's voice was small, her Swedish intonation slight, but alluring as hell. Carlson loved that sexy accent, loved hearing it in his ear, a mere whisper. "I know you are the real thing, Dick. I do believe in you. I just don't feel right about the seminars. At least in private sessions you were able to come up with some of your own…"

"I have to do it this way," he interrupted. She was getting uppity. She hadn't even been working with him a year yet. He saw a faint pink flush glow on her cheeks and he wondered if her nipples were the same shade. *No*, he told himself again. *Too complicated.* "This way, I can help so many more people overcome their grief. That's all they care about. They just want to know that their loved ones are at peace."

"I want the opposite," Ingrid muttered under her breath.

"What?"

"I want to see your apartment," she said.

Tears were streaming down Ingrid's delicate face, dripping off the tip of her pert nose, as she pulled her sweater back on. "I can't do this. I'm sorry."

Carlson got up from the couch and took her in his arms. "What is it, Ing? Is it me?"

"No, no. It's not you. It's my mother."

"Huh?"

"Oh, it's nothing. Can we just forget this? Please? I'm so ashamed."

"Of course," Carlson said, already thinking ahead to raiding his online porn collection and finding a nice, infantile Swedish model to relieve his pent-up passion. Ever since the arch-feminist movement had hit Hollywood, he was hitting it less and less often.

But then Ingrid did the unexpected: She kissed him again, fervently, passionately and with such force she bit his lower lip, drawing blood. Her blue eyes blazed for a moment after she drew away, licking at the drops that stained her own lips. Then she was crying again. "No. No. No, I am so sorry. I can't let this happen. It's evil."

"But do you want to talk about it? Hmmm…? I can help you. I'll even give you the employee discount, huh?" He cracked a half-smile, though he wasn't kidding. Ass, grass, gas, psychotherapy—nobody rides for free.

She shook her head. She sniffled back the last of her tears. "No, thanks. I'll be fine."

"Okay, Ingrid. All is forgotten. See you Monday—and have a nice weekend," he said, his lower lip throbbing.

Ingrid had not been gone ten minutes before Carlson was at his girlie cache. He went directly to the site he'd been thinking of and downloaded Ursula, a Scandinavian scorcher with white-blonde hair, black eyebrows and shaved pubes. As her image gyrated jerkily on his monitor, Carlson stroked his crotch. And stroked again. Gripped. Tickled. Rubbed.

Nothing.

For the life of him, he could not get it up. Was he feeling rejected by Ingrid? Was he too stressed out? Was he getting old? Was he… psychoanalyzing himself again. He had to stop that and just relax.

He felt that familiar rush and just as he did, he heard a whisper in his ear. "Ingrid… Don't touch Ingrid…"

The curtains by his bed fluttered. Carlson tensed.

But it was only the wind.

"Oh, fuck," were the first words Carlson uttered on Saturday morning.

He felt as though he'd been hit by a freight train. He'd suffered the strangest nightmares. He couldn't quite remember what happened. Something about sex and someone chasing him. A fight, bloody hair. He shook his head.

"What I need is a cup of coffee."

Carlson got up and went into his kitchen. The autotimer had worked perfectly and he could smell the pumpkin-spice holiday blend all ready for him. He took a deep breath, mouth closed. It was vaguely metallic… time to clean the maker. He got a cup and filled it. Took a tentative sip to test the temperature. And immediately spilled it.

The cup clattered to the floor, shattering, and the coffee splashed everywhere. Carlson peered at the stained floor. Only coffee. But when he brought the cup to his lips, he could have sworn he tasted… blood.

He was definitely stressed out. First striking out with Ingrid, then online Ursula, the nightmares and now this. He vowed he would just have a nice, relaxing weekend at home for a change. No going over his accounts. No working on his book. No meetings. Just Netflix and chill.

Carlson cleaned the coffee up, put the shards of the mug into his trash compactor and poured himself another cup. It was fine, just fine. He sat at the counter, sipping it slowly as he read yesterday's paper.

Two downings later, it was time to answer nature's call. As he approached the bathroom, Carlson felt an inexplicable stab of fear. He paused. The bathroom was shadowy, but innocent-looking enough. He could see the edge of the sink, the john, the opaque shower curtain.

The shower. *Psycho.* The hazards of living in Hollywood: Everything went back to the movies.

He chuckled to himself and entered the small room. He flipped on the lights and stood in front of the commode. He eased himself out and took a leak. He'd often wondered at that expression; wouldn't you rather *leave* one? Yawning, he reached down to flush the toilet.

The *blood-filled* toilet.

Gasping, he stumbled back, hitting the wall. He stole a quick glance at The Little Doctor—all good. Tucking himself away, heart pounding, he checked out the bowl. It had flushed and clear, perfectly normal water was swirling back in.

"Stress, stress, go away…" he whispered. Time to break into the old medicine cabinet, for sure. He went to the sink and opened the hinged mirror. He had several drugs and assorted sundries on the shelves there, but he knew exactly what he was after. He gobbled two tablets without water and shut the cabinet.

What was that?

Carlson would have sworn on his mother's grave he saw a female figure walking quickly by the open doorway. Only, he couldn't swear on his mother's grave. His mother wasn't dead. Another silly expression.

Had someone gotten in? Carlson peered cautiously out the doorway, into the hallway. No one.

But then he heard a girlish giggle, coming from his bedroom. *Ingrid?* It sure sounded like her. It had to be. She, being his assistant, did have a key to his apartment.

Tiptoeing, moving very slowly, he went to his bedroom. He turned the knob, then threw the door wide open. "Ah-ha!" He jumped in, grinning. He knew she couldn't resist him for long.

But the room was empty. There was nobody in his bed, no one smiling at him. Then he heard the feminine laughter again. The sexy titter. "Mmmm... that tickles."

Then he saw the glow—the glow of his monitor. The computer was on. He must have left the Scandi-Babes site on all night. That would explain his strange dreams, which he knew had something to do with sex.

No computer today. He was going to just relax in bed and try to get some more sleep. As Carlson reached for the power button, he saw a real beauty on the screen. A nubile blonde, maybe thirteen or fourteen years old, doing an awkward striptease.

She was smiling and blushing hotly. "I can't do this." The camera pulled back, revealing a young man sitting on a bed. The girl who had been dancing in front of him stopped.

Strange. Carlson had never seen any males in the scenarios. He sure as hell hoped his credit card hadn't been charged all night long for this—especially not with guys in the picture. Carlson liked having his women all to himself.

"I can't do this." Sounded familiar... he took a closer look. It was Ingrid! Holy Mary, Mother of God on a corndog stick. It was his *assistant*! Moonlighting as a cam porn star.

Unbelievable.

But cool.

He pulled up his chair and sat. Her knockers were every bit as magnificent as he'd imagined. He'd almost gotten her bra off last night and he had seen a promise of heaven there.

Why did she look so young? Granted, he did have a glare on the monitor, but he could see what was what. Then he saw something else. A mature, buxom and slender redheaded woman walking into the room. A threesome. *Hmmm...*

"Vaat are you doing?" the older woman screeched, her accent so heavy as to be a parody.

That didn't sound right. The "what are you doing?" was angry. Carlson kept watching.

"Mamma, I..."

The woman ignored the girl and advanced on the boy. He scrambled from the bed and fell to the other side. Carlson heard the thud of his body hitting hardwood. Ingrid, still naked, ran to him.

The redhead was pummeling the boy now, yelling something about how wicked he was, how he had ruined her daughter. Ingrid was saying nothing happened, but the woman called her a whore. Carlson couldn't see what was going on on the floor beside the bed, but he heard gagging sounds as if the boy was being strangled. Then he saw Ingrid reaching for the bedside lamp. She whacked her mother across the throat with it.

The two struggled, but Ingrid was stronger. She seemed possessed. Savagely she choked her meddling mother harder and harder, pounding her into the wall with her efforts, then slinging her across the room. The woman crumpled to the rug, still.

This wasn't like any porn Carlson had ever seen. This was some sick…

He was thrown back by the explosion. Instinctively, he shielded his eyes from the glass as pieces of the monitor flew like shrapnel shards.

He scrambled to his feet and scooted backwards. All was quiet, except for the hiss of what was left of his screen.

I guess it wasn't such a good idea to leave the laptop on all night, he thought.

He had to get out for a while. Leaving the mess on the floor, not even thinking about the fire hazard, he got dressed and went out to get a pastry, pick up the L.A. Times and maybe take a walk on the pier.

Every moment he was gone, Carlson felt an overwhelming desire to return home. He couldn't get back fast enough.

It didn't take him long to discover his computer in perfect condition, or the once-shattered coffee cup sitting innocuously in the dish-draining rack.

He was seriously losing it. He took two more of his pretty red pills and climbed into bed with his almond-crusted bear claw and his paper.

"Swedish Immigrant Murdered," screamed the headline on the front page. "Daughter confesses," in the smaller sub-head. Carlson glanced at the date in the top righthand corner... why didn't it surprise him? Today's date, but the year—a decade ago.

He read the story about how Sussana Siggurd, 33, was strangled to death, then stabbed, by her daughter, Ingrid, 13. Sussana was a widow and she and her daughter were starting a fresh life in L.A. When Ingrid's boyfriend went to the police, they took his claim seriously. Sussana was found lying across the floor, dead on a cheap throw rug. A stalk of IKEA brass lamp-stand was sticking out from between her collarbones. Her daughter, Ingrid, was nowhere to be found.

When the girl was caught several hours later, hiding in the basement, Ingrid was sent for psychiatric evaluation. She was an abused child, she told investigators. Her mother was insane. Her mother was into black magic and other weird stuff. Her mother had killed her father. Her mother wanted Ingrid all to herself.

The story went on to say that the delusional young woman would be committed to a mental hospital. She would be released with a clean slate when she hit the age of eighteen.

How did the paper get all this? Carlson wondered. Then he shook his head. His brain was steeped in a druggy haze, but even he realized the paper couldn't possibly be real. But could it be that was why Ingrid had rejected him? Had her traumatic first sexual experience scarred her for life?

How about killing her own mother—that would scar even Hitler for life.

His mind was wandering again. The drugs were slithering through his bloodstream like serpents.

Blood. So much blood.

"The lost weekend," Carlson muttered as he got dressed on Monday morning. He only remembered fragments and bits and pieces. He shouldn't have raided the candy cabinet. That had been stupid.

But he felt fine now, just fine.

He took a hired car to his office, sipping a to-go cup of coffee on the way. Despite the ever-present Westside congestion, the ride didn't take long. He could have walked, actually, but it was Indian summer. Another silly old saying. And politically incorrect to boot. *Can't say anything anymore*, he grumbled to himself. Regardless, it was the most stifling, hot, humid time of the year in the city. He gave the driver a generous tip, then made his way to the building.

He rode the elevator up to his office and walked to the door. Locked. *Hmmm. Ingrid must be running late.* He took the keys from his pocket and unlocked it. He flipped on the lights. The answering machine was beeping insistently.

The first message was from Ingrid, telling him she wouldn't be in on Monday. It was about what happened between them on Friday night, she said. She quit.

"Fuck me sideways!" Carlson whispered explosively. He could see the headlines now. Not only would she tell about the scam, but she might even sue for sexual harassment. "Me too," Carlson mocked.

She might do anything. The girl was obviously unbalanced.

Or was she? Had he imagined it all? The murder? The paper? Of course, he had. *Thanks a lot, Oxy. Thanks a lot, Xanax. And you too, Vicodin.*

He picked up the phone to call Ingrid. He had to talk her out of it. A raise. A big, fat raise would get her attention. Secure her loyalty.

There was another message. Maybe it was her, changing her mind. He replaced the receiver and let the second memo play. It was the LAPD. Something about his assistant, Ingrid Siggurd, having committed suicide on Friday night. The last call she placed was to *him*. Could he please phone them back as soon as possible?

The next few days were surreal. Ingrid had indeed killed herself. She was found lying in her bathtub with a gunshot wound to her once-pretty head. She left a note in meticulously looped cursive, explaining that the guilt of killing her mother had been too much for her to bear.

So, she really *had* killed her mother. Maybe Carlson's childhood gift was coming back. Through a cam-girl site. *Huh. Well, whatever.*

Whether it was or it wasn't, he still had a business to run and a book to write. He needed a new assistant.

A mature, discreet assistant, his ad said. Of course, the ad didn't reveal his identity. Everyone wanted to work for a Hollywood psychic celebrity. Still, in spite of the blind listing he'd gotten *a lot* of responses.

"Your next applicant is here. She's early." It was the temp, using the speaker function on the phone.

"Send her in," he returned.

He was looking for her resumé, which the temp had printed out for him. His back was to the hopeful, but he could see her reflection in the window. A smartly dressed redhead, busty, slender and composed.

"Have a seat," he offered. "I'm just trying to find your CV."

"Take your time," she said softly. Nice voice. He would enjoy listening to it in the earpiece.

He heard the chair cushions settling with her weight. "So, tell me about your skills," Carlson said, rifling through the neatly filed sheets. Where the hell was that resumé?

"I'm mature," she said. "I'm discreet. And I can communicate with the dead. I do it all the time. You won't even need that little earpiece anymore, Dick."

Dick? And was that a Swedish accent? Ingrid come back for her job? He was afraid to turn around now. No, those were crazy thoughts. He wasn't crazy.

"How do you know about the earpiece?" He said sharply. Ingrid had told someone his secret before she died. That was it. All perfectly logical. He was dealing with a blackmailer. He turned around.

She was a picture. Her face was like porcelain and she sat elegantly poised, with her hands folded in her lap. Every inch a lady. Her tailored suit was of the highest quality and her skirt was just short enough. Her hair was a titian flame of silky waves.

Too bad she'd chosen to wear white, though. The blood dripping from the gaping hole in her neck was ruining the jacket.

That old movie trope came to his mind unbidden: *The only way you can kill a zombie is a gunshot to the head.*

Sussana bared her jagged, rotten teeth.

"Nine-one-one, what is your emergency?"

"Uh, I'm calling from the Palm Towers. The office of Dr. Dick Carlson. I was just temping here," the voice broke. "I... I buzzed into his office to let him know his job applicant had canceled her appointment and — and," a sob. "A few minutes later I heard a gunshot. I know he kept a pistol in his filing cabinet... I... I think he killed himself."

The Case of the Butchered Bombshell

From mashers to slashers and peepers to pedophiles, I thought I'd seen just about everything in my storied stint as a private dick. My bones begged for respite and I had my eye on a nice, soft retirement. On my last birthday, the candles cost more than the cake. It was time to hang my fedora on a peg and put on my captain's hat—I'd bought a small houseboat, The Lucky Break. I planned on spending my weekends drifting between Marina Del Rey and Catalina Island.

But I hadn't seen it all. Not yet.

It was a series of stories in the newspaper that piqued my interest. Women were being cut up. That was nothing new. But folks couldn't get enough of the sordid and salacious. Hell, The Black Dahlia case was twenty years old and fresh as ever. This slew of slayings stood out because the victims weren't bag-ladies or pro skirts—they were upstanding citizens. They were rich. Rich enough to drive a Rolls Royce and have enough left over to pay for their phony smiles.

Yes, "They had faces then" —but making the most of them usually required a little work. Miss Marilyn Monroe's perfect nose wasn't always so perfect and, according to Confidential magazine, Carmen Miranda's maracas weren't always so perky. Gary Cooper's facelift almost undid his career and after a losing battle with the Big C, Cooper's widow tied the knot with his surgeon.

In case you're wondering, I'm not handsome. My looks haven't improved with age. The last time I was somebody's type, I was donating blood.

That afternoon I was in my office. It wouldn't be my office for long. I'd let my girl go, shredded my files and all but my blower was boxed up. My loafers were up on the desk and my schnoz was between the pages of the Los Angeles Times. I was reading an op-ed with a baiting headline: *Hollywood Wives Go Under Beverly Hills Knives: Dying To Be Beautiful.* It was written by some feminist, probably a dyke. The world was changing. I figured I was taking a powder just in time.

There was a curt knock on the glass of my office door, then my one-eyed landlord, Bernie, let himself in. "Hey, Ryker," he snapped. "You ain't retired yet."

I slowly removed my feet from the desk and folded the paper closed. I yawned for effect. "As good as."

"You sure about that?" he asked. A smile sat strangely on his withered face. If there was anyone older and uglier than me in this town, it was him. His glass eye stared straight ahead, independent of the real one which was scanning the few folders left on my desk. "You're paid up till the end of the month."

"What are you getting at?" I asked.

"You haven't heard," he stated. The strange smile came again. "Maybe you *should* retire then."

"Spit it out, Bernie."

"It's Lola. Your girl. She's croaked. Murdered."

I gave a low whistle. "Poor kid."

"She was offed by The Surgeon," Bernie said excitedly. "Did you know she was one of them silicone sisters?"

I nodded.

"Bet you did," Bernie went on. The worm was verbally incontinent—and he had a nose for gossip. "In fact, I know you did. Maude and Lola talked. They talked *a lot.*"

So, I'd gotten dizzy with the dame. Sue me.

Maude manned Bernie's front desk. I pitied her but I didn't like her spilling my private business to Bernie. Well, maybe Lola's death wiped out the bond of confidentiality.

I fixed Bernie with an expressionless stare.

He took my silence as a request to keep talking. "Her melons was taken clean off with a scalpel," Bernie said with a grimace. "And once again, the killer got away. And once again, he sent a note to the cops. Anyway, just thought you knew… The brass ain't been here to see ya?"

I shook my head.

"Well," he went on. "They will be. I mean, you was her boss an' all. Didn't know you paid so good, Ryker. Since when can a secretary pay for bigger bazoongas?"

I merely shrugged in response. Actually, Lola hadn't paid for her silicone injections. Her ex-husband—a mobster type who owned the clip joint where she waitressed before marrying him—did. The divorce was still fresh. Maybe it was him, getting his investment back. But the police had received a note. That fit the M.O.

He always signed his notes "The Surgeon" and added a crude sketch of a scalpel. The first killing that we know of happened on January 12, 1965. That was eighteen months ago and a baker's dozen of once-beautiful bodies had been put on ice since. It didn't take long for the local gestapo to figure out they had a real psycho on their hands.

The Surgeon was targeting people who'd had plastic surgery or enhancements. Then he was *undoing* the work. Stiffs turned up missing noses or eyelids. Facelifts were… reversed. It was gruesome. Rumors ran rampant through Hollywood's elite circles about who it could be. Was the Black Dahlia Killer back? Was it some new, even sicker twist? My money was on the latter. But I wasn't that kind of P.I. No, murder wasn't my business. If you had a cheating spouse, a missing kid, or a pervert to catch, I was your guy.

But what about now? Lola was a sweet kid. She didn't deserve to die like that.

"So, whatchoo gonna tell the cops?" Bernie asked, still standing in front of my desk. The two client chairs had already been picked up by St. Vincent's—the desk and my chair would be sent to my houseboat. I was sentimental like that.

"The truth," I replied. "I let her go on Friday, gave her some severance pay and that was that."

"No horizonal hokey-pokey for old time's sake?" Bernie asked, eyebrows wriggling like Groucho Marx. He thought he was being funny.

I swallowed bile. "Nope."

The phone on my desk rang.

Bernie grinned. "That must be them. The cops."

I let it ring as I fixed him with a pointed stare. He got the hint and hightailed it.

Once I heard the door shut, I picked up. "Max Ryker Private Investigations. If persons are missing or trinkets are lost, I'll find them for you at reasonable cost."

"Lay off the B.S., Max. I know you're retired." I recognized the voice. It was the District Attorney of this fine City of Angels, Griffin Davies. Davies had used me as an investigator once or twice. He was a police officer before he passed the State Bar and worked his way quickly up the ladder of prestige.

"I'm not retired yet," I returned. "Still got four days left."

"Sorry about Lola," Davies said, his tone turning serious. "Sad thing."

Lola hadn't been with me long. Only about a year. But everyone who met her, loved her. Well, *almost* everyone. "Yeah. Any leads?"

"Chief Dempsey should be calling on you soon. The papers reported there was another note but not what was in it. I trust you'll be discreet?"

"Scout's honor," I said. "Look. I'm gonna save Dempsey the drive. I'll head over to the clubhouse now. Bye."

But I didn't plan on going directly to the station. The sight of Lola's forgotten scarf hanging on the coatrack gave me an idea.

II.

I met Mellie in '63. She was dangling off a pole at Delilah's Den. She reminded me of a filly I'd once bet on at Hollywood Park who broke early and finished dead last.

Now she was eighteen years old and working at The Book & Bean. I got her the job a couple of years ago. I'd been hired by Mellie's parents to find her. I did find her. Like most runaways, she didn't want to be found. She had her reasons. Those reasons had to do with her stepfather diddling her, she said. I believed her. I told daddy-dear she was in the wind and returned most of what he'd paid me—minus expenses.

Ever since, Mellie and me had been pals. She was pretty. Blonde. Stacked. And smart.

She was jailbait and she'd been hurt, so I never tried to be anything other than Uncle Max to her. I got her out of Delilah's Den. Got her a better fake I.D., so she wouldn't get flagged. Sometimes she worked at the bookstore-café and sometimes she worked for me. I guess I'd call her an investigator. Others—including herself—would use a different word: Psychic.

I never did believe in all that mumbo-jumbo swami swill, but I had to admit the girl had a gift. Whether it was intuition, good guesses or bona fide help from the beyond, she'd never failed me. She couldn't just turn it on though. She had to touch something that had belonged to the person in question. That's why I'd grabbed Lola's scarf on my way out the door.

The Book & Bean was tucked away on Third, not far from the Santa Monica Pier. It was owned by one of my ex-wives—Helga. Believe me, she didn't look like a Helga when I'd married her. She still didn't, but the alimony payments colored my view. Helga was a good egg. She'd given my little foundling a job, no questions asked and let her live in the studio apartment above the store. Mellie had been there two years now and had made herself indispensable. But now I needed to borrow her.

The bell above the door chimed when I entered. I shook the rare Southern California rain from my trench coat as I removed it and stuck it on a hook. I headed to the back of the long, narrow store.

As expected, Mellie was there. She was the only one there. I ordered a black coffee and a buttered roll and took a seat on one of the threadbare velvet sofas. Before I could read more than a paragraph of the book I'd slid from the nearest shelf, she brought my food and drink.

"Have a seat, sister," I said, patting the cushion next to me.

"What's up, Max?" she asked.

Mellie could always tell when I had more than just small talk on my mind. Intuition is a bad quality in a woman, if you ask me. But it can be useful. Hers had helped solve more than a couple of my cases. Not that I wouldn't have solved them anyway, but she had a shortcut to the finish line.

I looked at her for a beat before answering. I was proud of Mellie. Her dark blue eyes were shadowed by mascara and jadedness and, yeah, she looked a few years older than she was but now there was hope in her crooked smile. Laughter came more easily to her as time passed. Nobody was looking for her anymore.

Now that she was eighteen, she was truly free. I'll admit I wasn't fond of the hippie types she hung around with, but I guess I'd always be a little overprotective. Uncle Max. That was me.

I reached into the pocket of my pinstriped jacket. I produced a small silver flask I'd had since W-W-2 and spiked my coffee with some cheap Irish whisky.

"Max!" Mellie admonished, looking around the café. We were still alone. "You know we don't have a liquor license."

"If you don't tell, I won't," I said and took a pull.

She laughed. This was our routine.

I reached into another pocket and produced a fine silk kerchief. Lola's old sea green scarf felt warm to the touch, as if it had only just left her lovely neck. I could smell her perfume still on it.

Mellie looked at it. "A new case?"

I nodded and handed it to her.

The moment the fabric touched Mellie's hand, she screamed.

I nearly spilled my coffee. I'd never seen her react this way.

I put the cup on the end table. I glanced around the café. We were still alone.

Mellie clutched at the delicate chiffon, then gripped it in an irate fist. Her eyes were screwed shut at first, then they opened but all I saw was white as they rolled back. Her breaths were coming short and fast.

"Mellie!" I put my hands on her shoulders and gave her a firm shake. I was old but I was still strong. She tried to wriggle free, but I held her fast. "Mellie!" Another shake. The girl was wailing now. Eyes still white as cue balls.

I grabbed Lola's scarf and pulled at it. Mellie's grip tightened. A death-grip. The fabric tore as I continued to pull. Finally, I got it.

The moment the scarf left Mellie's hand, her blue eyes were back and she quieted. Before I could catch her, she crumpled. She slid off the sofa and landed on the hardwood floor, tailbone-first. The poor kid was out like a light.

I stood and dragged her back onto the cushions. I slapped at her cheeks until she came around.

Mellie sobbed as she came to. "What the hell was that?" she demanded. She wiped her tears away and sat up. "Ow," she said softly as her caboose undoubtedly protested the move.

"It was Lola's scarf."

"Was?" Mellie was quick on the uptick.

"Yeah," I sighed. "She's dead."

"Why didn't you tell me first?" she sniffled. "That was awful."

I didn't think to warn her, honestly. It was true I didn't usually handle murder cases but I hadn't a clue Mellie would be affected like that. I scoffed at myself. *A gumshoe without a clue.* Maybe it *was* time I retire.

I handed her my spiked brew and she sucked it down in a single gulp.

"Sorry, kiddo," I said.

Mellie was getting better by the second. She stood and said, "Hang on. I'll put the closed sign on the door." When she returned, she took the easy chair that sat across from the couch. She gave me a grave look. "Lola isn't just dead. She got bumped off."

"I know," I said. "What did you see?"

According to Mellie, she could catch glimpses through the eyes of the victim when she touched something that belonged to them. She saw the lovers of cheating spouses and she saw the addresses where thieves were hiding. She saw how gamblers cheated. And once she even saw the face of a dog-napper. I wasn't proud of being reduced to finding lost dogs, but the reward money helped keep the lights on. And Mellie always got her cut. She was saving up for a car. One of them foreign jobs.

Mellie closed her eyes and recalled the vision. "I saw… mirrors."

"What kind of mirrors? Like, in a dressing room?"

"No. Not like that. More like a rearview mirror. I saw Lola's eyes in the reflection. They were full of terror." Mellie's shoulders sagged. "Poor Lola. She was always so sweet to me."

Maybe I'd overstepped. I should have told Mellie what was what. Up to now, she'd never known any of the victims.

She continued. "Where was she found?"

I didn't know yet. I had no details to give her, but maybe that was better. I couldn't influence her answers this way.

Mellie reached across the narrow coffee table that bisected the sofa and the chair. "Hand it to me again."

I hesitated. She was still pale. "Are you sure, Mel?"

She bounced her hand slightly. I placed the kerchief into her palm and her fingers gripped it. Her eyes closed and sweat bulleted her forehead.

I watched her like she was the late-night picture show. She was still and quiet. But I could see her trembling. Then she opened her eyes and let go of the scarf.

"I saw him," she said, voice soft. "The Surgeon."

III.

The precinct was bustling. But behind Dempsey's closed door it was quiet as a nun's cooch. The late afternoon sun coming through the blinds lit his face in long slats. It gave him a mysterious quality. But the man himself was being anything but mysterious. He was telling me everything I wanted to know. We'd fought together, seen a lot, been through a lot.

"I'm sorry you had to come into the case this way," Dempsey said. He lit a cigarette. Proffered the pack to me.

"I quit," I said.

"I hear you're quitting lots of things. Closing your doors, eh?"

"The door's been open a long time," I sighed. "It's time to move on."

"But not now. Now that The Surgeon's made it personal."

"Look, Demps," I said. "I'm not officially on the case."

"Since when have you been official?"

"Touché," I dipped my chin in a single nod.

Dempsey and me, we'd been through hell and back. But he never did approve of me going into private practice. He didn't like rule-bending. At least, not on the books. Paperwork never mentioned me, but I'd been around the clubhouse a time or two.

I met his gaze. "So. This most recent note. What's it say?"

Dempsey opened a brown manila folder and slid out a piece of torn white paper with heavily inked lettering on it. The note was in a plastic bag. He handed it to me and I took it.

The smell of the burning Pall Mall and the tang of my own sweat came into sharp focus as I read the typed taunt.

"Mr. Policeman," it began. They all started like that. Ended the same, too: "The doctor is in." But it was the middle that interested me. The killer wrote, "She wasn't a good girl. I had to teach her a lesson. She learned that beauty is only skin deep. If you don't stop me I will kill again." Then there was his usual sign-off and, the only hand-drawn bit, a childlike scrawl of a scalpel.

"Can I borrow this?" I asked.

"You know I can't let you do that," Dempsey sighed and sucked his gasper down to a nub. He stubbed it out in a heavy green glass ashtray and watched as I set the note back onto the desk.

Since I had been only a bystander on the case up till now, the Chief brought me up to speed. Their biggest lead, one that they were keeping secret, was that the same plastic surgeon had performed all of the procedures on the fatalities.

"What in blazes!" I exclaimed. "How long have you been sitting on this? Do his patients know?"

"Don't worry," Dempsey said, holding his palms up. "We have surveillance on the ones who still live in the jurisdiction. And we've suggested to the Doc he take a vacation until we catch this S.O.B."

"Who is it?" I asked.

Dempsey hesitated for a split second, but he decided he was all-in and replied, "Dr. Ralph Rasmussen."

I felt my jaw drop before I could stop it. Even I knew the name. He was the surgeon to the stars. He even had his own daytime television series. It came on right after the Jack LaLanne Show. LaLanne shared his fitness secrets with bored housewives, while Rasmussen extolled the virtues of the knife to those who were too lazy or too rich to bother with sit-ups.

Dempsey lit another cigarette. In the moment he looked down, I quietly slid the note off the desk and tucked it under my jacket. If he saw me, and I think he did, he didn't mention it. "So," he continued. "That makes several citizens in the cemetery and me with no leads."

"You don't consider the Doc a suspect?"

"Where's the motive?"

"Maybe he doesn't need one. I mean, the man cuts people up for a living. Maybe it's his hobby too."

Dempsey shook his head. "He's got alibis. That man is on a tighter schedule than an assembly line. Murder before last? He wasn't even in town. He was in Chicago for a medical convention."

"You said 'no leads'," I pressed. "What have you got on your pen-pal?"

"No fingerprints. The stamp is stuck on with a glue-sponge. Everything's typed, except for his artwork. He's a wise head." Dempsey took a deep breath. "Tomorrow, we'll have plainclothes at Lola's funeral. Sometimes these sickos like to attend the services, you know."

I nodded. "I didn't get an invite. When and where?"

Dempsey rifled through some of the papers on his desk. It was darker now, the window slats letting in less light. He yanked the chain on his green desk lamp. I hoped the newly illuminated area wouldn't reveal the lack of a certain note. But Dempsey was single-minded if nothing else. He found what he was looking for and read the time and place aloud.

"Thanks," I said, standing. I tucked my left arm tight, holding my pilfered prize in place. Then I took it on the heel and toe.

IV.

It was early evening now, part sun and part rainclouds. My 1949 Buick Roadmaster gleamed beside an expired parking meter. I glanced at the windshield for a ticket, but all I saw was the reflection of palm trees on the glass. The meter maids around here knew better than to ding a pal of the Chief's.

I got behind the wheel and navigated the big boat to my favorite Chinese takeout joint, picked up dinner and headed home. I lived in a small apartment on Franklin— La Belle Tour, they call it. Legend says it's haunted. All I ever heard was the spirits of cockroaches. But it was cozy and cheap. Suited me fine.

After I ate my dim sum and then some, I made myself a gin and tonic. Strong. I turned on the radio. There was a low hum of static, but Dave Brubeck's *Take Five* was just starting so I left it. I mulled over the day's events.

I thought back to what Mellie told me. Her visions were usually clear. I mean, the girl could see whole addresses, license plates and phone numbers. It was uncanny. She could make a fortune with that gift of hers. But she wasn't ready to come out of the shadows yet. She may be legal, but she was still daddy's little hostage in that pretty noggin of hers.

"I see mirrors. I see Lola's face in them," Mellie said. "Small, like a compact. But there's two of them."

As she spoke, the story became clearer. There were details. Gruesome ones. I severed my mind's thoughts from my heart's fondness.

According to Mellie, this is what happened. Lola was out back, pulling her trashcans to the alley when she was grabbed from behind. The person was big, over six feet tall, heavy-set and strong. He levered his forearm across her throat, stopping the scream. The arm was clad in black. He wore dark gloves. Leather. New. Lola's mules slipped off her feet and she could feel the rough, painful scrape of pavement on her heels as she was dragged to a secluded corner. Her attacker let her go just long enough to reach for something. Then she felt a thin jab in the corner of her eye. She watched as the hypodermic withdrew from her skull.

She'd been drugged. Her heart raced. But she didn't pass out. She watched, eyes fixed open, as she saw the masked figure loom toward her prone body. The man was a black shape from head to toe. Black except for the two mirrors over his eyes. Sunglasses like a highway patrol cop. Reflecting her own face back at her.

"Look at yourself," the attacker growled. It was a husky sound. Not really a distinct voice. "Watch yourself die."

Somehow, Lola was able to do just that. Mellie said she, as Lola, was fully awake. But completely paralyzed. She couldn't move. Couldn't scream. But she could watch. And she could feel.

I shuddered and took a belt. Refilled my tumbler with straight gin. Kept going over the story.

Lola watched in mute dread as the killer ripped open her blouse and cut her bra off with a scalpel. He put a knee in her stomach and went to work. The pain was immense. So much that all she could really feel was the weight of this man on her body. Her lungs sucked at thimblefuls of air. All the while, she watched herself in the twin barrels of the mirror glasses. She saw her face get pale as she lost blood.

As quickly as he'd appeared, the killer was gone. Lola felt bliss in her solitude. And then, there was no more to know. "Just emptiness," Mellie said.

Good as she was, even Mellie couldn't see to the other side. I thought of something Faulkner had written: "The reason for living was to get ready to stay dead a long time." But Lola had hardly lived. The kid was only twenty-six.

Why should an old wretch like me survive the war and still be here, while a sweetheart like her gets snuffed for no reason? It wasn't fair. I glanced at my empty glass. The ice was half-melted. The eel juice was making me maudlin. I poured myself another.

V.

A hangover hugged me like a hot, heavy sweater. But I had to get up. The library opened at 8 a.m. and I wanted to be the first one there. I had a big day ahead of me. I made a pot of coffee. Drank a cup, hot, black, and forced a buttered roll down. In time, I felt human. Well, almost.

As the Buick turned over, the roar of its engine stabbed at my head. I ignored it and pulled from the curb into traffic.

The Regional Library was on Ivar. Nobody was there yet. It was just me, an elderly librarian and the microfiche. I pored over all the newspaper stories and magazine articles I could find on Dr. Ralph Rasmussen.

I'd heard he was one of one of the most notorious philanderers in L.A. In this town, he had stiff competition—but came out on top every time. Mrs. R stayed by his side. She knew where those mink stoles came from.

The papers didn't report anything on their private life. Mostly it was puff pieces on red carpet events the couple attended. Or his TV show. His latest polo pony purchase. Nothing about the murders of his patients. I figured he must have paid off the paper moguls because news hawks may be annoying but they aren't dumb. If what the Chief had said was true and the victims really were limited to Rasmussen's patient roster, word would have to come out sooner or later. Sooner, if I had anything to say about it.

I went back in time, scanning stories until I got to the very first one. It was dated June 12, 1952. Rasmussen had just set up his practice on Rodeo Drive in the hale Hills of Beverly. There was an extensive interview with him and it revealed a detail I didn't know before: He and his wife had a daughter. She died shortly after birth. Apparently, the infant was disfigured and couldn't survive. Like the

Thalidomide babies. But this was over fifteen years ago. Before that drug's short and horrifying heyday. I read a quote from the doctor. "I've decided to devote my career, in part, to helping those less fortunate." He went on to say he'd be traveling to third-world countries to perform charitable reconstructive surgeries to deformed villagers.

I jumped ahead for other stories. There was nothing more about his promise to do good for others. Instead, he'd fallen into the local constellation of stars. He made them prettier than they had any right to be. And made himself richer than he had any right to be. Greed was an ugly thing.

After I'd learned all I could, I headed to the Book & Bean to see if Mellie could help me out a little more. I had the killer's note with me.

Helga was there. She stood behind the cash register in the Book section. Mellie was toward the back, in the Bean section. She was making cappuccino. I could hear the frothy screech of the machine. I glanced at Helga without saying hello. "How can you stand that noise?" I asked. The hangover was still hanging over.

Helga shrugged. "I'm an old bag now. My ears are purely ornamental at this point."

I stepped up to the counter. I leaned over. I nuzzled her ear. "Very pretty ornaments they are."

She grinned and gave me a playful shove. "Go on now. Dolly's in the café."

When I'd found Mellie, she was dancing under the name Dolly Danger. Dolly Danger in Delilah's Den. Decadent. The moniker had become an in-joke between the three of us, but Helga was the only one who stuck with it. Helga always did have a hard time letting things drop. Maybe that's why we were kaput.

I covered the length of the shop in long strides. Mellie was serving the cappuccino to a couple seated on the sofa.

She smiled when she saw me. "Hey, Max."

"Got a minute?"

"If the boss says it's OK," she said. Then she took off her apron and laid it on the chair behind the counter.

"Let's take a walk," I said. Truth was, I had to get some fresh air. The smell of coffee and musty books was making my stomach do a rumba.

We headed for the door. Mellie said she was taking a break. Helga nodded. Then she asked, "Hey, Max. Why the black suit on a sunny day?"

"Funeral," I replied.

Once we were outside, Mellie said, "I didn't mention it to her. You know, about Lola."

Helga knew about Mellie's gift. But she didn't like me... what'd she call it? *Exploiting* the girl.

I took a deep breath. Yesterday's rain had washed away some of the smog. As we walked, I slipped the note from my pocket. It was still in its plastic bag.

Mellie took it. Read it. Kept walking. Her hips swayed like she could still do the old bump-and-grind if she wanted to. "Hmmm," was all she said.

"What?" I asked.

"Interesting note, Uncle Max, but unless I touch it, I can't tell you anything about who wrote it."

"Let's sit," I said. We'd come to a small park with some benches.

I took the letter and gripped it carefully at the edge with the nails of my thumb and forefinger. I slid it out just a little. "Don't leave prints," I warned her.

She set her wrist on the exposed paper and shut her eyes for a moment.

"This is not from the killer," she finally said.

I slipped the note back into its protective plastic. "You sure?"

She gave a look. "Yeah. I'm sure. Whoever wrote this letter never killed anyone. I'm sensing a piano."

"Piano?" I repeated.

"That's all I got," she said definitively. She paused, then added, "Well, not all. I've been doing some thinking. You know, Lola's feelings when she died reminded me of something. Succinylcholine."

"Sucks-a-what?" I queried. But the word did seem oddly familiar.

"Succinylcholine," she repeated. "It's been all over the news. You know: The Carl Coppolino case. The doctor's murder trial that just ended. He was found guilty of inducing a heart attack in his wife with that drug. The one that paralyzes patients during surgeries."

"Right," I said. I remembered a tawdry headline I'd seen just last week: *Wife and Death! Deadly Doc Gives Murder a Shot.* Apparently the swarthy S.O.B. had been out for strange and wanted the Mrs. out of the way. He used succinylcholine chloride, a muscle relaxant used by anesthesiologists. In its intended dosage, it just sends folks into la-la land. But too much and it's lights out forever.

Mellie had done some digging. She told me that the beauty of the drug as a murder weapon is the fact it's rapidly metabolized by the body, sometimes within five minutes. It would be impossible to detect in an autopsy, because it was already long gone.

"In surgeries," she continued, "It's used with sedation, so you go to sleep. But if you're hit without sedation, you'll spend those minutes before death in a state of waking terror, realizing there is nothing you can do. You cannot move. You are a helpless witness to your own death."

"I can see why Coppolino did it that way," I said. "Clever. Covert. But The Surgeon doesn't try to pass off these killings as anything other than murder."

"I felt what she felt," Mellie shuddered. "He does it to *torture* them."

VI.

Lola's funeral was small and sad.

Bernie and Maude were there. So was Dempsey. I returned the note. He took it without a word. I saw some people there I didn't know. An older man and woman were crying. Probably her parents. The three guys in grey suits standing in back were clearly plainclothes.

One mourner caught my interest: It was a heavy-set woman, tall. She had on a long, loose black dress. She wore a wide-brimmed hat with an opaque veil over it. It covered her face. I heard her stifle sobs as the preacher read from Genesis 3:19. "In the sweat of thy face shalt thou eat bread, till thou return unto the ground; for out of it wast thou taken, for dust thou art and unto dust shalt thou return."

As the casket was being lowered into the ground, a Yellow cab pulled up. The mysterious mourner got in.

"Whaddaya make of that?" I asked the Chief.

"What?"

"Her." I jutted my thumb at the retreating hack.

"Creepy. But she's not our man. Our man is a man. Got to be."

I nodded. Mellie said a man killed Lola and I was inclined to agree. I still hadn't ruled out Rasmussen. Enough money could buy a hundred alibis.

Dempsey and I walked over to the gift shop. I wanted to buy some flowers to put on Lola's grave. As the gravel path crunched beneath our feet, I presented Mellie's theory on the drug as if it were my own. I knew the kid wouldn't mind. She didn't like to get involved with the police.

"Hmmm," Dempsey nodded, absorbing the idea. "I'll run it by the coroner."

"If the victims were poked, say, in the corners of their eyes, needle-marks would be hard to find," I added.

I bought a dozen yellow roses. Dempsey didn't bother. As we exited the shop, I went my way and he went his.

When I returned to the gravesite, Bernie and Maude were about to leave. I wished I'd been a minute later. Maude hugged me. She let go, but her perfume didn't. I was drenched in a cloud of dime-store lavender. Bernie shook my hand. Limp. Offered his condolences. Fake.

Maybe Maude was there for the right reasons, but not Bernie. Bernie was a parasite. I was glad I wouldn't be writing him any more rent checks.

"So, Max," Bernie said conspiratorially. "Are you going after The Surgeon now? Are you looking for him here? You know they say the perp likes to return to the scene of the crime. Funerals, too. Likes to see what he's done."

I looked at him. Saw my own face reflected in the lenses of his Wayfarers. Not mirrored. I looked at him some more. He started shifting from foot-to-foot. Bernie didn't like to be looked at. He wanted to be the one looking.

Finally, I spoke. "Yes, they do. How do we know the killer ain't you?"

He sputtered. "Don't even kid about that, Max. The cops are here."

"They are?" Maude craned her neck. "Where?"

"Plainclothes, baby," Bernie said, putting his thick, hairy hand on the small of her back. His tarnished silver wedding band glinted in the sun.

Bernie told me he had to get back to his office and said goodbye. As he and Maude left, his mitt still on her, I could hear him say, "Didya know I used to work security? Wore iron and everything…"

I hadn't met Lola's parents. I didn't want to meet them. Tears made me jumpy. I put the roses on the grave and breezed off.

After the funeral I went home and caught some shuteye. I woke up in the early evening. I felt restored. But I had an itch. I had to keep digging. The only way to solve Lola's murder was to cut the head off the snake. In this case, the snake was Dr. Rasmussen. I needed to talk to him. Maybe more.

His home address was in the White Pages. I drove there. Parked out front. Bold-like. I had nothing to hide.

The house was big. Bigger than any house I'd ever live in. I saw a brand-new black Jaguar in the driveway. Someone was home.

I went to the door. I saw a doorbell, but I wanted to knock. I rapped the dark wood hard with my knuckles. A servant opened the door. No, I wasn't expected. No, Dr. Rasmussen didn't know me. The servant closed the door. But not fast enough—I wedged my foot in. Then I wedged myself in.

"Dr. Rasmussen!" I called out.

An older man, dressed classy but casually, appeared. "I say. Who are you and what do you want?"

"I'm a friend of one of your patients. One of your patients who won't be coming back for a checkup. Lola Stewart. And she wasn't the first to get deep-sixed, was she?"

Rasmussen's eyes widened in alarm. He wanted to keep me quiet in front of the help. "Come with me," he hissed.

The doc led the way to his study. It was lined floor-to-ceiling with books. The ceilings were so high a ladder was required to reach the books at the top. I saw some classic novels. Mostly medical textbooks, though. The floor was of the same dark wood as the front door and the window was covered in heavy russet drapes. There was a fire lit. I saw Rasmussen's pipe smoldering in an ashtray on his desk. He took a seat behind that desk. I took the chair in front of him.

"Now who are you and what are you doing here?" he demanded. "You want money?"

"I want answers."

"Who are you?" he asked again. He didn't like me. Or maybe it was the stink of lavender. Whatever it was, Rasmussen wouldn't answer until I did.

I reached for my inner breast pocket. He tensed. I had a gun. But that's not what I was going for. I produced my photostat and slapped it down on his desk. "P.I." I said.

He glanced down at the I.D. His eyes met mine. "I don't even remember that girl. Or—I didn't, until I heard she'd been murdered. I've been working with the police on this matter. It's confidential."

"She was my secretary," I said.

"Sorry for your loss," he replied.

"You got enemies, Doc?" I asked. "Any disgruntled employees? Dissatisfied customers?"

"That's none of your business, Mr. Ryker." Rasmussen stood.

He expected me to do the same. I didn't. "Here's how it works," I said. He sat. "I'm not a blackmailer. But I do like to talk. If you don't talk, then I will. How would it look if your rich friends knew that your clientele was being picked off one-by-one?"

Rasmussen sighed. "Look. I don't know who it could be. This is wrecking my life. Sure, nobody knows—yet—that the victims are all on my patient roster. My wife—"

"Rosemary," I said. "Read about you two in the society rags."

"My wife is terrified. What if the killer comes after her?"

As he spoke, my gaze landed on something behind him. A coatrack. On the floor beside the coatrack was a pool of black silk. A wide-brimmed hat with a veil on it, if my guess was right. I let him keep on blabbering about his troubles. I took him in. He was tall. Sturdy. The mysterious mourner *could* have been him.

I heard a woman's voice coming from behind. At the doorway. "Ralph?"

I turned to look. It was Rosemary Rasmussen. Almost as pretty as she was in the social columns. She looked at me. With recognition. I saw an inner switch flick on. "I have to go run some errands," she said to her husband.

I stood. "Nice chatting with you, pal," I said to Rasmussen. "Good afternoon."

Mrs. R walked quickly across the floor, her high heels making click-clack sounds on the varnished wood. She was in a wiggle dress and she had a small clutch-purse tucked under one arm.

I followed her out the front door. She got into the new Jaguar. She backed hurriedly out of the drive. I watched as she made a left on Camden. It was only after she disappeared from sight that I fired up my Buick and gave chase.

VII.

Chase may be too strong a word. I was following. At a discreet distance. She never made me. I hung back as she came to a stop in front of a swanky cocktail joint in West Hollywood. It was one of those upscale places with ironic names—this one was called The Town Pump.

A valet took her white-gloved hand and helped her out of the deep bucket seat. She entered the establishment.

I parked my car on a side-street. I was grateful I was still wearing my funeral suit. It was slightly rumpled from my catnap but it would do. When I entered the bar, I was immediately asked for I.D. As the maître d pondered my fate, I peered into the darkness beyond.

I saw a handsome cat playing bop piano in the center of the room. The place wasn't crowded. Happy hour was over and dinner service hadn't yet begun. The song ended. I saw Mrs. R approach the young man. She was crying, it looked like. He got up and put his hand on her arm. I was enjoying the show. But I wouldn't be able to see how it ended.

"Sir," the maître d's voice busted in. "I don't see your name on the reservation list. Perhaps we can fit you in next week?"

"Don't bother, mac," I said. "I prefer Chinese takeout."

I exited back through the front door. I headed for the alley. I was in luck. The piano man and Mrs. R were out there, having a smoke. They were sharing it. Cozy. I couldn't hear what they were saying, but I gathered they weren't talking about the weather. They went back inside.

I went back to the Buick. I staked out the front, but not for long. Mrs. R collected her high-priced crate within minutes. She was carrying a white paper sack along with her clutch purse. I saw her take a right turn, headed toward Sunset. She wasn't going home.

Relying on the street lights, I tailed her as closely as I dared. She sped up on Sunset and swerved onto Laurel Canyon Boulevard. In what can only be described as a suicidal left turn, I followed. My big Buick protested, burning rubber. Still, she didn't seem to notice me. The lady must have had a lot on her mind.

There were fewer cars up here. Laurel Canyon Boulevard sat perched above Sunset and Hollywood, just a stone's throw from the glitter of the Strip, but it was a world away. Quiet, secluded. Hills and trees, bungalows and mansions sitting side-by-side.

Mrs. R took a right on Mount Olympus and her slinky sports car nearly shook me as she shimmied up the steep incline. But there was only one way up and I kept going, even after her red taillights disappeared into darkness. I flicked on my beams just in time to see her hastily park and dash toward a nondescript house. I drove on by.

I parked a few houses up and walked down the steep shoulder of the narrow road. I wasn't sure what the doctor's wife was up to but I knew it was no good. Was she covering for her murdering husband? Or maybe her lover, piano boy, was the slasher. What was she doing here? Was it her secret love-nest? A place to stash evidence? My mind went to the paper sack and what might be inside it. Could have been a scalpel or the drugs. Or hush money.

I knew I had to be careful. And quiet. I practically tiptoed up to the house. I peered into a side window. There was a light on in the hallway and I saw an open door next to the kitchen. I didn't see anyone. But then another light went on in the room next to the kitchen.

I went to the front door, hoping Mrs. R had been too distracted to lock it. She wasn't. So I took the Diner's Club card from my wallet and jimmied the lock while twisting the brass knob. Easy as 1-2-3, I was inside. I shut the door and listened. I could hear voices coming from down the hall. Hugging the wall and grateful for the cover of darkness, I made my way toward them.

Light shone from the dome light in the hallway, but not much. Clinging to the dimness, I stopped before the open door. The voices, murmuring, came from below. I took a quick peek beyond the jamb and saw unfinished pine stairs leading down into a basement.

I caught a word. "Baby…" It was Mrs. R. "Shhhh."

Then I heard someone crying softly. Definitely another female.

A paper bag rustled. Mrs. R said, "I brought you some fried chicken fingers. Your favorite. Come on, baby. You need to eat."

Using the sound of her voice as cover, I crept onto the first stair. I peered down into the sparsely furnished room. Mrs. R's back was to me. I could see her holding food out to someone. Or something.

A huge, hulking creature sat cross-legged on the bed, the weight of it bowing the mattress. Its face tilted up to accept the hand-fed treat. I felt my blood run cold. The vaguely female face was a mass of lumps and suppurating boils. I didn't know what her problem was, but I bet it was hard to pronounce. One glinting greenish eye was visible, while the other was sunken into folds of flesh. She wore a long black dress… the same one I saw on the mysterious mourner at Lola's funeral earlier in the day. I juddered silently.

But not silently enough.

"You might as well come down here," said Mrs. R, turning to face me. It gave me a jolt. The gun in her hand gave me another.

As I came carefully down the rickety stairs, the thing on the bed shriveled into the shadows. It whimpered.

"It's OK, honey," said Mrs. R to the disfigured woman-child.

Mrs. R was staring at me hard and so was the barrel of her Colt Python revolver. I put my hands in the air and gave her a watery smile. "OK, sister. Don't shoot. I'm just trying to find out what happened to my secretary. Lola. Lola Stewart. She was murdered and she was a patient of your husband's."

I reached the bottom of the stairs and the doctor's wife closed the gap between us. "I don't know what you're talking about. And I don't like being followed," she snapped.

I put my hands down. I reached for the roscoe tucked inside my coat, but I wasn't fast enough. I felt the cold steel of her gat slam against my right temple. I slid down the wall into three dimensions of blackness. I felt a pinprick. Then it was as if my entire existence had been annulled.

I think I opened my eyes. Or maybe shapes just came into focus. I don't know. But I knew I couldn't move. My arms and legs were heavier than my Buick. I couldn't move them if I tried. I was behind the eight-ball. Paralyzed. Panic seized my ticker and squeezed like a vise. I felt sweat trickling down my face. Or was it blood?

A face, blurry at first, loomed into view. The brow was knit with concern. Not with concern that I was dead, but that I was alive. A sound swam to the surface. A voice. "Don't fight it, Max."

My lungs felt like hot water bottles, but I knew I could breathe. I took in my surroundings. I was still in the basement of the house on Mount Olympus Drive.

Who was talking to me? It was a man. Dr. Rasmussen? No. I strained to make out his face. It was the gigolo piano player from The Town Pump. Was he the killer? No. He was too scrawny.

"Esteban." Now it was Mrs. R talking.

"Yes, dear?" Esteban turned from me and went to her side.

"What are we going to do with him?" she fretted. "Baby won't... do what she usually does."

Esteban took both of her hands in his. Oh, goody. That meant she wasn't holding her gun anymore. They weren't sure what to do with me. But they planned on rubbing me out somehow, that much was clear. Since I was dead to them anyway, they spoke freely.

I got the gist that Ralph and Rosemary's disfigured daughter had not died. She had been kept here in this basement for sixteen years. The thing on the bed was the killer, Mrs. R was protecting her and Esteban was writing letters to the cops. The sap seemed to believe that someday soon his squeeze would ditch the M.D. and they'd both be rich. Nobody said anything about what would happen to Baby. But somebody did say I had to kick off. And quick.

I saw Mrs. R take an unladylike belt of whisky straight from the bottle. She was working up her courage. I tried again to move. No dice.

She picked up the Colt Python. Steadied it with both delicate hands. I noticed she had one of those fancy French manicures. And—BAM! I heard the gunshot. Loud. Deadly.

Then I heard a thud. I was already down, so it couldn't have been me.

I willed my vision to sharpen. Mrs. R was lying on the floor beside Baby's bed. Baby began to wail. She threw herself to the ground and took her mother into her clumsy, clutching embrace. I saw the round, black bullet hole between Mrs. R's eyes. I saw Esteban standing, stunned. He was looking toward the staircase, mouth slack.

Then I spotted someone gazing down at me. It was Mellie and she was holding my pistol. "You dropped this," she said, then patted my cheek. "You're going to be OK, Uncle Max."

VIII.

Within seconds, I heard sirens caterwauling through the quiet neighborhood. I tried moving again and this time I could. I was woozy, but I sat up.

I was standing by the time the buttons arrived. Dempsey led the charge.

The Surgeon and the Pen-pal were taken into custody without busting up the furniture. Mrs. R was zipped into a body-bag.

Soon the press was there, then Dr. Rasmussen. They—the news hawks and the physician—demanded answers. I didn't hear any. But I provided one: I'd fogged the doctor's wife in self-defense.

The roar of the siren added insult to my injured head as I was transported to Cedars-Sinai Medical Center. A few hours later I got a somewhat clean bill of health and some happy pills. Mellie drove me home in my car.

The kid was shaken up. She hadn't gone to the house with the intention of killing anyone. She saw the address in a vision, she said. It came to her after she touched Esteban's note. She had a hinky feeling, she said. She called me at home and at the office. When I didn't answer, she got scared. Decided to do some digging. When she saw my car outside, but no me inside, she went to the house. The door I'd jimmied was still unlocked, so she let herself in. After that, she said, "It's a blur."

Over the next few days, secrets would come to light. Ugly ones. Turns out Baby had been through several unsuccessful reconstructive surgeries at her father's otherwise talented hands… and she carried a grudge against her father's pretty patients. She was horrendous and she was sick in the head, but she wasn't dumb. She read his medical books. She knew how to steal. How to get information, and how to hail a cab. Lovesick Esteban had written the letters to the police to throw them off. But he wasn't a killer. That left Mrs. R to take care of me and obviously she would do anything to protect her child.

But we didn't know any of that yet.

Mellie wiped a tear with the back of her hand and I poured her a tall one. "Thank you, Mellie. You saved my life," I said.

"Like you saved mine," she replied. "Now we're even."

I wondered if that was a goodbye. No, I decided. Just a clean slate.

Abracadaver

Minerva's ancient Peugeot puffed up the hilly driveway that led to The Magic Castle, spewing diesel exhaust strong enough to stun any bird that may have been perched in one of the nearby trees.

She patted the envelope containing her invitation. She'd placed it on her lap to make sure she wouldn't lose it. She was getting old, she feared. So old, in fact, she'd nearly ignored the party invitation. She rarely went out anymore.

But there was something irresistible and compelling about the mysterious invite that was hand-delivered to her door a few days before. She'd even had to sign for it.

"The pleasure of your company is requested for cocktails at Hollywood's most mystical and esteemed historical landmark, The Magic Castle. This private party will be held at 9 p.m.

on the dot. For this night only: Free admission, open bar. Costume required. There will be an unprecedented séance in the Houdini Room. No guests… unless they're ghosts."

As she rounded the final corner, a tire hit the curb. The heavy Peugeot protested, and she thought she heard something crack. Minerva knew she was getting too advanced in years to drive; she could barely see anything, especially at night.

The rust bucket rattled into the valet area. There were no other cars and she saw only one employee standing there. Had she come to the right place?

Minerva glanced over at the towering structure to her left. Yep: It was a castle, alright.

The odd-looking valet opened her car door and took her by the upper arm to help her out. The bony hand was encased in a thick velvet glove, but the coldness of the flesh beneath could not be concealed. Minerva shivered as she watched the masked person get behind the wheel, and without handing her a slip of paper or anything, drove the car away.

Lu Fang had never been to The Magic Castle before. Even though he was a native Angelino, he'd just never gotten around to it.

Besides, he wasn't interested in cheap parlor tricks. As one of the top agents in Hollywood, he was much more interested in *pricey* parlor tricks.

But now, pulling his Koenigsegg CCXR Trevita into the valet area, he was mildly intrigued. The castle was so timeworn and tacky—this could be a fun way to slum it on Halloween night. Being newly-single, his choices were: A) Wallow in self-pity at home, or B) Chase tail at the annual West Hollywood carnival on Santa Monica Boulevard. Neither appealed to him, so when the unexpected invite turned up, Lu Fang decided it must be a sign from the universe.

He glided to a smooth stop and exited the car. A valet dressed as an undead bellhop stepped up to him and Lu Fang scrutinized the costume for any sign of fake blood or makeup. The valet would be dead for real if he soiled the agent's pride and joy.

Satisfied, Lu Fang handed over his keys. The zombie gestured to the front door and without a word, whisked the luxury vehicle away.

Brock roared up to the front entrance on his sick Harley. The lone valet was there, waiting for him.

"I'll park it myself," said Brock, blipping the throttle of the beast.

The valet shook his—or was it her?—head. It was hard for Brock to tell. The figure was slight, quite tall, dressed in a red bellboy uniform complete with gloves and the silly chin-strapped hat one saw on performing monkeys.

The face was obscured by a rubber mask made to resemble something out of *The Walking Dead*. Brock had been on that show for a season, playing a semi-regular character. Then he was killed off and no one seemed to care.

"You ride?" asked Brock.

The valet nodded solemnly.

"It's your funeral," said Brock, chuckling. This, he had to see.

He dismounted and the valet scrambled aboard.

"Keeping the helmet," said the actor. "It's part of my costume."

Brock stepped back, watching with amusement as the bike wobbled toward the hidden parking lot located beyond a steep descent.

He shrugged and headed toward the closed door. The Magic Castle was one of his favorite haunts and he couldn't wait to see what was in store this Halloween night.

"This is sooo basic," said Sofia to herself in flat monotone, as she came to a halt in the valet area. The nineteen-year-old spoke in frazzled vocal-fry, even when there was no one else around to hear.

"Oh wells," Sofia continued, "The invite said open bar. And, like, Halloween is a total drag. Might as well get wasted. For, like, free-ee."

The zombie bellhop valet approached Sofia's souped-up Mini Cooper. She got out inelegantly, flashing her crotch and not caring. "Wait a minute," said Sofia to the grave-faced attendant. "I gotta get the rest of my costume out of the trunk."

Once Sofia's costume was complete, she handed her keys over to the valet who silently gestured to the closed front door. The girl headed to the entrance, tottering on her leopard-print high heels.

"This sucks," Sofia deadpanned. "Where are all the hot guys? There's no one even here."

But the lights were on inside and the invitation Sofia got *did* say it was an exclusive private party not open to the public. She'd crashed more parties and gotten beyond more red velvet ropes than she could count, so actually being invited was novelty she wanted to explore.

Lu Fang, Sofia, Minerva and Brock were standing in the lobby area of the venerated landmark, invitations in hand, not quite sure what to do next.

"Do you think there will be a costume contest?" asked Lu Fang, who was dressed in rented swashbuckler attire. It had cost him a good chunk of change, and if there was a competition, he'd win for sure. No one else had gone to the trouble he had.

The bimbo had on a 1940s cigarette-girl getup, with the requisite tray strapped on by a sturdy red ribbon that went behind her neck. Inside the tray lay an assortment of fake body-parts including fingers and eyeballs. She sported leopard cat ears and matching heels. She took a selfie, pouting duck-lips.

The washed-out old woman wore a threadbare full slip with the word "Freud" handwritten in Sharpie across the chest. On her feet were house-slippers and over her shoulder was slung a small purse.

Lu Fang knew black-haired Brock from being in the biz, but only peripherally. The small-screen stud was decked out as Ghost

Rider from the comics. He watched Brock staring openly at the babe and wondered at the young man's lack of taste. Anything with a pussy and a pulsebeat would do, it seemed.

Brock replied to Lu Fang's question about the costume contest. "Nah, they usually hold open auditions on Halloween night." He looked at the girl. "Know any tricks?"

Sofia gave him her most smoldering look, one she'd perfected and posted on YouTube in dozens of self-shot videos. "A few."

Brock winked at her. "I guess we should go in, then."

"Like, how?" asked Sofia. "The only door goes back outside."

"That's the first bit of magic," Brock said. He walked up to a bookcase, waved his arms and said dramatically, "Abracadabra!"

The bookcase swung slowly outward, opening into a dimly-lit bar.

"Free drinks," said Sofia, the first one in.

Once the small party was inside the main Magic Castle, the bookcase door closed. From this side, it looked like just another wall.

Sofia tottered toward the bar and looked around. "Where's the mixologist?"

"Where's... anybody?" asked Minerva.

A Gen-Z bottle redhead seemed to appear out of nowhere. The girl was dressed as a classic magician complete with satin cape, ebony top-hat and fetish-style livery boots; but instead of slacks, she wore shiny gold hot-pants.

"Whoa, cool costume," said Sofia, introducing herself.

"I'm Winston," replied the girl. "I was just checking out the stage in there," she gestured toward a closed door to their left. "It's empty. I was beginning to think I was the only one here."

Suddenly, a voice boomed from unseen speakers. "Welcome!"

The partygoers looked at each other, then up toward the ceiling as the intonation continued.

"Your drinks await you in the Houdini Séance Room. Please: Look to your right, where you will see a magnificent staircase. Follow the stairs, pass the mirror and turn left. See you soon."

"Whoa, that's sketchy," muttered Sofia.

"V," Winston agreed.

With a petulant scowl, Sofia added, "This place stinks, too. It's, like, a hundred years of cigarette smoke." She did not care for the dark wood paneling, heavy chandeliers, stained glass and all those old portraits staring at them. She should have gone to that party on the Strip instead, she thought to herself. This was lame. And it was so quiet. In her life of constant stimulus, the absence of sound really triggered her anxiety.

"Kind of weird there's no music," muttered Lu Fang.

Just beyond the bar, as if on request, a piano began to play an archaic song no one recognized. The group followed the sound with quizzical expressions.

"That's Irma," supplied Brock.

"You know her?" Lu Fang asked, cocking his head. He didn't see anyone playing. Must be one of those odious automated gizmos.

"She's the resident ghost. Supposedly. I come here a lot," Brock explained. Then he looked at Sofia and Winston, grinning. "Nerdy. I know."

They did not smile back.

"Um, shouldn't we go upstairs?" Minerva prompted, wondering if only she had been informed in advance of the séance. She had to admit, she was intrigued by the notion.

"Whatever," replied Sofia, leading the way toward the gothic staircase with its deep mahogany banister and well-worn carpet runner.

As the group climbed the stairs, they looked at themselves in the huge mirror that hung on the wall before them. The deep shadows on their faces made them look like ghouls.

"Almost here," the disembodied voice said, its timbre gender-neutral. "Come, come. Now to your left."

They saw a huge, empty restaurant to their right and then a comparatively small room just opposite.

Lu Fang gawped. The séance chamber was stunning. Alight with candles, round in circumference with an oval table inside and decorated with ancient art, including a magnificent oil portrait of its namesake, it truly was an awesome sight to behold.

Sofia entered the room first. "Basic," she declared flatly. She looked around with disdain. "Where do we sit?"

A candelabra in the center of the table self-lit, revealing each of their names written in red paint on the off-white tablecloth.

Brock, ever the gentleman, seated himself first and let everyone sort themselves out.

While Brock put on his motorcycle helmet to complete his costume, Sofia dismantled hers. She couldn't sit at the table with her cumbersome cigarette tray. She laid it gently on the floor, then took her seat. Immediately, she began to fret. "Where's the drinks? They said open bar."

"Alcoholic much?" asked Winston.

Sofia sniggered. "Hella."

A shiny silver ice bucket with two bottles of champagne appeared from the ceiling, lowered down on a black nylon rope which did not seem to be attached to anything above. A basket of glasses followed, landing lightly on the tabletop. There were only four glasses, so Brock swigged straight from the bottle.

The group made small talk as best they could, but it was awkward.

Within just a few minutes, Sofia stood up and said she wanted to go. "Let's bounce, Win. This party is, like, the lamest party in the history of parties. Wanna hit the Strip?"

Winston nodded and stood. "Yeah. The struggle is real, yo."

"Not so fast," came the voice from the speakers.

Before they could react, a luminous and unusually lanky creature entered the room in an old-fashioned cane wheelchair.

Winston's eyes grew wide. "Slender Man!" She stumbled backward, toward her chair and sat back down.

The pale thing in the wheelchair chuckled. "No, no. Please. I'm supposed to be Nosferatu." It scoffed. "Kids today."

The partygoers took in this new development as it came deeper into the room and closer to the candlelight. There was a latex mask over its face, but no amount of makeup could mimic the horror of its emaciated body. That *had* to be real.

It spoke, revealing the same unisex voice heard over the speaker system earlier, but there was an undeniable feminine quality to it. "I'm Robin. Your host."

Minerva squinted. "Do I know you?"

Robin didn't reply. Instead she reached behind the chair and brought out five orange and black trick-or-treat bags. Robin brought the rolling chair to the table's edge and handed the bags out to the guests, one by one, ending on Winston.

Brock peered at the individual. "Hey, aren't you the valet? How'd you change so fast?"

Robin, who already had a glass of bubbly, took a slurpy sip through her twisted mouth and ignored the questions. "You'll notice the bags are empty, except for a sealed envelope. Written inside each envelope is an item you must collect for tonight's scavenger hunt. And—"

"What!?" Lu Fang interjected. "I thought it was just a party. I don't want to go traipsing around some dirty dust-bucket. This getup cost me five hundred bucks. It's a rental."

"And what about the séance?" Minerva pressed.

Winston half-stood. "Nice try, hunty," she spat at Robin. "We're gone."

"No." Robin's tone was dead-serious. "No one leaves."

Everyone stared at Robin like chastened children.

Robin chuckled lightly. "I mean, come on. The party's just getting started. Let us join hands and begin the séance."

"How does this work?" asked Minerva.

"We link hands and I invite the spirits to join us." Robin's long, knotty fingers flexed. Those were hands no one wanted to hold. "There are several living here within these walls, in the basement, the attic and the belfry. Who will answer the call?" Robin paused. "Could it be Marie Antionette, or perhaps even King Tut?"

Brock perked up. "I did a Lifetime movie set in ancient Egypt. It's called *Love on the Nile.*"

"One of my clients was up for that," said Lu Fang.

"Are you an agent?" asked Sofia, perking up. "I have seven million followers on YouTube."

Lu Fang rolled his eyes. "Of course you do."

"Let us join hands," Robin prompted.

Everyone did so.

"O spirits of Lane Mansion, ghosts of the Holly Chateau and phantoms of The Magic Castle… *arise*!" commanded the host.

One of the windows in the next room opened, letting a breeze rush through the séance room. The candles flickered, then went out. All except for the candelabra in the middle of the table.

"The spirits have a request," said Robin. "Please place all of your devices on the table."

Reluctantly, the guests did so. Then watched in abject horror as the screens all cracked in unison.

"What the actual F?!" shouted Sofia. "That's a two-thousand-dollar phone!"

"Not to worry," said Robin calmly. "This is just one of the many illusions and wonders you will witness here tonight."

"Swerve," Sofia replied acidly. "I'm out of here!" Her body tensed, but the young woman didn't—or couldn't—move. "What's going on?" she whined, eyes wide.

Robin reached out. "Please. Let us join hands once more."

As if moved by unseen forces, Sofia's arms lifted and placed her hands into those seated on either side of her.

Everyone was quiet. The only sound was that of the wind gusting through the open window.

After a moment, Robin said, in an oddly altered voice, "The Child wishes to speak."

A young female voice rang out. "Hi, Minerva!"

Minerva's mouth fell open.

"Oh, snap," said Sofia. "The ghost knows you."

A falsetto sob rang out, then the voice came again: "I'm scared."

"Where are you?" asked Minerva, alarmed and excited at the same time. How did the spirit know her name?

Robin replied in a deep, menacing voice: "The Child is in purgatory because of *you*!"

"No... no..." Minerva stammered. "I didn't do anything." Unbidden tears sprang to her eyes.

Robin, back to her neutral tone, said, "You've all done *something*. Each and every one of you. Now it is time to reach into your trick-or-treat bags and discover the objects of your hunt. Read them to each other aloud or suffer the consequences. Whoever finds the most objects wins."

"Wins what?" asked Lu Fang.

"You'll see." With that, Robin's wheelchair whooshed backward and disappeared into the darkness. The host was gone.

"OK. That was creepy," said Brock, reaching into his bag and pulling out a small, square black envelope. He tore it open, revealing a red card with gold embossed lettering on it. "Gun."

Lu Fang went next. "Rope."

Minerva, wiping her tears away, opened hers and read, "Ax."

Sofia followed suit. "Knife," she said. "Lame."

Winston took the card from her. "Mine's blank. Guess we have to share, Sofia."

Winston stood and addressed her fellow scavengers. "I don't know about you guys, but I'ma start searching." She took Sofia's hand and headed into the restaurant area. "Come on, Minerva," she added. "We ladies should stick together."

Minerva followed them, while Lu Fang and Brock went their separate ways.

The women headed into the kitchen where there were bound to be plenty of knives.

The smell of fresh food was on the air, but the room was dry and deserted.

Since it was a working kitchen with gas stoves, Minerva figured there had to be a fire extinguisher. Where there were fire extinguishers, there were usually fire axes. At least, she thought so. She'd seen them encased in glass on the walls of public buildings, but maybe they didn't do that anymore. She cursed her foggy memory.

She saw Winston taking the biggest butcher knife from the wooden chef's block.

"Got it!" crowed Winston proudly.

Then Winston looked around. Her eyes settled on Minerva. "Where's Sofia?"

Minerva shrugged. "She was here a minute ago."

Her eyes scanned the room and she saw it: A classic fireman's ax with a safety yellow handle and red poll propped conveniently against the refrigerator. "Hey, look," she said. "I found my item, too. Let's go back to the Houdini Room."

"But it's whoever collects the most items wins," said Winston. "Let's see if we can find a gun and some rope and beat the boys."

Minerva shivered in the semi-darkness, thinking that her Freudian slip costume idea wasn't so clever after all. "No... I really need to get back home."

Winston snapped, "Whatever," and headed toward the open doorway that led back into the restaurant. Then she gasped.

Minerva's gaze swung to the shrouded figure rushing toward them at super-speed. Faster than any wheelchair should be going. Their host was heading right for them, full throttle and screaming like a skinned animal. Minerva jumped back, falling into a freestanding cart. She watched in shock as the apparatus slammed into Winston. Her distress intensified as Robin met with Winston's knife.

Winston went into a fear-fueled frenzy, stabbing and stabbing until the wheelchair-bound beast had ceased shouting and stopped moving.

Brock heard a distant scream. "Women," he muttered, as he stepped down yet another flight of stairs, leading him deep into the bowels of the mansion.

There were only a few lights on and they were strategically placed for maximum disorientation, he thought. He removed his helmet, but still it was hard to see anything even inches in front of his face. Feeling the walls and knocking off several framed photos of revered magicians as he did so, Brock made his way to the basement.

He figured the gun had to be here, because when he turned the small card over he saw a hand-written clue: Go below.

When he'd reached the final stair of the final staircase, he found himself facing a heavy wooden door. He turned the crystal doorknob. It didn't budge. Locked. *Dammit!* He kicked at the door, cursing, then jiggled the knob. Nothing.

Now he had to go find the key. Brock turned around angrily and felt warm flesh. He'd run smack-dab into someone.

Lu Fang had noticed a clue on the back of his card and he was following it. The vague handwritten hint led him to the magicians' dressing room, where he saw all kinds of trick paraphernalia piled around. Including lots of ropes. *Perfect,* he thought.

They were all coiled in one corner by a rolling wardrobe stand. He assumed any rope would do. As he reached for one, a hand snaked out of nowhere and slapped a handcuff on his wrist.

When Lu Fang saw what was on the other end, he shrieked.

Winston was backed against the wall, sobbing quietly with the knife in her lap. "It was coming to get me," she kept repeating. She held her hands protectively to her throat.

Minerva noticed something odd about the cloaked, blood-soaked figure, though. It was the feet. More specifically, the shoes. These were the designer leopard-print pumps of a fashionista, not the wasted crone they'd met in the séance chamber. Minerva tiptoed toward the wheelchair, terrified that the corpse would somehow come to life. Gently, she tugged at the corner of the thin black blanket.

As it fell free, it revealed Sofia who was tied to the chair. Even in death, she puckered perfect duck-lips.

"Omigawd!" Winston wailed, craning her neck for a better look. "Oh, no. No, no, no!"

"Robin or whatever her name is, tricked us," said Minerva. "This is no game. We've got to get out of here. Now."

Winston wedged herself deeper into the corner and now she was rocking back and forth. "This can't be happening," she said. "I don't want to die. I'm too young to die."

"Come on," Minerva said, covering Sofia back up with the cloak. "We have to leave. Now."

"I can't," sobbed Winston. "Can't..." She sniffled loudly. "Go to the phones. Call 9-1-1."

"OK," Minerva replied. "I'll be right back."

The Houdini Séance Room where she'd left her phone wasn't far, but to Minerva it felt like a thousand leagues. Not only was she freezing in her stupid little slip but her lumbago was acting up thanks to her collision with the cart. She carried the ax, but she was terrified.

Sofia certainly hadn't tied *herself* to that wheelchair. It must be Robin, who probably wasn't handicapped at all. Definitely wasn't. Brock was right; the valet and the host were one and the same.

But why target me, Minerva wondered. Why any of them? Was it all just some kind of sick game? And how was it that The Magic Castle, a famous public place, was deserted? None of it made any sense.

Every shadow was a potential assassin and every creak of the floorboard a demon, but Minerva made it back to the room without incident.

She entered the chamber and saw the phones, still in the center of the table by the flickering candelabra. She barely registered the phones, though—it was their recently-deceased owners that commanded her attention.

Sofia, a bloody mess, was at the table and still tied to the wheelchair. Next to her was Lu Fang, an angry red rope-burn just beneath his chin and his neck quite obviously broken. Handcuffed to him was Brock, who'd been shot in the forehead. They were propped up in sturdy chairs but looked as though they could topple at any moment.

A voice came from the speakers. "Join them, Minerva. Take their hands. The séance is not quite over."

"No way," said Minerva, backing toward the door.

The door slammed shut, shutting her in.

"Now!" One of the chairs was pulled out by unseen hands.

Minerva, shaking with terror and stupefied by the seemingly supernatural shenanigans, took the seat. She clutched the ax in her lap. What else could she do?

From the shadows, Robin emerged. Bony, sickly and horrid… the unmasked face barely female. She wore a long black gown and on her forehead were two sixes drawn in blood.

Robin sat beside Minerva and took her hand tightly to the point of pain. The host lifted her head and shouted, "O spirits of Lane Mansion, ghosts of the Holly Chateau and phantoms of The Magic Castle… *arise!*"

Even though the room was closed, a gust of wind shot past the seated guests, lengthening the candle flames to the point just before extinguishment. Shadows danced, making the dead faces of Minerva's barely-known companions seem to grin at her.

Minerva turned to Robin and asked meekly, "Where is Winston?"

Robin ignored her. "O spirits, please enlighten this oblivious and wicked woman." Thunder crashed in the distance and the room grew even colder. "Child, please show yourself."

In the far corner of the room, near the huge oil painting of Houdini, the gloom began to take shape. Eddies of dust took on the form of what looked to be a teenage girl.

She stepped forward, swirling and indistinct.

"Winston?" said Minerva softly.

As the redhead came into focus, Minerva saw a bloody number six on her forehead. She shuddered.

"My daughter," Robin supplied. "You killed her."

"What?" Minerva huffed. "No, I didn't… I left her in the kitchen… but… she was alive."

"You *all* killed her, twelve months ago to the day."

Minerva quivered as the corpses of Sofia, Lu Fang and Brock stirred and moaned. They opened their eyes, but they most certainly were not alive.

The ghostly figure flew across the room and the candle-flames flickered and went out. It was dark as dark could be.

Minerva tried to get up, but Robin held her fast. The ax fell to the floor with a thud.

"Watch," said Robin, whispering. "All of you, watch."

Minerva saw Houdini's portrait melt. A new painting emerged from beneath. A moving picture, showing what had happened on October 31st a year in the past.

Life had never been easy for Winston. She'd grown up in a commune in Chatsworth called The Brothers of Beelzebub. It was not far from The Spahn Ranch where Charles Manson had done his thing back in the 60s and the area was believed to be tainted by evil. In fact, their leader regularly weighed the pros and cons of how they'd leave the world when doomsday came—would it be by gunshot, hanging, or stabbing? There was a monthly drill in which the followers would explore different exit scenarios.

Winston hated being there. The vivacious redhead longed to live in the city, to go to school with other kids and to watch Netflix whenever she wanted. She had big dreams and high aspirations. But she was stuck. Until one day, when her prayers were answered.

Winston's dad abandoned her and her mom, leaving no trail of any kind. Without a male to vouch for them, Robin and Winston were excommunicated from the cult.

At first, things were not bad. Thanks to low income housing assistance, Robin rented a modest ground-floor apartment in the slums of Hollywood. She quickly went into the fortune-telling business. She put a neon sign in the window and she drew desperate sooth-seekers by the dozens. Winston sometimes helped with the séances. Those were her favorite.

Then when Robin got sick, she had to stop working. There was no money to pay for the medicine she needed. Not the good stuff, anyway. The state provided some crappy generic substitute but Robin eventually wasted away to nothing. Her breasts had shriveled and her neck was so thin her Adam's apple stuck out like a man's. She couldn't walk on her own, even with braces. Winston found her a vintage wheelchair at the Salvation Army, but Robin rarely had the strength to use it.

Between spoon-feeding her mom and changing her bedpan, Winston practiced illusions night and day. She watched instructional videos online and joined a Facebook group for aspiring prestidigitators. Whenever she could get away, she would walk several blocks from the cramped apartment to the stunning, sprawling castle. She would stand as close as she could get and stare at the magnificent structure beyond the gates. She had to know what was inside. Photography was banned, adding to the mystery and allure.

Winston wanted nothing more than to be a magician. In her childlike mind, she thought that if only she could become a famous headliner at The Magic Castle, she could pay for her mother's treatments and everything would be wonderful.

She found out that open auditions were being held on the best day ever: Halloween.

But on the big day, Robin was sicker than usual. She begged her daughter to stay with her.

Winston felt guilty about leaving, but it had to be done. So Winston gave Robin a double dose of pain pills, figuring they would put her in dreamland long enough for the tryouts. She would be back long before her mother woke up.

Winston put on the magician's costume she'd been collecting piece by piece from thrift shops over the past few weeks, gathered up her props and headed out the door.

As she crossed the intersection of Orange and Franklin, Winston heard a man whistle at her as he whizzed by on his Harley Davidson motorcycle. The traffic light on the Franklin side turned yellow as the bike peeled onto Orange toward Hollywood Blvd. A Chinese man who was texting while driving a pricey Koenigsegg CCXR Trevita looked over at the motorcycle, distracted, then punched it, running the light. He narrowly missed sideswiping a teenage girl behind the wheel of a Mini Cooper, who swerved and in turn almost hit a woman in a smoke-spewing Peugeot. The elderly driver veered toward a passel of pedestrians, making them scatter. That was the final straw.

Winston felt a tug at her cape, pulling her by the neck. The next thing she knew, she was being trampled underfoot. As the tourists shouted at the oblivious driver of the passing Peugeot, Winston felt a high-heeled shoe pierce the hollow of her throat. The last thing she saw, as she lay faceup, was the top turret of The Magic Castle.

The candelabra flickered on. The painting dissolved back into shadow.

Minerva remembered that day. Sort of. She didn't know any harm had been caused though. And certainly, it wasn't *her* fault! It was just a random chain reaction starting with Brock and ending with her.

"But it *is* your fault. It's the fault of all of you," snapped Robin. "Winston never came home and I died. For that, your punishment is reliving my daughter's last wish over and over again. This, my guests, is her audition."

Minerva heard something from behind. The whoosh of an ax cutting the air. There was a blinding pain. As her skull cracked she heard Winston giggle and say, "Sorry, not sorry!"

The last thing the old woman experienced before succumbing to the vacuum of oblivion was an unbearable, biting and all-consuming coldness in her bones.

Meanwhile, in the true and present dimension of the living, The Magic Castle was full of partygoers watching the open auditions of aspiring magicians.

A woman shivered out of the blue. She snuggled closer to her boyfriend and asked, "Did you just feel a chill?"

At that moment, the couple heard a screech of brakes in the distance followed by the wallop of a collision.

Later, when they left The Castle, they were rerouted through a back-exit because there had been horrific car crash at Orange and Franklin involving four fatalities.

Alice on Wonderland

An old Switchblade Symphony song oozed from the speakers. Strobe lights pulsated, freeze-framing the slow-moving, black-clad crowd on the postage stamp dance floor. The bar was packed. The tables were all taken.

Alice stood paralyzed in the doorway for a moment, trying to decide which way to go.

"Move it, ho!" The bossy woman behind Alice decided for her.

Alice stumbled into the club, veering left and nearly falling off her skyscraper heels. She moved aside and clung with her back to the cool wall. She'd never been to a nightclub before.

Alice was twenty-six, but she was immature. She felt awkward and ancient amongst the overly made-up, scantily-clad teen clientele. When she saw the ad for a new dance club posted on the telephone pole outside her new apartment, she thought it would be fun to go out and explore Hollywood.

She'd moved from Bakersfield, hoping to make it as a screenwriter. If nothing else, she thought, maybe there would be a good story here. But looking around, she saw only childrens' faces. She shouldn't have come here.

Alice turned back toward the door.

"Hey, where are you going?"

A hand was on her elbow.

The hand had frosted, glittery fingernails. The girl, probably all of fourteen, was tall and impossibly thin. She wore red velvet hip-huggers, a silver lamé kerchief top and wildly exaggerated hoop earrings. She had white-blonde hair with bright pink bangs, and a friendly smile.   "Leaving so soon?" she asked.

"Well, I think I'm a little out of my element," Alice replied apologetically.

She mentally appraised herself and compared the image with the one that stood before her: Alice was short. Dumpy, even. She was on the heavy side, so she wore a longish, loose-fitting dress to hide her culinary sins. She had a round, chubby face and short brown hair. She wasn't hideous by any means, but nor was she one of the Beautiful People. And she never would be. She'd forced herself to accept that fact long ago. She had never used the front-facing camera on her phone, not even once.

"Nonsense!" the waif snorted. "I make it my personal business to meet and greet all newbies." She gripped Alice's right hand. "I'm Nova Tackysex."

"Huh?" Alice thought she'd misunderstood. The DJ was now playing an even older Concrete Blonde tune at top volume.

"Nova Tackysex," the girl repeated. "Not really, but it's my glam name."

Alice stared perplexedly.

"It's really fun," Nova explained. "You go to this place on the Dark Web. You type in your real, boring name. Then it translates it into a cool new glam name. You know, like Ziggy Stardust or Iggy Pop."

Alice shook her head. She'd never heard of it.

"That's okay," said the blonde with a toss of her asymmetrical bangs. "Come on over and meet my band."

Alice followed the willowy form through the crowd. She felt an odd mixture of hot and cold—warm bodies radiated dance and drunk heat, while high-powered fans blew a gale from all four corners of the matchbox disco.

There were two other embryonic girls seated at the table. They looked up at Alice and smiled. Maybe it wasn't such a bad idea to have come, after all. At least they seemed to be accepting her.

Nova sat and indicated the fourth, empty, chair. Alice hoisted herself up on the high stool, praying that her heels wouldn't twist out from under her. Nova introduced her friends. "This is Star Purpleplume and Glossy Glittertwist."

"Hi," Alice said, feeling too shy to use their tongue-twisting names. "So, you guys are in a band? What kind of music do you play?"

Glossy giggled. Nova answered, "We're not in a band, *really*. I just say that. It's like they're my squad or my posse."

"Oh." Alice fell silent. What did she have to say to these kids? She could hardly understand a word they said. They were friendly, though. She scanned the crowd.

"See anything you like out there?" It was Glossy Glittertwist, winking and nodding toward a trio of girls huddled by the bar.

Alice laughed. "Sure, and go to jail?" Actually, she liked the young ones. Not that she'd have a chance with any female, let alone a teenager—she was painfully shy around other lesbians. They seldom gave her a second look. But she wanted to change that. That was why she'd bolstered her courage, left her partially finished screenplay behind and headed to the club.

"You thinking statutory?" Nova asked. "How old are you?"

Alice told her.

"No way!" all three glam-gals burst forth at once.

"You look so young," said Star, soft spoken.

Flattery would get them everywhere. Alice blushed. "Really?"

"Really," Nova said. "And besides, those girls are easy. You should go talk to them."

Several seven-and-sevens later, Alice did just that.

"Hi, I'm Alice," she said, poking her round face into the ladies' conversation.

The blonde she liked looked her up and down, then burst into fake laughter. "Twat's that?" she burst out, cupping her ear. "I cunt hear you."

She shouldn't have gone over—she was out of her league. Alice slithered away in shame.

Nova didn't look surprised. "You know what you need, baby-girl? Confidence. Confidence is very sexy."

"What about looking like a heifer? Is that sexy?" Alice downed what was left of her drink in a single slug. An attentive server immediately replaced it.

When Alice looked up, Nova's open hand was in front of her, palm up. In it were three brightly colored pills. "These will give you the boost you need."

Alice cocked her head and looked down. The pills were huge and each one seemed hand-painted with a portrait. She struggled, forcing her scotch-saturated vision to focus. The bright red pill had a regal queen painted on it, the white one had a rabbit in Victorian clothing, and the sky colored one had a pretty, pigtailed blonde girl in a blue pinafore on it. Characters from the Lewis Carroll book, obviously.

"What are they?" she asked.

"Wonderland, Alice," Nova replied, giggling at her play-on-words. "Better than Ecstasy, Bath Salts and Viagra combined!"

Alice shook her head, then regretted the action as the room began to spin. "I don't do drugs." But the pills were so pretty. She plucked one—the Alice—from Nova's slender palm.

"That one's on the house," Nova said. "Just try it."

Before she could think twice, Alice popped the pill into her mouth and chased it with a seven-and-seven slug.

Within seconds, she was violently ill. "Bathroom?" she croaked, knocking her chair backwards as she rose. Glossy Glittertwist pointed and Alice was off and running.

She bolted into a stall and heaved. Nothing came up, but her stomach felt like it was full of Pop Rocks. And then, without further ado, it settled. She felt fine. Alice rose and went to the sink. She splashed her flushed cheeks with cold water from the tap, then assessed the damage in the mirror.

She could not believe her eyes.

She was *gorgeous.* No. She was drop-dead gorgeous!

The face that gazed back at her with absolute wonder was dewy peaches and cream, framed with long, lush honey-blonde hair. The eyes were doe-brown, with impossibly long lashes under fashionably thin brows. The mouth was full and stained a sexy siren red. Alice smiled and the mouth did, too. It *was* her! She turned and looked behind herself, just to make sure. She was alone.

They've given me LSD! she thought. But she was too drunk to care. She glanced at her comely reflection once again. *A nice hallucination, at least.*

She walked through the crowd, making her way back to the table. How embarrassing. Her new young friends were probably laughing their asses off at her inability to hold her booze and pills.

"Hey, bae, are you new here?"

Alice felt a hand on her waist. She turned around. It was one of the girls who'd blown her off just minutes before. She was smiling. Genuinely. Alice said nothing.

"Are you new here?" the woman raised her voice, thinking her quarry couldn't hear over the music. "I'm totally crushing on you. What's your name?"

"Uh," Alice stammered. She looked down. She saw her own body, much thinner and dressed in a tight, black sparkly sheath. Could she really look like that to other people, too? It was impossible. But she decided to go with it. "My name is Bambi." She thought it sounded like she looked.

Within moments, Alice and what's-her-name were doing the nasty in the parking lot. Not the most romantic place Alice could have wished for, but something had come over her. She felt like a tigress, ready to conquer all.

Afterward, she found her friends again and she bought the whole bottle of Wonderland.

When Alice got home much later that night, the first thing she did was look in the mirror. The blonde beauty smiled back at her and winked.

When Alice got up the next morning, she felt like shit on a shingle. She hauled herself out of bed.

"Wonder-what-the-hell-happened-last-night-Land," she muttered to her puffy, blotchy face in the bathroom mirror. She looked like her old self again and she felt much worse than she ever had. What a total loser she was—screwing strangers, scoring pills. This had to be the "comedown" as dope-addicts called it. She would never, ever do drugs again!

By 8 p.m., Alice was climbing the walls. She opened the bottle of incredible, edible dreams-come-true.

Every night brought a new and exciting adventure, depending upon which pill she took. Each one had a perfectly-rendered, miniature work of art portrait on it. If she swallowed Alice, she could live an evening as a beautiful blonde babe-magnet; if she swallowed the Red Queen, she was brilliant and powerful; if she swallowed the White Rabbit, she could be faster and wilier than any human. She felt she was changing for the better, forging a future she never could even have imagined before.

But it never lasted. Every morning, it was all gone. And then one night, Nova Tackysex and her friends were gone, too. Chunky, brown-haired Alice searched the club frantically, hyperventilating and crying. They were nowhere to be found. Nobody knew where they were. No one had a drug for sale called Wonderland.

She was asking too many questions.

"Narc!" one of the nubile dancers screamed, pointing at Alice. About a dozen phone cameras came up, seeking her image in the strobe lights. Before a single synapse could fire in her brain, the kids dogpiled her, punching, kicking, pulling her hair. She managed to get away with her life, but she was a bruised pulp by the time she did.

She couldn't even get up the next morning. All she could do was lie in bed and cry, the salty tears stinging the broken skin on her face. She cringed, imagining the video of her being beaten going viral.

By evening, her withdrawal pains were much worse than anything she'd suffered before. Her stomach was on fire and her muscles were twitching as if hooked up to electrodes. She rolled out of bed, falling to the dirty floor. She struggled to her feet and staggered into the bathroom, desperate to see what she had become.

The face that looked back at her with small, beady eyes was that of a man. A pimply-faced, greasy-skinned, balding weasel with a pencil mustache and a rumpled suit—the stereotype of a card-carrying pedophile. Unable to stop herself, Alice went out into the twilight, searching for children.

With Wonderland, Alice was something beautiful and adored. Without it, she was something ugly and reviled. And it got worse with each passing night.

She could do nothing but wallow in her cramped apartment all day, dreading the coming darkness. If only she had saved one pill—she could have had it analyzed maybe and somehow made more. She cursed her stupidity endlessly. All she could hope for was that once the withdrawals went away, she'd be back to herself.

But the withdrawals didn't go away. They grew and grew.

Alice couldn't bear to turn the lights on, but she could still see herself in the soft glow of the bathroom mirror. Her long ears hung, droopy, dejected. Her yellow eyes glinted in the darkness, as if lit from within. Her protracted snout wriggled, as if trying to sniff out prey.

"So, it's come to this," she muttered, trying to keep her tongue away from her sharp fangs. "All because I wanted to be beautiful… *was that so wrong?*" Wasn't vanity one of the Seven Deadly Sins? She couldn't remember. Her brain was so foggy now.

The days passed in a dull blur and as she lay there just passing time until the dreaded night, she heard snippets from the news on her droning TV set… When did she last turn it off? When did she even turn it *on*? Her memory was failing her more and more.

The reporter said people in Hollywood were being killed in the most heinous, animal ways. A few days ago, two people were found ripped to shreds in Hancock Park, as though attacked by coyotes. The night before last a convenience store clerk was found lying behind the counter, drained of every last drop of his blood. There were two perfectly round holes puncturing his jugular vein. And just last night, the reporter said, an elderly man out walking his dog was clawed to shreds.

That night, facing the mirror, Alice saw the worst nightmare she could imagine: She was tall and thin, her hair bleached a blizzard blonde with hot pink accents and, on her body, she wore red velvet hip-huggers and a silver lamé kerchief top. She looked familiar but she couldn't place the face.

"You have mail." It was the electronic voice of her computer. Had she turned it on? She couldn't remember having done so. Alice dutifully answered the computer's call and stumbled on her spiky heels to the hutch in the corner of her den.

An envelope flashed on the screen, insistently. She clicked on it and it opened. Imitating a real letter, the pixels onscreen pulled a lined piece of notepaper from the envelope. Written in a girlish cursive were the words, "You know what you have to do." It was unsigned. At the very bottom was an unusual-looking URL. An electronic voice came through the tiny computer speakers, whispering, "Click me."

Alice did as she was told. A web site came up. There was a bright purple banner across the top that said, Glam Name Generator. Alice typed her name into the blank space.

The club was packed. Alice sat at a small round table by herself, watching the door.

Finally, someone came in alone. A newbie. The stranger looked shyly around, not sure how to proceed.

Alice felt inside her fluffy pink faux-fur handbag. The bottle of Wonderland was there, ready and waiting. She hated to do it, but it was the only way she could free herself. She now knew that this wonder drug had come from Hell's own pharmacy.

Taking a deep breath, Alice got up and made her way to the woman's side.

"Hi," she said with a friendly smile. "I make it my personal business to meet and greet all newbies. I'm Nova Tackysex."